The Man Who Read Mysteries

The Short Fiction of William Brittain

The Man Who Read Mysteries

The Short Fiction of William Brittain

Edited and Introduced by

JOSH PACHTER

Crippen & Landru Publishers
Cincinnati, Ohio
2018

For information contact:

Crippen & Landru, Publishers

P. O. Box 532057

Cincinnati, OH 45253 USA

Web: www.crippenlandru.com

E-mail: Info@crippenlandru.com

ISBN (softcover): 978-1-936363-34-6

ISBN (clothbound): 978-1-936363-33-9

First Edition: November 2018

10 9 8 7 6 5 4 3 2 1

CONTENTS

INTRODUCTION
THE BEST OF BRITTAIN

Although he's best known to the world at large for his four YA fantasies set in the made-up New England village of Coven Tree (the second of which, *The Wish Giver*, won a Newbury Honor Award in 1983) and his 1979 book *All the Money in the World* (which became a 1983 episode of the television series *The Adventures of Teddy Ruxpin*), William Brittain is remembered by readers of mystery fiction for his eleven "The Man Who Read" and thirty-two "Mr. Strang" stories, which appeared in *Ellery Queen's Mystery Magazine* (*EQMM*) between 1965 and 1983.

Born in Rochester, New York, in 1930, Brittain earned college degrees from Brockport State Teachers College (now the State University of New York at Brockport) and Hofstra University. In 1954, he moved to Long Island with his new bride Ginny, where he took a job teaching English at Lawrence Junior High School.

For a period of almost twenty years, Brittain was not only a teacher but a mystery writer, publishing regularly in *EQMM* and *Alfred Hitchcock's Mystery Magazine* (*AHMM*).

He sold to *AHMM* first: his "Joshua" appeared in the October 1964 issue and was followed by another eighteen stories over the next twelve years, ending with "Historical Errors" in February 1976.

Although his first publication in *EQMM* came a year later than his *AHMM* debut, it was certainly an auspicious beginning, with both "The Man Who Read John Dickson Carr" and "The Man Who Read Ellery Queen" appearing back-to-back in the December 1965 issue. Over the next eighteen years, forty-four more stories followed, culminating with "Mr. Strang Takes a Tour" in Mid-July 1983.

That's a total of sixty-five stories in nineteen years, an average of three and a half stories per year across the two publications.

Up to this point, I've been referring to the man who wrote

the "Man Who Read" and Mr. Strang stories as either "William Brittain" or just "Brittain," but now I'm going to start calling him Bill, because that's how I knew him.

My own first published piece of crime fiction, "E.Q. Griffen Earns His Name," appeared in *EQMM*'s "Department of First Stories" in December 1968. As a professionally published author, I was eligible for membership in the Mystery Writers of America, and I joined that organization in '69 and began attending its monthly cocktail parties at the Hotel Seville in midtown Manhattan. I wasn't old enough to drink the cocktails, since I was only seventeen, but I was old enough to attend the parties, and I was taken under the wing of four lovely couples who made me feel not only that I was welcome but that I belonged: Ed and Pat Hoch, John and Barbara Lutz, Stan and Marilyn Cohen ... and Bill and Ginny Brittain. I had many very friendly conversations with Bill and Ginny over the next couple of years, at cocktail parties and other MWA events — and, after I moved to The Netherlands in the late '70s, Bill and I stayed in touch for a while. We didn't have email then, not yet, so we passed what would now be called "snail mail" (but were then called, simply, "letters") back and forth across the Atlantic. He wrote warm, chatty, informative and inquisitive letters, did Bill, keeping me up-to-date on his activities and always interested in mine.

In 1986, after his retirement and right around the same time as the birth of my daughter Rebecca, the Brittains moved to Asheville, North Carolina, and somehow we lost touch. Bill wrote the third and fourth of his Coven Tree books (*Dr. Dredd's Wagon of Wonders* in '87 and *Professor Popkin's Prodigious Polish* in '91), and a few short stories for younger readers, and then retired from writing for publication in 1994. He died in Weaverville, North Carolina, on December 16, 2011 — his eighty-first birthday. Not long after that, Ginny moved back to New York to be closer to her daughter and son-in-law, Susan Brittain Gawley and John Gawley.

In 2017, Dale Andrews and I began putting together a collection titled *The Misadventures of Ellery Queen* (Wildside Press, 2018), and we wanted to include Bill's "The Man Who Read Ellery Queen." To obtain the proper permission to reprint the story, I had to track Ginny down. She didn't — and doesn't — use email, but, thanks to EQ scholar Kurt Sercu, I was able to get a snail-mail address for her and wrote her one of those "letter" things I mentioned previously.

I included my phone number, and on August 5, 2017, we spoke for the first time in some forty years. We had a lovely conversation, and she was delighted that I remembered "The Man Who Read Ellery Queen" and gladly agreed to allow Dale and me to use it. She was, in fact, so pleased that her husband's work was still remembered that I suggested perhaps it was time for someone to put together a collection of Bill's stories. Ginny was not only agreeable but enthusiastic. As soon as I hung up the phone, I emailed Doug Greene and Jeff Marks at Crippen & Landru to sound them out about the idea — and before I went to sleep that night they'd written back to say that they were on board.

So here we are.

My original suggestion for this volume was to include all eleven of Bill's "Man Who Read" stories and all thirty-two of the Mr. Strangs. That would have resulted in much too thick a volume to publish at a sensible price point, though, so Doug and Jeff and I agreed to include all the "Man Who Read"s and a sampling of the Strangs, and it was left to me to decide which of the latter to select.

I've chosen Mr. Strang's first recorded case ("Mr. Strang Gives a Lecture," from the March 1967 *EQMM*) and his final appearance ("Mr. Strang Takes a Tour," from the Mid-July 1983 *EQMM*), and to those I've added "Mr. Strang Performs an Experiment" (June 1967), which is Bill's daughter Sue's favorite, "Mr. Strang Versus the Snowman" (December '72), which is my favorite, and, nostalgically and selfishly, "Mr. Strang Takes a Field Trip," because it was in the same December '68 issue of *EQMM* which contained my own first published story. Since that adds up to three stories from the '60s, but only one each from the '70s and '80s, I've added "Mr. Strang, Armchair Detective" (December '75) and "Mr. Strang Interprets a Picture" (August '81) for a better balance.

As I worked on gathering the material for this collection, I had many warm email exchanges with Susan Brittain Gawley and a number of delightful follow-up phone calls with Ginny Brittain. At one point, I asked Ginny why her husband stopped writing short crime stories. "After his retirement," she told me, "his mind and his heart went to the children's books. If he hadn't been so successful with those, he probably would have gone back to Mr. Strang."

We also talked at length about Bill's passion for education. Even after he retired from the public schools, she told me, he continued teaching, volunteering to instruct courses in mystery writing and old-time crime films through the University of North Carolina's Asheville campus' College for Seniors from 1993 to 2010.

"When he died," Ginny told me, "the funeral was packed with people who were his students."

Bill Brittain was a good friend, a good man, a good husband, a good father — and a good writer. Here are all eleven of his "Man Who Read" stories and seven of the Mr. Strangs. I hope you'll enjoy reading them as much as I enjoyed them when they were new ... and enjoyed them again as I was putting together this collection.

Josh Pachter
Herndon, Virginia
April 2018

PART I

THE "MAN WHO READ" STORIES

THE MAN WHO READ
JOHN DICKSON CARR

Although he did not realize it at the time, Edgar Gault's life first gained direction and purpose when, at the age of twelve, he idly picked up a copy of John Dickson Carr's *The Problem of the Wire Cage* at his neighborhood lending library. That evening after supper, he sat down with the book and read until bedtime. Then, smuggling the book into his room, he finished it by flashlight under the sheets.

He returned to the library the following day for another of Carr's books, *The Arabian Nights Murder*, which took him two days to finish — Edgar's governess had confiscated the flashlight. Within a week, he had read every John Dickson Carr mystery the library had on its shelves. His gloom on the day he finished reading the last one turned to elation when he learned that his favorite author also wrote under the pseudonym of Carter Dickson.

In the course of the next ten years, Edgar accompanied Dr. Gideon Fell, Sir Henry Merrivale, et al. through every locked room in the Carr-Dickson repertoire. He was exultant the day his knowledge of an elusive point in high-school physics allowed him to solve the mystery of *The Man Who Could Not Shudder* before the author saw fit to give his explanation. It was probably then that Edgar made his momentous decision.

One day he, Edgar Gault, would commit a locked-room murder that would mystify the master himself.

An orphan, Edgar lived with his uncle in a huge rambling house in a remote section of Vermont. The house was not only equipped with a library — that boon to mystery writers, but something few modern houses possess — but the library had barred windows and a two-inch-thick oak door which, opening into the room, could be locked only by placing a ponderous wooden bar into iron carriers bolted solidly to the wall on both sides of the door. There were no secret passages. The room, in short, would have pleased any of Carr's detectives, and it suited Edgar perfectly.

The victim, of course, would be Edgar's Uncle Daniel. Not only was he readily available, but he was a believer in Ralph Waldo Emerson's philosophy of self-reliance, and, in order to help Edgar achieve that happy condition, Uncle Daniel had decided to cut the youth out of his will in the near future.

Since Edgar was perfectly prepared to wallow in his uncle's filthy lucre all the days of his life, it was up to him to do the old man in before the will could be changed.

All of which serves to explain why Edgar, one bright day in early spring, was standing inside the library fireplace, covered with soot and scrubbing the inside of the chimney until it gleamed.

The chimney, of course, was Edgar's means of escape from his locked room. It was just large enough to accommodate his slim body and had an iron ladder that ran up the inside for the convenience of a chimney sweep. The necessity of escape by chimney somewhat disappointed Edgar, since Dr. Gideon Fell had ruled it out during his famous locked-room lecture in *The Three Coffins*. But it was the only exit available, and Edgar had devised a scheme to make use of it that he was sure John Dickson Carr would approve of. Maybe Edgar would even get a book written about his crime – like Carr's *The Murder of Sir Edmund Godfrey*.

It didn't worry Edgar that he would be immediately suspected of the crime. Nobody saw his preparations – Uncle Daniel was away on business, and the cook and gardener were on vacation. And at the time the crime would actually be committed, Edgar would have two unimpeachable witnesses to testify that neither he – nor, for that matter, any other human being – could possibly have been the murderer.

Finishing his scrubbing, Edgar carried the pail of water to the kitchen and emptied it down the drain. Then, after a thorough shower to rid his body of soot, he went to the linen closet, took out a newly washed bed sheet, and returned to the library. Wrapping the sheet around him, he got back into the fireplace and climbed the iron ladder. Reaching the top, he came down again, purposely rubbing the sheet against the stones at frequent intervals.

Stepping back into the library, he walked to a window, removed the sheet, and held it up to the sunlight. Although wrinkled, it had remained gleamingly white. Edgar smiled as he put the sheet into a hamper. Then, going upstairs, he unlocked the window of a storeroom beside which the chimney rose. After that, in his own room, he dressed in clothing chosen especially for the crime: white shirt, white trousers, and white tennis shoes. Finally, he removed a long cavalry saber from the wall, took it to the library, and stood it in a shadowy corner.

His preparations were nearly complete.

Early that evening, from his chair in the music room, Edgar heard his uncle's return.

"Edgar? You home?" The nasal New England twang of Uncle Daniel's voice bespoke two hundred years of unbroken Vermont ancestry.

"I'm in here, Uncle Daniel — in the music room."

"Ayah," said Daniel, looking in through the door. "That's the trouble with you, young fella. You think more o' strummin' that guitar than you do about gettin' ahead in the world. Business first, boy — that's the only ticket for success."

"Why, Uncle, I've been working on a business arrangement most of the day. I just finished about an hour ago."

"Well, I meant what I said about my will, Edgar," Uncle Daniel continued. "In fact, I'm going to talk to Stoper about it tonight when he comes over for cards."

The weekly game of bridge, in which Edgar was usually a reluctant fourth to Uncle Daniel, Lemuel Stoper, and Dr. Harold Crowley, was a part of The Plan. Even the perfect crime needs witnesses to its perfection.

Later, as Edgar arranged the last of three armloads of wood in the library fireplace — and added to the kindling a small jar from his pocket — he heard the heavy knocker of the front door bang three times. He took the opportunity to set his watch. Exactly seven o'clock.

"Take the gentlemen to the music room and make them comfortable," said Uncle Daniel. "Give 'em a drink and get the card table ready. I'll be in presently."

"Why must they always wait for you, Uncle?" asked Edgar, his assumed frown almost a smirk.

"They'll wait forever for me and like it, if that's what I want. They know where the biggest part of their earnings comes from, all right." And still another part of Edgar's plan dropped neatly into place.

Entering the old house, Lemuel Stoper displayed, as always, an attitude of disdain toward everything not directly involved with Uncle Daniel's considerable fortune. "White, white, and more white," he sneered, looking at Edgar's clothing. "You look like a waiter in a restaurant."

"Don't let him get to you, boy," said a voice from outside. "You look fine. Been playin' tennis?" Dr. Crowley, who reminded Edgar of a huge lump of clear gelatin, waddled in and smiled benignly.

"No need to butter the boy up any more," said Stoper. "Dan'l's changin' his will tonight."

"Oh," said Crowley, surprised. "That's too bad, boy – uh – Edgar."

"Yes, Uncle's already spoken to me about his decision," said Edgar. "I'm in complete agreement with it." No sense in providing too much in the way of a motive.

In a small but important change from the usual routine, Edgar led the men to the door of the library on the way to the music room. "Uncle," he called, "Dr. Crowley and Mr. Stoper are here."

"I know they're here," growled Daniel. "Wait in the music room. I'll be along in a few minutes."

The two men had seen Uncle Daniel alive and well. Everything was now ready.

In the music room, Edgar poured drinks and set up the card table. Then he snapped his fingers and raised his eyebrows – the perfect picture of a man who had just remembered something.

"I must have left the cards upstairs," he said. "I'll go and fetch them." And before his guests could answer, he left the room.

Once through the door, Edgar's pace quickened. He reached the door of the library eight seconds later. Ignoring his uncle's surprised expression, Edgar took the saber from its corner and strode to the desk where Daniel sat, a newspaper still in his hand.

"Edgar, what in – ?"

Without a word, Edgar thrust the sword violently at his uncle. The point entered Daniel's wattled neck just below the chin and penetrated to the back of the chair, pinning the old man to his place. Edgar chuckled, recalling a similar scene in Carr's *The Bride of Newgate*.

He held the sword in place for several seconds. Then he felt carefully for a pulse. None. The murder had been carried off exactly as planned – in seventy seconds.

Hurrying to the fireplace, Edgar picked up the small jar he had placed there earlier. Then, shuffling through the generous supply of paper among the kindling and wood, he pulled the tall fire screen into place and began to climb the chimney. Reaching the top, he glanced at his watch. Two minutes had gone by since he had left Stoper and Crowley.

Standing on the roof beside the chimney, Edgar removed several small pieces of blank paper from the jar. He had prepared the paper himself from a formula in a book on World War II sabotage operations. These "calling cards" were designed to burst into flame shortly after being exposed to the air. During the war, they had been dropped from planes to start fires in fields of enemy grain. Edgar, who had shortened the time needed to make them ignite, knew the pieces of paper would start a fire in the library fireplace.

Dropping the papers down the chimney, he waited a few seconds, and finally was rewarded with a blast of warm air coming up through the opening. Three minutes and ten seconds. Right on schedule.

Edgar moved along the slanted roof to a large decorative gable in which was set the storeroom window. Carefully inching along the edge of the roof, he raised the window and scrambled inside, taking care not to get dust or dirt on his clothing. He went to his own room, took a fresh deck of cards he had left there earlier, then trotted loudly down the stairs to the music room. He rejoined the two guests a little less than five minutes after he had left them — again exactly as planned.

Edgar apologized for his short absence, privately gloating over the unsullied whiteness of his clothing. Surely he could not have just climbed up the inside of a chimney from which smoke was now issuing.

Soon Stoper became restless. "I wonder what's keepin' Dan'l?" he grumbled.

"Mebbe we'd better fetch him," said Crowley.

As they rose, Edgar attempted a yawn while his heart pounded wildly. "I believe I'll wait here," he said, trying to act nonchalant.

John Dickson Carr would be proud of me, thought Edgar, as Stoper and Crowley left the room. He hoped that the investigation of his crime would not include any theories involving the supernatural. He remembered his disappointment at the ending of *The Burning Court*, with its overtones of witchcraft.

Odd, he thought, that there was no shouting, no crashing sounds as the two old men tried to batter down the heavy library door. But there was no need to worry. The plan was perfect, foolproof. It was —

In the doorway of the music room appeared the figure of

Lemuel Stoper, looking tired and beaten. In his hand he held a revolver from Uncle Daniel's desk.

"Did his money mean that much to you, boy?" Stoper asked, his voice trembling with shock and rage. "Is that why you did it?"

For only a moment, Edgar wondered how Mr. Stoper had gotten into the library so fast. And then suddenly he knew. For a fleeting instant, he wondered if a plea of insanity would help. But then nobody would appreciate the perfect crime he had devised.

What would Dr. Fell think of him now? What would H.M. think? What would John Dickson Carr himself think?

What could anyone think of a locked-room murder in which the murderer had forgotten to lock the door?

THE MAN WHO READ
ELLERY QUEEN

To make the transition to institutional living easier, each resident of the Goodwell Senior Citizens Home was allowed to retain one item of personal property. Some of the old men kept their stamp collections, others preferred to treasure voluminous photograph albums. One senior citizen, Gregory Wyczech, had a 1907 ten-dollar gold piece that was almost as precious to him as life itself. Aside from the single personal item, all the necessities and luxuries — food, clothing, bedding, and recreational material — were furnished by the home.

The only thing that Arthur Mindy brought with him when he entered the Goodwell Home was a complete collection of books by Ellery Queen.

Shortly after his admittance, arranged by a daughter who had grown weary of ministering to the constant needs of an eighty-year-old man, Arthur Mindy sat in his small room, discussing his choice with Roy Carstairs, the first-floor attendant.

"I read my first Ellery Queen mystery at the age of forty-five," said Arthur, finishing his meager lunch. "It was at the beginning of the Depression, and I had plenty of time for reading. For a long time, I dreamed of solving a mystery just the way Ellery does."

"What's so different about the way he solves mysteries?" Carstairs asked.

"The pure logic of his solutions is beautiful," Arthur answered. "He uses only the smallest wisps of evidence, and from these he is able to arrive at the only possible solution. Take *The Roman Hat Mystery*, Ellery's first novel. I read it thirty-five years ago. It was solved when Ellery made deductions from an opera hat found near the body of the murdered man. In other books, the pivotal clues have been things like a shoelace, a bottle of iodine, a collar, a packet of matches — all so insignificant! And sometimes the vital clues are things that should be there but aren't, what Ellery calls 'invisible clues.'

"It's always been my ambition," Arthur went on dreamily, "to solve a mystery using only the one or two seemingly vague clues that Ellery Queen finds sufficient." He looked at the light brown walls of his tiny room and sighed. "But now I guess I'll never get the chance."

"Yeah, but Mr. Mindy," Carstairs said, "you got to remember that — "

Whatever it was that Arthur had to remember may never be known. At that moment, a shout — the thin cracked voice of an old man — came from the hallway outside the door.

Carstairs sprang from his chair and through the half-open door, followed at a more leisurely pace by Mindy. They were brought up short by the scene in front of them.

In the middle of the thickly carpeted hall, Gregory Wyczech, dressed only in the light green pajamas and robe which were almost a uniform at the home, was engaged in a boxing match with another similarly dressed resident. Although the sparring form of both men would have done mild credit to a Jack Dempsey or a Joe Louis, each man was standing well out of reach of the other.

While Carstairs stepped between the two combatants, Arthur Mindy looked at Wyczech's opponent. Eugene Dennison had been admitted to the home some time before Arthur. After a short but unsuccessful attempt on the part of the other men to become friendly, Dennison had been classified as a "cold fish." He never had any visitors, and his haughty manner repelled even the most amiable of advances. He refused to take part in any of the home's recreational activities. Television bored him. In the crowded world of the Goodwell Home, he walked aloof and alone.

Dennison stood stiffly just outside Gregory Wyczech's door as Wyczech circled him, chattering like an angry monkey. "He stole my eagle," Wyczech repeated, over and over.

"Your what?" Carstairs' eyebrows shot up.

"My eagle. My ten-dollar gold coin. He stole it!"

"Mr. Carstairs." Dennison spoke for the first time. His imperious tone brought silence to the hallway, which was beginning to fill with old men. "Mr. Carstairs, I have not stolen his eagle or whatever it is. I was on my way to the dispensary to renew my supply of pills. I took the elevator down, since at my age the prospect of three flights of stairs is appalling. Congratulating myself for not having picked up a sliver from the wooden floor of that infernal machine, I came out the elevator door — which, unfortunately for me, is next to Mr. Wyczech's door. Then this idiot came around the corner, entered his room and burst out again, striking out at me. Naturally, I fought back."

"You stole it," Wyczech said again.

"I didn't."

"You did!"

"I did not."

"Wait a minute," said Carstairs. "How do you know he stole it, Mr. Wyczech?"

"Here's what happened," said Wyczech, catching his breath. "I'd just gone down the hall and around the corner to wash my hands. My gold coin was in its envelope on the table, and I wanted to wash before handling it. When I got back, just a minute later, the gold piece was gone, and this — this thief in the night was walking away from the door of my room. So I took a swing at him."

"You must have hit him fairly hard. I see you cut his cheek quite badly." Arthur pointed to a rather long, deep wound on Dennison's cheek, from which fresh blood was oozing.

"To lapse into the vernacular," said Dennison, "he never laid a glove on me. I cut myself shaving this morning."

"Could anybody else have taken the coin?" asked Carstairs.

"Nobody would have had time," said Wyczech. "I wasn't gone that long. And no one else was around."

Dennison looked at the many pairs of accusing eyes turned in his direction. Then he opened the front of his robe and spread it dramatically. "If I submit to a search, will that satisfy everybody?"

Dennison shrugged off the robe and flung it at Wyczech. He removed the tops of his pajamas, loosened the bottoms, let them fall to the floor, and shuffled out of them. He stood on the green carpet, naked as a jaybird, without losing a particle of his massive dignity.

The clothing was quickly searched, even the seams and buttonholes. Nothing. No gold coin.

"He must have swallowed it," sputtered Wyczech.

"Mr. Carstairs, I leave it to you," said Dennison, in the manner of a parent speaking to a dull-witted child. "You know the condition of what's left of my stomach. Considering that my diet for the past several years has consisted only of oatmeal and milk, could I have swallowed a piece of salami, much less a gold coin?"

"That's true, Mr. Wyczech," said Carstairs reluctantly.

Wyczech examined Dennison's hair and the inside of his mouth without results. Then he shrugged. "I still say he stole it. He was the only one who could have."

"Mr. Dennison," said Carstairs, "you go back to your room. I'll take care of Mr. Wyczech."

With a shrug, Dennison reclaimed his clothing and, not bothering to put it on, shuffled to the carpeted stairway across from Wyczech's room.

"Just a moment, please!"

The men in the hallway looked to see who had spoken, and Arthur Mindy stepped forward and faced Carstairs and Dennison.

"If you gentlemen would indulge me, I think perhaps I might be of some assistance. This case is reminiscent of 'The Black Ledger,' a story in *Q.B.I. — Queen's Bureau of Investigation.* In that story, Ellery kept a long list of known criminals on his person the entire time he was being minutely searched by some desperate individuals who were determined to find the list. Ellery was stripped to the buff, just like Mr. Dennison here."

"Where did Ellery hide it?" asked Carstairs.

"That would be telling. I'll lend you the book sometime."

The attendant shook his head sadly. He was sure something had snapped in Arthur's mind.

"Now," Arthur continued, "if Mr. Dennison did take the coin, what did he do with it? Where did he hide it? Unless we can find that out, he's innocent by default. Let's see if the problem will yield to logic."

"Like Ellery Queen?" asked Carstairs, attempting to humor Arthur.

"Precisely. I ask you to consider two pieces of evidence, Mr. Carstairs. The first is that long, deep cut on Mr. Dennison's cheek."

"He cut himself shaving, Mr. Mindy," said Carstairs. "What about it?"

"And the second is that Mr. Dennison is now preparing to climb the stairs to his room," Arthur concluded.

"So what?" moaned Wyczech. "Come on, great detective. Where's my coin?"

Arthur smiled. "You know," he said, "in Ellery Queen's earlier novels and in many of his short stories, there's a point at which the reader is challenged to solve the mystery using only the facts given in the story. I'm sorely tempted to use that device right now."

"Mindy!" screamed Wyczech. "You can't torture me like this! Where's my gold eagle?"

"Very well," said Arthur, "let's first consider the cut on Dennison's cheek. He said he cut himself shaving this morning. That would have been at least two hours ago, since lunch was just served. But you all see that the cut is bleeding again. Fresh blood. Why?"

"Because Mr. Wyczech hit him?" Carstairs suggested.

"By Dennison's own admission, Wyczech never laid a glove on him. But tell me, Mr. Carstairs, what do you do when you cut yourself shaving?"

"Use a styptic pencil."

"But suppose the cut is long and deep?"

"I'd stick a piece of adhesive plaster over it."

"Exactly. Adhesive plaster. And if Dennison had just torn a piece of adhesive plaster from his face, it would have re-opened a long deep cut. Right?"

"Right," said Carstairs.

"So we have Dennison provided with a piece of adhesive plaster. But where is it now? Evidence Number Two: what did he just do when he was told to leave? He went to the stairway, in spite of the fact that there is an elevator waiting right here for him. What is so attractive about the stairway?"

"So he wanted some exercise," said Wyczech. "Get to the point."

"The point," said Arthur, "is that the stairs are carpeted, while the floor of the elevator is bare wood. When Dennison left the elevator and noticed the door to Wyczech's room open, he walked in – probably just out of curiosity – and saw the coin. He couldn't resist taking it, but, as he went back into the hall, he heard Wyczech returning. So he had to conceal the coin in a place where it could not be found, even if he were searched, but where it would be available to him as soon as he was allowed to leave."

"I don't get it," moaned Wyczech. "Why didn't he go back to his room by the elevator?"

"He would have clicked."

"Clicked?"

"Clicked. Logically, the only place the coin could be is the one place on his person that we failed to search."

Arthur savored the silence of the men in the hall. At the age of eighty, he had finally been given his golden moment.

"You'll find it taped to the bottom of his foot."

Dennison was quickly forced to sit on the stairs, and on the ball of his right foot was found the gold coin, held there by a thin strip of adhesive plaster – just as Arthur Mindy had deduced. Dennison's face was now a mask of hatred. And then the mask came apart.

"I didn't mean to do it!" he cried out. "I just wanted something all to myself — something that belonged to me and not to everybody else, too. You men — you have relatives to come and see you. They bring you gifts and tell you about their families. You don't know what it's like to be really alone. I've got nobody — nothing." His thin body was racked by sobbing.

Gregory Wyczech sat down on the bottom step and put his arm around Dennison's shoulders. "I tell you what," he soothed. "You and me, we're gonna be partners. I'm giving you a half interest in my gold coin, see. Every other week you get to keep it all to yourself."

The two old men stood up and crossed the hall, while Carstairs gazed at Arthur Mindy in awe.

"Thank you, Mr. Queen," he heard Mindy murmur.

THE MAN WHO DIDN'T READ

Monty Reeser brushed cement powder from his clothing and wiped his brow as he watched the green station wagon come up the long drive, a cloud of dust in its wake. It lurched past the front of the enormous brick house, missed a tree stump by inches, and screeched to a halt with its rear end at the spot where he had laid out his building materials.

"I brought over some cinder blocks like you asked me to, Monty," said the driver. "I think, with what you've got there, we'll have enough."

"Thanks, Ford," Monty answered. "Living way off the main road here, it's hard for me to bring in heavy stuff, especially in that little car of mine. And I appreciate your being willing to help me, too. I'm afraid I haven't had much experience mixing cement and laying blocks."

"The pleasure's all mine," said Ford Donato. "Tell the truth, Monty, I'm kind of glad you asked me. I didn't figure you'd feel very kindly toward me after — well, you know."

Monty was silent for a moment. His eyes glistened with tears. Then he wiped one arm brusquely across his face. "It was an accident, Ford. They said so at the hearing. Being angry at you won't bring Helen back, so forget it. Life's got to go on."

"I'm glad you feel that way," said Ford. "You know how sorry I am about it. Most men wouldn't be as reasonable as you are." He looked at the pile of cinder blocks, the bags of cement, and the mixing trough. "What's the project, Monty?"

Monty pointed to the small windowless room that projected from the back of the house, facing a deep woods in the rear. "I had a man build this for me last week," he said. "I'm going to use it for a darkroom. I was away when he came to lay the blocks, and, when I got back, I found he'd put in an extra door just where I don't want one."

He led Ford to a rectangular opening in an exterior wall of the room, and they peered across the gloomy interior to a wooden door on the opposite side. "That goes into the house," he said. "But this opening shouldn't be here. I'm afraid, if I put a door here, I might leave it unlocked, and somebody might open it while I'm developing film. So, to be on the safe side, I thought I'd wall it up."

"Well, I don't spend all my spare time reading books like you do," said Ford, "but what I don't know about masonry just isn't worth knowing, if I say so myself."

"How about a drink before we start?"

"I thought you'd never ask."

"Bourbon okay?"

"Sure. On the rocks?"

Monty went around to the house's side door and into the kitchen. He returned with a half-full bottle, a glass, and a bag of ice cubes. Ford took the bottle by the neck and held it up.

"Connoisseur's Choice. That's my brand. Where'd you get it? I didn't know they sold it around here."

"They don't. A man I know brought it when he came out to see me one day."

"Aren't you drinking?"

"No. I did too much of that after Helen's funeral."

Ford half filled the glass, dropped in one ice cube, and gulped down the liquor before it had a chance to cool. "Ah," he sighed, "just the thing to start off an afternoon's work."

"I'll leave the bottle here," said Monty. "Help yourself."

Ford showed Monty how to mix cement and sand in the trough and supervised the adding of the water. Then, while Monty puddled the mixture with a hoe, Ford snapped a chalk line across the doorway. He laid down a coating of wet cement with his trowel and placed a row of cinder blocks into place, testing each one with a level.

"Got to get 'em straight at the beginning," he said. "Otherwise the whole thing'll be out of line."

The rows of blocks rose quickly, until they were nearly waist high. Ford prepared another batch of cement and then reached for the bottle. He put it to his mouth and tilted it up.

"Man, that's good," he grinned. "I hope it'll last until the job's done."

"There's more where that came from," said Monty, who had walked over to Ford's green station wagon and was now circling it. He stopped by the right front fender, which, in spite of its coating of dust, was obviously newer and shinier than the rest of the car.

"Was this where it hit Helen?" he asked, pointing to the fender.

"Yeah, Monty. They had to put on a new one."

"Isn't it lucky a fender can be replaced that easily," mused Monty, a faraway look in his eyes.

"Look, Monty," said Ford, trying to change the subject, "I'm gonna need some help getting the rest of these blocks into place. I think it'll be easier if one of us stands on each side."

"Okay, Ford. Why don't you go inside? It'll be cooler in there, out of the sun."

"Fine. But this goes with me." He gripped the bottle tightly.

"Be careful going over the wall. Don't knock any of the blocks loose."

"They're solid now. Whoever sold you this cement gave you the quick-setting kind."

Ford climbed into the room, and Monty handed across a pail of cement. Then Monty stared at the man on the other side of the wall for a long moment.

"Ford?"

"Yeah?"

"How did it happen?"

"The accident?"

"Yes. You never told me about it — except for what you said at the hearing."

There was a gurgling sound inside the vault-like room, and then the clink of the bottle as it was set down. "It was just after sundown," Ford said. "I was driving along the road in front of your house, and, just as I was passing your driveway, she suddenly ran out, right in front of my car."

"You couldn't avoid hitting her?"

"You saw where her body was lying, Monty. It was almost in the middle of the road."

"The policeman testified that you'd been drinking."

"I'd had one drink over at Pete's Place. The bartender testified that all I had was the one — you remember he said that? I wasn't drunk, Monty — it was just an accident."

"It's okay, Ford. I was only asking."

As the afternoon wore on, the wall rose, until there were only two more tiers to be set. Monty passed Ford another pail of cement, which Ford nearly dropped. The bottle of Connoisseur's Choice was almost empty.

"Ford?" called Monty.

"Yeah, Monty boy? Wha's trouble?"

"Do you want to finish the wall from out here?"

"Naw. 'S a lot easier with one of us on each side. Blocks slide right inna place. Squish — in they go!"

"You'll have to go in through the house when we're finished."

"'S fine. I'll meet you inside, an' we'll have a li'l drink. Say, ain't you got no lights in here?"

"No, I haven't put the wiring in yet."

"Oh. Well, gimme 'nother block."

Finally, there remained only a single block to be put into place. While Monty rested, Ford finished the bottle and dropped it out through the opening.

"On'y one more block, Monty boy," he mumbled. "Give 'er here, an' I'll finish yer job fer ya."

"Ford?"

"Wha' ya need?"

"The day after the accident, I went down to the spot where it happened. Just for something to do, that's all."

"So?"

"I found paint on the post that holds our mailbox, just off the road. Green paint, Ford. Like on your station wagon. It wasn't there two days earlier, when I gave the post a coat of whitewash."

"Wha's 'at got to do with me?"

"It makes me wonder, how paint could have gotten on the post, if you were on the road, the way you said you were. You see what I mean, Ford?"

"Wha' would I be doin' off the road by your mailbox?"

"You were drunk, Ford."

"Look, Monty, the bartender at Pete's said I had one drink — jus' one. How could I be drunk on jus' one drink?"

"You could have had a bottle in the car."

"The police searched the car. They din' find no bottle."

"No, but I did. You threw it into that pile of rocks on the far side of the road. But it didn't break, Ford. I found it there the next day."

"Aw ri', wise guy. Where's 'at bottle now?"

"It was half full when I found it. You've been drinking out of it all afternoon."

Ford stared through the last opening in the wall at the bottle glinting in the late-afternoon sun. He licked his lips as Monty put his face up to the opening.

"You were drunk when you hit Helen, weren't you, Ford?" said Monty. "Not from what you had at Pete's, but from the bottle you had with you in the car. Helen didn't run out in front of you. You swerved off the road and hit her while she was standing by our mailbox. Then you carried her body to the middle of the road, so the police would think it was her fault. And it would have worked, if the bottle had shattered when you threw it away. But it didn't, Ford. I found it. Connoisseur's Choice, your brand."

Ford was silent for a moment. Then a smirk crossed his

face. "Yer gonna have a tough time provin' any of that, Monty boy."

Monty smiled gently. "I don't have to prove it, Fordy boy."

"Whaddaya mean?"

"Earlier today, you said you weren't much of a reader," said Monty. "Don't you ever read books, Ford? Not even an occasional mystery story?"

"Naw. Readin's a waste of time."

"That's too bad."

"Look, I ain't gonna stan' here and listen to you no more. I'm goin' home. I din' tell my wife I was comin' up here. Besides, this wall's jus' about finished."

"You're right, Ford. It's just about finished. But you can't get out this way, through the wall. You're way too big to fit through that little opening."

"Did ya forget about the door into the house, Monty boy? Tha's my escape hatch. An' if you locked it, I'll jus' break it down."

"You do that, Ford. You go right through that door. I didn't lock it."

Ford's face left the hole in the wall. There was the sound of a door opening, followed by the smack of a fist against a brick surface.

"It's a phony! The door's a phony! There's nothin' behind it, 'cept a brick wall!"

"That's right, Ford. I hung the door yesterday — right against the solid wall of the house."

Ford's face reappeared at the tiny opening. "Wha' do you wan' from me, Monty?"

"Do you know how long we'd been married?" Monty replied. "Eleven days, Ford. Eleven days, we had, to plan a future — and then you came along with a belly full of booze and wiped it all out in a split second, and you thought you'd got off scot-free. There are a lot of names for what I want, Ford: justice, satisfaction, revenge. Take your pick."

Monty took up a cinder block and began to put cement on its edges. Ford watched, his mouth opening and closing soundlessly. Then Ford screamed, "For the love of God, Monty!"

Monty smiled. He approached the opening, holding the final block in both hands. "Yes," he said, "for the love of God."

The block slid smoothly into the opening. Monty braced it with a length of board so that it could not be pushed out before the cement set. When the block was immovable, Monty went to Ford's station wagon and slid behind the wheel.

It would take him ten minutes to drive to the place where he had left his own car the previous day. Even allowing plenty of time to wipe his fingerprints from the station wagon, he ought to be back home in less than an hour.

As he looked again at the small room, now completely sealed, it occurred to him that, one day, he might be able to make an excellent darkroom of it, after all. Of course, it would be a long time before he got around to that.

Monty shook his head sadly. "It's too bad you never developed an interest in mystery stories, Ford," he muttered. "If you'd ever read Edgar Allan Poe's 'The Cask of Amontillado,' you might have been in a better position to appreciate what was happening to you."

He started the motor, and the station wagon moved slowly forward. As he passed the sealed doorway, his eyes glittered coldly.

"*In pace requiescat*," he said.

THE WOMAN WHO READ REX STOUT

The first time I saw Gertrude Jellison reading a Rex Stout detective novel, I laughed so hard it made me weak inside. She didn't pay any attention to me, though. She just sat there on the platform with her nose buried in that book. It was called *Over My Dead Body*, and the jacket had a picture of this big fat guy, Nero Wolfe, scowling as if he had stomach trouble. I'd look at Gert, then I'd look at the book jacket again. That combination would break anybody up.

You see, Gert Jellison weighs over five hundred pounds.

Gert and I both work in a Ten-in-One, a carnival sideshow. My name's Robert Kirby. I'm Gert's partner, which means I stand beside her on the platform during the shows. A pretty easy way to make a living, but I'm not strong enough to do much else. I got the job because, although I'm as tall as Gert, I only tip the scales at seventy-five pounds. Fat lady, thin man. Get it?

To return to the Nero Wolfe books, it was Mel Bentner got up the idea. Mel owns the show, and he's our magician and spieler. He stands out in front and tells everybody about the wonderful sights inside the tent. Then, when he's turned the tip and everybody is inside, he comes in and does his act. Mel saw the Nero Wolfe book with the picture on the jacket in a store and thought it would be a good gimmick to have Gert reading it during the show.

After Gert finished that first book, she read her way right through all of Rex Stout's Nero Wolfe novels, starting with the earliest one, *Fer-de-Lance*. And pretty soon she began to act like Nero Wolfe. Wolfe liked beer, so Gert developed a yen for pink lemonade. Wolfe raised orchids, and Gert got her tent so full of carnations she hardly had room to sit down. She took those mysteries seriously, all right. It didn't surprise me much. Gert's serious about her reading. For all her weight, she's got a really sharp mind. She told me she was once up for a job teaching psychology at a college, but the first time those profs got a look at her, they started laughing so much she ran away and joined the carney the same day.

As I say, we all thought it was pretty funny to see Gert reading those books about that fat detective. But then Lili was murdered. I didn't laugh at Gert after that.

We should have known something was going to happen. First, one of our trucks broke down, so the Ten-in-One had to stay behind while the rest of the carnival headed for the next set-up. While Mel was trying to fix the truck, he burned his hand on a soldering iron and had to put salve and a big bandage on it. That meant his magic act was out of the show for at least a week.

Well, they say misfortune comes in threes. The third thing was what happened to Lili.

Lili was our snake charmer. She came on the lot one day last season and asked for a job. Just for a joke, Mel told her to feed the snakes our last charmer had left behind when she took off with a whole night's receipts. We all waited for Lili to start screaming, but she handled those snakes like so much garden hose. Within two weeks, she had her act ready, Gert had made her a costume, and Ferdinand Hanig, our strongman, was in love with her. Ferdie had competition, though. Zeno the sword swallower thought Lili was pretty nice, too.

But Gert kept both men at a distance. She mothered Lili, sewed clothes for her, and made sure she got to bed on time. She even let Lili water her carnations, when nobody else in the carney was even allowed to sniff them. And both Ferdie and Zeno knew that, if they tried any hanky-panky, Gert would clobber them. I guess Lili became the daughter Gert would never have.

Mel was the one who found Lili's body, but I guess we all got to her trailer pretty fast when he started yelling. All but Gert, that is. Gert was just too heavy to walk that far. It's all she can do to waddle from her living tent up onto the bally platform. So I knew it was up to me to tell her what had happened. That's another thing about Gert: she gets me to do her errands for her. She says she got that idea from Nero Wolfe, too — something about a guy named Archie.

I went into her tent while the rest were still over by the trailer. She looked up at me slowly and poured herself a glass of lemonade. "What's all the caterwauling outside?" she grumbled. "It spoiled my beauty sleep."

I knew how she felt about Lili, but I didn't see any way to break the news gently. "It's Lili," I said, "She's dead."

"Dead? Pfui. I just saw her an hour or so ago. She was waving to the rest of the carney when it departed."

"Gert, she's been — somebody killed her."

She just sat there staring at me with her mouth open. Then it hit her. I hope I never see anything ever again like that great fat woman in a big lacy pink dress sitting there and crying. She buried her face in her hands and sobbed, shaking all over.

At last she looked up at me. Her expression wasn't sad any more; it was angry. It was the same look Nero Wolfe had on the cover of that book.

"How was she killed, Bob?" she finally asked.

"Strangled. Somebody took a scarf — one of hers, probably — and tied it around her neck. Then he put a tent stake through the loop of the scarf and twisted. I'm glad you didn't have to see her face, Gert. It was terrible."

"Garroted," she said. "What kind of person would choose that way to kill?"

"Whoever it was must have knocked her out first," I continued. "Mel says her head was bruised, and there was blood in her hair."

"Does anyone have any idea who did it?"

"Mel's still over at the trailer, looking around. He told me to come and tell you. I don't know if he found anything."

"I did." The tent flap behind me opened, and Mel came in. "This was under Lili's body." He held out his hand.

Gert and I both looked at the object on Mel's palm. It was a flat piece of metal about two inches long. It was almost semicircular in shape, except that the edge that normally would have been straight had a series of notches in it.

"It looks like a piece of that slum jewelry the old man with the ring-toss concession used for prizes last year," said Gert. "He gave me one before he left the carney."

"Yeah," I said, "but that doesn't prove anything. I used to have one, too. He gave 'em to just about everybody who was working with the show then."

"I don't remember seeing one before," said Mel.

"This is just half of it," said Gert. "When both halves are fitted together, it forms a complete circle. He engraved a name on each half, and the boy got one and gave the other to his girl."

Mel smiled wryly. I figured he was just trying to take Gert's mind off Lili. "Whose name did you have put on the other half of yours?" he asked her.

"Don't be facetious at a time like this, Mel," she said. "He put my name right across both halves, if you must know. Is there anything special about this medallion?"

"Just proves that whoever killed Lili must have been nuts. Look."

He flipped the metal plate over in his hand. On the polished surface were engraved four letters, two above and two below:

BY
BY

"What kind of a screwball would murder a girl like Lili and leave a message like that?" I asked.

Gert took the medallion into that huge palm of hers and looked at it for quite a while. "Whatever happened to that ring-toss man, Mel?" she asked. "Is he still around?"

"No, he's with an outfit down south somewhere. I hear from him occasionally."

Gert dropped the medallion onto her dressing table among some of the carnation pots and slid farther down into her reinforced chair. She closed her eyes, and pretty soon her lips started working — pushing out, drawing back, pushing out again. We knew her brain was busy, and finally she turned her head slowly to look at us.

"Mel, have you called the police?" she asked.

"No, but I'm on my way right now."

"I don't want you to tell them yet."

"I've got to, Gert," Mel said. "This is murder."

"No! Trust me, Mel, I want to see the murderer apprehended probably more than anyone else on this lot. But he's mine, Mel. I want the person who did this to know that I caught him."

"Oh, Gert, you've been reading too many of those Nero Wolfe stories."

"I've never been one to ask a favor," said Gert. "But now I ask this. Just have everybody here in an hour. At that time, I will prove to your satisfaction who murdered Lili."

Mel thought about it. Then he scratched his head. "I believe you will, Gert," he said. "Okay, I'll do it."

He turned to me. "Come on, Skinny, let's round up the others." He walked out of the tent.

I watched him go and then banged my fist on the table, nearly mashing one of Gert's flowers. "Why does he keep calling me that, Gert?" I scowled. "He knows I can't stand that nickname!"

She laid her heavy hand on my arm. "Easy, Bobby," she said. "He's just jumpy, like the rest of us. He probably forgot."

"He didn't forget. He knows I hate people calling me that."
I took a few deep breaths to calm down and then went outside, leaving Gert sipping at her everloving pink lemonade.

It took us a little more than an hour to get everybody in
the show together. Cal Lynn, our Flatbush-born swami, had
taken his car into town to get a part for the truck, and Sam-
my Marsh had gone with him to buy some cotton wads for
his fire-eating act. Finally, though, we got everyone crowded
inside Gert's tent. Nobody thought she'd really be able to
figure out who had killed Lili, but we thought she deserved
the chance.

She looked up at us from her chair with that angry,
grouchy expression still on her face. "Ladies and gentlemen,"
she said, "a member of our company has been murdered.
I ask you to indulge me for a few moments, during which
time I will attempt to ascertain the identity of the murderer.

"I am going on the assumption," she continued, "that the
murderer is one of us. Lili was alive early this morning, when
the rest of the carney left. Since that time, nobody has been
on this lot with the exception of ourselves. Ergo, one of us
killed Lili."

We all turned to look at Ferdie and Zeno, who were standing off to one side. Gert held up her hand.

"Suspicion without proof is pointless," she said. "But I
intend to provide that proof. First, consider the method of
murder: a scarf, twisted tightly with a tent stake. But, we
must ask ourselves, why was a stake used as a lever? Surely
this would indicate that, for some reason, the murderer —
unlike most of us here — was incapable of strangling Lili
without mechanical help."

Now there was an eye opener. Maybe Gert was getting
something out of those Nero Wolfe books, after all! There
was a murmuring of voices, and everyone turned to Mel
Bentner, who was trying to hide his bandaged hand behind
him.

"Wait just a minute!" said Mel. "Maybe the murderer used
the lever in order to kill Lili more slowly and make her suffer
more."

"I must reject your hypothesis, Mel," said Gert. "You said
that Lili was struck on the head before being strangled.
Therefore, the killer was strangling an unconscious girl."

"But what about that medallion?" someone demanded.
"Why would anybody leave a crazy thing like that near the
body?"

"Leave it? Pfui! Are you asking me to believe that the killer had jewelry especially engraved for the occasion?"

It did sound ridiculous, the way Gert put it.

"Well, then how did it get there?" Mel asked.

"The murderer dropped it accidentally, of course."

"Accidentally? You mean the murderer just happened to be carrying a piece of jewelry that said 'BY BY' on it?"

"I think so, yes. Have you stopped to consider what was written on the other half of that medallion?"

Mel looked puzzled, but Gert went on. "It is my belief that the triangle of Lili, Ferdinand, and Zeno recently became a quadrangle. This morning, the fourth person had a rendezvous with Lili and offered her his love — and Lili rejected him. She probably did so in such a way that he became furious and hit her, perhaps with the same stake he used to tighten the scarf. Then, fearing Lili would tell what he had done, he killed her to keep her quiet."

Ferdie Hanig lumbered up in front of Gert. "Who did it?" he asked menacingly.

"Who is the person in this show who would find it impossible to use a scarf as a strangling cord without increasing his strength through leverage?" Gert asked. "Who takes umbrage at a simple remark that others would consider a joke? And, finally, who has a name that, in its diminutive form, could be written across both halves of a piece of jewelry in such a way that the right half would contain only the letters 'BY BY'?"

So that's it. It all happened just the way Gert said. Everything would have been okay if only Lili hadn't of called me "Skinny." Or if Gert hadn't of spent so much time reading those Rex Stout mysteries.

Just for the record, the policeman in charge of the case has asked me to put my name at the bottom of this page in a special kind of way. He says it'll help them, and that it's better for me to cooperate.

I hereby acknowledge that the above confession was freely given, without coercion, and that I have been offered no promise or inducement of any kind in order to make it.

(signed)

BOB-BY
KIR-BY

THE BOY WHO READ
AGATHA CHRISTIE

In the weeks following that insane Monday in Larkin's Corners, there were many versions of What Really Happened. The village gossips were generally agreed, however, that the first person to be approached by the young madmen when they entered the town was Rad Simpson, the proprietor of the drugstore.

It was shortly after eight in the morning, and Rad had just unlocked the cash register. He heard the bell jingle on the front door, and two youths entered. Rad put on his best smile: they were strangers, and, from the look of their clothing, they were used to spending money freely. College boys, he thought.

"Got any razor blades?" asked one. "I want the injector kind."

"Yep," replied Rad, tossing a container on the counter. "Ten blades for a dollar. Special this week."

Without a word, the boy drew a razor from his pocket, fitted the container to it, and clicked in a new blade. Then he tossed the container and a dime on the counter. "I only need one," he said.

"Hey, wait a minute!" Rad yelled. "You got to buy the whole thing. I can't sell somebody else nine blades when it says ten on the box."

"But I only need one," the youth repeated.

"That don't make no difference, son," said Rad. He came out from behind the counter. "Take the blades or leave 'em, but you owe me ninety cents, regardless. And either you pay up or I'm callin' the police."

The boy's companion walked up to Rad and smiled blandly. "Excuse me, sir," he said, "but is there any way I can purchase nine injector razor blades? You see, I only have ninety cents and — "

Immediately, Rad was all smiles. They were playing a joke on him. He gave the second young man the container. Like the first, the second boy took a razor from his pocket and put in a fresh blade. He walked to the soda fountain at the front of the store, took a tube of brushless shaving cream from his pocket, and began to apply it to his cheeks. Then, facing the window, he started to shave.

Rad picked up the phone and called the police.

At about the same time, another young man entered the Acme Hardware Store, two doors down the street. He purchased a mop and a bucket, requesting that Larry Nash, the owner of the store, fill the bucket with water. When the request was granted, he began — with great diligence, but without Larry's permission — to mop the store's floor.

Larry picked up the phone and spoke to the operator in a low voice.

Within twenty minutes, the main street of Larkin's Corners was in a state of shock.

Item: In the firehouse, two college-age boys were hard at work polishing the already gleaming brass fittings on the trucks.

Item: Fedder's Grocery was in a turmoil, because one lad was busily carrying boxes of jelly donuts to the diet foods section while another was just as busily replacing them where they belonged.

Item: In the bank, a boy was repeatedly going from teller to teller, getting a nickel changed into five pennies from one and exchanging the pennies for a nickel at the next; he kept this up for fifteen minutes before the bank president decided to call the police.

In his office at the rear of the village building, Max Cory, the town cop of Larkin's Corners, was as yet unaware of the deluge of calls about to descend on him. He smiled across his desk at the boy who had come to visit him.

Jacques duMonde had arrived in Larkin's Corners from his home in Belgium six weeks before, as part of a student-exchange program. Although his command of English was excellent, and his tests had shown that he was perfectly capable of handling the work of a high-school senior, the school authorities had been somewhat shaken when they first set eyes on the boy. They promptly made a note that, hereafter, they would insist on knowing the age of any exchange student coming to their school.

Jacques duMonde was ten years old.

When spoken to by the school authorities, Max and his

wife Jean had agreed to let the boy live with them. And he was certainly no trouble. In fact, the neat and orderly condition in which Jacques kept his room embarrassed Jean Cory, who was inclined to let her housework slide at times. His stamp collection was painstakingly mounted, catalogued, and annotated in a manner to put an expert philatelist to shame. He was never late for meals or an appointment. Order and precision seemed to govern the boy's life.

The village librarian was fascinated by Jacques. On his first visit, he took out Darwin's *On the Origin of Species by Means of Natural Selection*, and returned it in less than a week. When the librarian asked him how he had enjoyed the book, she was treated to a short lecture on Darwin's system of classification, including improvements he might have made. Jacques was impeccably polite, but it was obvious to the librarian that he had gained more from the book than she could have ever hoped to.

And then Jacques discovered Agatha Christie's stories about Hercule Poirot. In his fictional countryman, Jacques found a kindred spirit. He read and reread the stories, discussing the techniques of detection with Max. That was the reason for his early-morning visit to Max's office.

"I have yesterday completed *The Murder of Roger Ackroyd*," said Jacques. "And surely, *mon ami*, you will agree that, to a person with the tidy mind of Hercule Poirot, it must have been clearly evident — "

"Wait a minute, Jacques," said Max, holding up his hand. "My main job here is giving out speeding tickets. We've never had any wild crimes in Larkin's Corners. Besides, I haven't read the book."

Max looked at the small figure sitting across from him. The boy's short blue pants had a sharp crease and were, as always, spotless. His shirt was so white it almost glittered, and below the knee stockings his patent leather shoes were dazzling in their brilliance.

But what was that odd movement Jacques made with his thumb and forefinger beside his nose? It looked to Max almost as if he were curling the end of a nonexistent mustache.

Then the telephone began to ring.

Over the next few minutes, Max Cory almost went out of his mind. From drugstore, hardware store, fire department, grocery, and bank came the same message: Main Street had gone berserk.

Max jotted down each complaint in his notebook. He

started to rise, looked once more at the notebook, then sat down again and reached for the telephone.

"Rad," he said, when the connection had been made, "I want you to do something for me.... Yeah, I don't know what's going on, either.... Look, I'll investigate, but let me do it my way. Now, here's what I want you to do. Close the store — that'll keep 'em out for a while. Then go find Larry Nash at the hardware store, Al Fedder at the grocery, and Sam Donohue at the bank. Bring 'em all down here to my office ... and stop worrying about losing business. You don't sell that much on Mondays, anyway."

Max hung up the phone and turned to Jacques. "Bunch of college boys pulling stunts down on Main Street," he said. "It's crazy. There's no rhyme or reason for — "

"Pardon, Monsieur Cory," replied Jacques. "There is always a reason. Are we to believe that these individuals, after being exposed to the glories of a higher education, have taken leave of their senses? I would like very much to hear what the merchants have to say. Of course, if you — "

"Sure, kid, stick around. The whole world seems to be nuts today. I guess a little informality around here wouldn't hurt any."

Ten minutes later, the four businessmen crowded into Max's office, muttering complaints about a policeman who wanted to do his job without getting off his big fat over-stuffed —

"Now, hold it!" shouted Max. "I'm just as concerned about all this as any of you. But tell me something. Just what horrible crimes did these guys commit?"

The men looked at one another in silence.

Max continued in a lower voice: "Look, Rad, a young man took a shave in your window. We got no law on the books against that." He turned to Larry Nash. "Larry, that store of yours has needed a good cleaning since you bought it; the boy was performing a public service. And as far as the grocery is concerned, you said yourself, Al, they put everything back just the way they found it." Max spread his hands. "I don't say you haven't got good reason to be annoyed. It's just, they haven't done anything I can arrest 'em for."

"Yeah," Al Fedder growled. "Well, why can't they do their fraternity initiation somewhere else?"

"No, I checked on that," Max replied. "They're from Cutler College, according to the stickers on their cars. And Cutler has its initiations in the spring, not the fall."

"Then why are they doing it?" asked Larry Nash.

"I dunno. But all I can do is keep an eye on 'em. Now, take it easy — at least nobody's been hurt."

The phone rang again. Max answered, and, as he listened, his eyes became grim. He hung up the phone and turned to the others.

"Come on," he said. "That was Les Kincaid at the post office. A couple of those guys just roughed up old Mrs. Nearing."

At the post office, Max found eight youths backed against a wall and guarded by Postmaster Kincaid, who was armed with an ancient shotgun. The boys' eyes were wide with fear.

Victoria Nearing had settled her trembling body into a chair. "They really didn't do much, Max," she said. "They just frightened me a little, that's all. I wouldn't want to see them get in trouble."

"Well, I would," snarled Kincaid. "They all came in here at once, Max — all eight of 'em. Stood looking at the bulletin board, they did. I figured they was up to no good, so I got my gun ready. Then one of 'em steps up to the window and orders a hundred and two five-cent stamps. A hundred and two. So I gives him a sheet of a hundred and tears off two more singles from another sheet. He no sooner gets out of the way than the next one wants the same thing. Why a hundred and two? Just to make more work for me, the way I see it."

"They've made work for most of us, Les," said Al Fedder. He filled the postmaster in on the events of the morning.

Kincaid nodded. "Bunch of troublemakers. Anyway, after the second one got his stamps, Mrs. Nearing come in. She wanted stamps, too — a dollar's worth — and, as she was leaving, one of these galoots grabbed her by the arm and whipped 'em out of her hand. That's when I grabbed my gun and called you."

"But they didn't hurt me," said Mrs. Nearing. "In fact, they gave me all the stamps they'd bought. I don't think they meant any harm."

"How 'bout it, Max?" asked Larry Nash. "You got enough to arrest them now?"

"I guess I can at least question them. As far as arrest goes, that'll depend on Mrs. Nearing. But I wish I knew why they —"

"Monsieur Kincaid." Jacques' voice could be heard over the general din. "I wonder if I might ask you something?"

Kincaid looked down at Jacques and smiled. "Say, you're the boy living with Max, ain't you? Sure, boy, ask me anything you like."

"Have you ever seen any of these gentlemen before this morning?" Jacques waved a hand at the frightened young men along the wall.

"Nope," Kincaid replied. "I don't — say, wait a minute! That one in the green cap. Yessir, by golly, he was in here Saturday, just before closing."

"Did he come behind your little window at any time?"

"He did not. That'd be against regulations."

"Then allow me to ask whether or not he assisted you in picking up the stamps you dropped?"

"Why, yes, that he did. When I was unpacking the sheets, I dropped a couple of 'em, and he — hey, wait a minute! How did you know I dropped any stamps?"

"Because, Monsieur Kincaid, that would go far in explaining why these gentlemen are acting in this ridiculous fashion. *Sont ils fou?* Are they crazy? I very much doubt it."

Jacques turned to Max. "While you are attending to these men, *mon ami*, I wish a few more words with Mr. Kincaid. Then perhaps I can assist you in explaining this little mystery."

Max threw up his hands in amazement. But he left, taking his eight prisoners with him, and Jacques turned back to Kincaid.

Half an hour later, Jacques walked into Max's office. Seated on the floor on both sides of the small room were the eight college boys. Jacques turned to the one Kincaid had identified as the boy who had been in the post office the previous Saturday.

"I know why you did these crazy things," said Jacques, "and I am a friend of Officer Cory. Now, if I can convince you that your work here is at an end, and if Mr. Cory gives his permission, will you agree to leave Larkin's Corners in peace and return with haste to your studies?"

The youth in the green cap shrugged. "I don't know what you're talking about," he mumbled.

"Perhaps I can convince you that I know all about your scheme. But what have you to say, Monsieur Cory? Will you allow them to leave?"

"Leave? I'd be tickled to death if they were gone now. But first I've got to know what they were doing. And what did you mean about convincing them their work was at an end?"

"*Un moment*," replied Jacques. He took a thick pencil from Max's desk and entered the small lavatory off the office. Returning a few seconds later, he faced the boys, who looked at him in astonishment and then at one another.

Jacques had penciled a huge, sweeping mustache on his upper lip.

Without a word, the eight collegians rose and left the office. Staring wide-eyed at the door, Max could hear the roar of their cars as they headed for the village limits.

"But it was simplicity itself, *mon ami*," said Jacques, as he and Max sat alone in the office. "As Hercule Poirot has taught me, there is a pattern in what is seemingly the most foolish of human actions. To determine that pattern requires only the proper use of the little gray cells.

"What have we in this case? These strangers entered the town and committed several pointless acts. Obviously, however — if they are not insane — one of these acts is not so pointless. The rest were designed to conceal the one deed they wished to accomplish in secrecy. They were — how do you say it? — red halibuts."

"I think you mean red herrings," said Max with a smile.

Jacques ignored the comment. "But where does one find the significant deed?" he continued. "Consider, Mr. Cory, that the boys began by spreading themselves all over the village. And yet all of them came finally to one building — the post office. Is it too much to assume, then, that the post office was the real place of interest to them?

"But what is of such great interest in a post office? Obviously the stamps. After all, Mrs. Nearing was set upon so that those gentlemen could look at the stamps she had purchased. This event told me that the boys were looking for a particular copy of the current George Washington five-cent stamp — which, incidentally, they themselves had purchased in such an odd manner."

"But how did you know one of them had been in the post office before?"

"I assumed that the postmaster did not know of the existence of the particular stamp that interested our eight friends. I asked myself how this could be, and there seemed but one answer. In some way, one of the boys had seen the stamp in question. Since I could think of only one manner in which this might have happened, I put the question that so amazed Mr. Kincaid."

"Sounds good so far," said Max. "But why didn't the boys

just come in and buy sheets of stamps until they found the particular one they wanted? Why panic the whole town?"

"Ah, Monsieur Cory, to understand this, one must have some knowledge of rare stamps. Perhaps the most famous example in United States postage is the 1918 airmail, which has an error showing the airplane flying upside down. Each such stamp is worth several thousands of dollars.

"But in the fall of 1963, in New Jersey, a similar mistake was found. In that case, there was an error in printing the colors. The person who purchased the stamps realized that they were a rarity but made the mistake of boasting about his discovery. At that point, the government printed many copies of the error, making the man's prize almost valueless.

"This is what the eight gentlemen were guarding against. They wanted the stamp, but they had to get it in such a way that attention would not be drawn to it. And who would suspect a purchase of stamps after the other fantastic events of the day?"

"That would explain why they grabbed Mrs. Nearing," said Max. "They wanted to make sure Kincaid hadn't sold her the stamp they wanted."

"To be sure. All the events of the day were for the single purpose of buying an improperly printed stamp without giving anyone reason to suspect that it existed. One of the eight — probably without any knowledge of the stamp's worth — saw it last Saturday. He mentioned it at college to a friend who realized its value. So they came back today to purchase it."

"Jacques, I've got to know," said Max. "What in blazes was the matter with that stamp to make it so valuable?"

"At times, the plate from which stamps are printed becomes marred or damaged. When this occurs, normally the plate is replaced, and the imperfect stamps are destroyed. But once in a million times, perhaps, an error escapes the examiners. Such an error I found on one of the stamps Mr. Kincaid so kindly allowed me to inspect after your departure from the post office. Observe, Monsieur!"

Jacques held up a sheet of five-cent stamps, each bearing the head of George Washington. At first, Max saw nothing out of the ordinary.

"The third stamp from the left in the second row, *mon ami*," said Jacques.

And there it was: on that single stamp in the sheet of one hundred, a flaw in the plate had caused the ink to print in such a way that the Father of His Country seemed to be sporting a magnificent mustache.

"So that's why they left when — "

"Precisely. They saw that I had detected their secret. Unfortunately, I must return this sheet to Mr. Kincaid. He will send it back to Washington, where it will be destroyed. Sad, *n'est ce pas?*"

"Yeah, Jacques. That would certainly be a great find for your own collection."

"That is so, but that is not what makes me sad." Jacques held up a book — Agatha Christie's *The Labors of Hercules* — which had on its jacket a picture of Hercule Poirot, his superb mustaches stretching from one side of the cover to the other. He placed the book next to the sheet of stamps. Max chuckled at the similarity between Hercule Poirot's and George Washington's mustaches.

Jacques passed his hand across his own hairless upper lip. "It is indeed a pity," he sighed, "that even one example of such magnificent facial adornment must pass into oblivion."

THE MAN WHO READ
SIR ARTHUR CONAN DOYLE

To most people, a letter with a Washington DC postmark wouldn't seem too exciting. But when you're the owner, editor, and entire staff of a small-town weekly newspaper, you can get pretty desperate for something besides apple-pie recipes and corn prices to interest the public and increase readership.

Walking down Main Street from the post office where I'd picked up my mail to the ramshackle building where I put out the *Spannersburg Herald* every Thursday, I tore open the envelope and began reading the scribbled words on the sheet of paper inside:

Dear Terence,

Once again your old college buddy comes to the aid of one of your subscribers-in-distress. In the "Questions & Answers" section of your issue of June 18, there was a query from a Virginia DeLong of 740 Marsh Street, NYC. You might drop her a line and tell her that the part of the quotation she's trying to remember is, "There's no police like Holmes."

Always glad to be of help. Maybe you can return the favor sometime.

Danny Blassingame

Sounds like a nice, straightforward letter to the editor, doesn't it? But I smelled a rat. Three of them, in fact. And, once I'd had a chance to go through our back files, the odor of a fourth filled the air.

Item: Nobody named Virginia DeLong of New York City has ever subscribed to the *Herald*. The farthest any of my four hundred and eighteen readers lives from Spannersburg is three miles outside town, at the end of a dirt road.

Item: There is not now, nor has there ever been, a "Questions & Answers" column in my paper.

Item: While I did attend the Durham University School of Journalism and might have met somebody there named Danny Blassingame, I didn't remember him. He certainly was not the "old college buddy" he claimed to be.

Item: My paper is a weekly, not a daily. And I hadn't put out an issue on a June 18 in the last three years.

I took another look at the envelope. It had my name on it, all right: Terence Watson. The address was correct, too. I reached into the bookcase behind my desk and located my old college yearbook. A few minutes later, I found what I was looking for. When I was a senior at Durham, there was a Daniel Blassingame in the sophomore class. His face looked vaguely familiar, but I couldn't remember much about him.

I jammed the letter and envelope into my jacket pocket. Then, on an impulse, I pulled them out again and took another look. I grabbed the phone, dialed the operator, and asked for New York City information.

Forty seconds later, I was talking to Virginia DeLong. After reading her the letter, I asked if she had any answers to the questions buzzing around inside my head.

She hung up on me.

I sat there for a minute, staring at the dead phone in my hand, then shrugged. You can't win 'em all, I thought. And I wasn't about to waste any more time chasing down a lead that would probably go nowhere. Leave that to the big-city dailies. I'd stick to reporting local farm auctions.

It was about one o'clock that same day when the stranger poked his head through the door of my office. He was young — middle twenties, I'd guess — and, unlike most of my visitors, he was wearing a well-tailored suit and carrying a smart-looking briefcase. "Mr. Watson?" he asked, in a flat, businesslike voice.

"That's right." I looked up at him and smiled.

He didn't smile back.

"Will you come with me, please?"

"Come with you? I don't even know you. Where are we going?"

"I'm sorry, sir. I thought they'd already told you about — I mean, I think this will explain everything."

He reached into an inner pocket, pulled out a leather folder, and flipped it open. I looked wide-eyed through the folder's clear plastic windows at credentials that would have opened any door in the nation — including Fort Knox, if he'd wanted to get in there.

"Look, mister," I said, trying to keep my hands from shaking, "I just run this newspaper. I'm not a foreign agent. And if this is about my income taxes — "

That was the nearest I ever saw him come to smiling. "You received a letter today from Daniel Blassingame." The way he said it, it was a statement, not a question. "Have you talked with anyone about it?"

"Just the telephone call I made to that gal in New York. She hung up on me."

"Anyone else?"

"Nope. Nobody's been in the office today."

"Good." He glanced at his watch. "We'd better get going, Mr. Watson. The plane's waiting."

"What plane?" I asked. "Where are you taking me? What's this all about?"

He shook his head. "I'm not allowed to discuss anything with you except the weather," he said, "but I guess I can tell you that you've been ordered to Washington."

"Ordered? Me? I'm not in the Army. Nobody can order — "

"According to the statutes governing national security — "

Fifteen minutes later, I was at Rockton Airport, getting into an Army jet. And two hours after that I was walking through the door of an office in Washington, DC. Nobody in Spannersburg had even had time to notice I'd left town.

Inside the office was a huge oak desk, and behind it a man was seated bolt upright, as if he had an iron bar welded to his spine. He had a face as hard as a clenched fist, and, when he glanced up at me, I knew he'd be a tough person to have as an enemy. According to the sign on his desk, his name was James Harbell.

"That'll be all, Akins," Harbell said to the man who had brought me. "Any trouble getting him here?"

"No, sir. He came quietly. He has the letter and the envelope in his pocket."

"Good. Close the door on your way out."

As Akins left, Harbell motioned me to a chair beside his desk. When I sat down, he held out a hand that looked as knotty as a slab of wood. "May I see it, Mr. Watson?" he said softly.

"See what?"

"The letter. Agent DeLong told us what it contained after you called her. I want to compare her report with the original."

"DeLong? You mean that girl I talked to on the phone was

_ "

" – one of our people? Of course. That's how we found out you'd received the letter. Agent Akins was sent to Spannersburg immediately. Now, may I have it, if you please?"

"No." I leaned back in the chair. "No, I don't believe you can." The look in Harbell's eyes almost made me wish I'd kept my mouth shut, but I went on. "Before I show you that letter – if I ever do – I'd like a few answers."

"Answers?"

"Yeah. This morning, I committed the apparently awful crime of opening a letter addressed to me. Then I committed the awful crime of making a phone call to New York. As a result, I've been yanked away from my work onto a jet plane by a man I don't know, and brought hundreds of miles without even time to pack a toothbrush and a clean shirt. But I've had it, Harbell. I don't give you that letter until I know just why you want it."

"I could take it from you by force," said Harbell, without raising his voice.

"Yes, and I could scream bloody murder. I don't think you'd like that, especially if I screamed to the newspapers. Whatever's going on, you obviously want to keep it hush-hush. And either I know what it is or I'm walking out of here and taking the letter with me."

I could see Harbell's face getting red. He took a deep breath and let it out slowly, giving himself time to cool off. When he spoke, it was still in that deceptively soft tone.

"Okay, Mr. Watson," he said. "As an American citizen, you've got your rights. I just wish you hadn't picked this time to exercise them so vehemently. But, as the recipient of the letter, you might be able to help us.

"I'd like to make one thing absolutely clear, however, especially since you're a newspaperman. Nothing of what is said in this office is to be spoken of or even hinted at outside. Not in the papers, not in private conversation, nowhere."

"Agreed."

"Very well. Let's take a hypothetical situation."

I smiled. Whenever somebody says "hypothetical" to a reporter, it means he's about to describe an actual situation, but, if he's quoted later, he'll call the reporter a liar. Okay, if Mr. James Harbell wanted to play it that way, it was all right with me.

"In my, er, hypothetical case," Harbell went on, "there's a certain embassy building here in Washington. The country that embassy represents is lined up with the USA in the Cold

War, but it could easily be tipped into going the other way."

He motioned to a map behind his desk that showed the Eastern hemisphere. "Inside that embassy, as part of its staff, are a group of people who would like nothing better — for propaganda purposes — than to put us in an embarrassing situation. This group, without the knowledge of the ambassador himself, has got hold of a list, Mr. Watson, a list of individuals living in that country who, from time to time, have passed on information to us. Nothing of great importance. It's just that the citizens of the country involved might have objections to a security network set up right under their noses."

"Security network?" I said. "That means spies, doesn't it?"

"We prefer the other term. At any rate, the list hasn't yet left the embassy. We can't search the place, because, technically, it's on foreign soil. But we have been able to get one of our men planted inside as an employee. He's been able to convince the group who have the list that he wants to join their little plan to make us look bad."

I nodded. "Would the man's name just happen to be Danny Blassingame?" I asked.

"You're very astute, Mr. Watson," said Harbell. "If you ever leave the newspaper business, we might have a place for you here. Anyway, he's the one who found out about the box."

"The box?"

"The list will be sent out of the USA in a metal box, Mr. Watson. It will not be given the immunity of the diplomatic pouch but will instead be sent by special messenger. Our job is to open that box and get back the list before the messenger leaves the country."

"Why not just grab the messenger and take the box away from him?"

"The group at the embassy would be delighted if we did that. Think of the headlines: *Foreign Messenger Waylaid by Government Agents.* From their point of view, that would be better than actually having the list. Remember, their whole purpose is to turn the people of their country against the United States.

"No, the only time we can get our hands on the box is just as the special messenger boards his ship in New York. Then we'll have about two minutes at Customs to open it and confiscate its contents without the messenger's knowledge before returning it to him.

"Now let me describe this box to you, Mr. Watson. It's about the same size and shape as an ordinary cracker box. On the lid is a small latch and three combination dials, each containing all the letters of the alphabet. The lid can be raised only when these three dials are set in the proper sequence. The inside of the box is divided into two parts. One section contains the list. The other contains a smoke bomb."

"A what?"

"A smoke bomb. And that bomb will go off the moment anyone turns the latch and tries to raise the lid — unless he has previously dialed the correct three-letter combination. And there is our problem. In two minutes, we have to find the proper combination, raise the lid, and remove the list. Otherwise, we must either allow the messenger to go aboard his ship with the list or fill the dock area with smoke, announcing to the world that we were searching an embassy messenger without permission. Either way, this country is placed in an awkward position, resulting in a propaganda coup for the other side."

"So Blassingame's job was to learn the three letters of the combination."

"That's right. And he did better than we expected. According to his last message to us, Blassingame himself was assigned to adjust the mechanism of the box — to choose the three letters, in effect."

"Then why didn't he tell you the ones he was going to choose?"

"He was afraid they'd change their minds at the last minute, so he was holding off until the box was actually rigged. But since that time, they've clamped tight security on the embassy. Nobody in or out. Blassingame hasn't had a chance to communicate with us in more than a week. We do know one thing, however. Blassingame told us that the three letters had to be in consecutive order: ABC or DEF or RST, you get the idea."

"So, instead of having an almost infinite number of choices, you now have one chance in twenty-six — no, one in twenty-four — of guessing the combination."

"Right. Once we have the first letter, the other two follow naturally. And we think the clue to the correct combination is in that letter you received. Blassingame couldn't contact us, but he took the chance they'd allow him to write to an old college pal who couldn't possibly be connected with anything like this. And now may I see the letter, Mr. Watson?"

I passed it across the desk.

Harbell read it carefully. "There's no police like Holmes," he mused. "That must be the operative phrase. And your name's Watson. Ever read Sir Arthur Conan Doyle, Mr. Watson?"

"Just some of the Sherlock Holmes stories," I said. "And call me Terry. Everybody else does."

"Fine, Terry. Too bad your name isn't John, like Dr. Watson in the stories. Then everything would fit perfectly."

"John was my roommate," I said.

"I beg your pardon?"

"In college, we were assigned to rooms alphabetically. I roomed with another Watson. His name was John — John Howard Watson. He's got a job in Philadelphia."

"John H. Watson. Damn it," said Harbell.

"Huh?"

"If Blassingame was trying to point us toward Sherlock Holmes, why didn't he contact John Watson, instead of you?"

"Maybe he wanted to indicate my first name."

"Terry? Terence? No, that's too vague. He must have meant the Holmes part."

"So now what?" I asked.

"So now we begin reading Doyle's Sherlock Holmes stories. There must be a clue in one of them."

Harbell lifted his phone and barked orders into the mouthpiece. Within twenty minutes, he not only had several volumes of *The Complete Sherlock Holmes* in his office, but he'd admitted and introduced me to two men named Klein and Dykeman who turned out to be members of the local chapter of the Baker Street Irregulars and well-known authorities on Sherlockiana.

And so we began. *A Study in Scarlet* had us puzzling for forty-five minutes over the word "Rache" before we gave up. By the time we finished *The Sign of Four*, I found myself more interested in the story than in any code it might contain.

"The Adventure of the Dancing Men" was promising, but finally yielded nothing. Nor did "The Five Orange Pips" or "The Red Circle." Klein had high hopes for "The Musgrave Ritual," but he was doomed to disappointment. There was nothing we could find that pointed to a series of three consecutive letters of the alphabet.

"That pun on the name of Holmes is what confuses me," said Dykeman, frowning. "It's not something Doyle himself wrote, you know."

"I know," said Harbell, "but it's not something Blassingame would throw in unless he had a reason. He's devious, but he doesn't have much of a sense of humor."

I just shrugged. I was still with Holmes and Watson, waiting for the Hound of the Baskervilles to come bounding out of the fog.

By midnight, the four of us in the room were all on a first-name basis. I had become something of an expert on Holmesian lore myself, ranging from the cocaine bottle and the VR punched in bullet holes on the wall of 221B Baker Street (and don't think we didn't give those numbers and letter a thorough going over) to Sebastian Moran's air gun and the gasogene (whatever that was) on the sideboard.

And we'd gotten absolutely nowhere. Why Blassingame had written to me instead of to John Watson — and why he had included that clever pun — nothing seemed to fit.

I was halfway through "The Lion's Mane," figuring it might have a clue because it was one of the few stories Holmes himself was supposed to have written, when I heaved the book into a corner and looked at Harbell through aching eyes.

"You know, Jim," I said, my voice shaking, "I'll never make a spy. What's the use of sending a message if the guy receiving it doesn't know what you're talking about? We have here the ultimate in secret codes — nobody knows what it means. If we were back in Spannersburg, where I come from, and Blassingame wanted to give you this information, he'd just walk up to you on the street and say, oh, 'IJK, Jim Harbell,' or — "

Klein and Dykeman both started to laugh. Klein whispered something to Harbell, who let out a chuckle that soon grew to a roar. For a few seconds, I sat there with a puzzled look on my face, until they explained the joke and I got in a few good yuks of my own. Klein and Dykeman were sent home, and I went with Harbell to his place to get some sleep.

Maybe you remember reading in the papers how some characters at a certain embassy in Washington were declared *personae non grata* and booted back home? But not a word was said about the box or the list that Harbell's agents found inside it — not only because we wanted to save face but also because that crew in the embassy still think Dan Blassingame is on their side and we just got lucky. But when our men got their hands on that box for the two-minute Customs inspection, they knew the right combination.

Maybe it was luck, at that. If I hadn't said what I did, we might still be reading Sherlock Holmes stories. But Blassingame's code, which explained both the pun and why he got in touch with me instead of my old roommate John, was based on the most familiar phrase connected with the

Holmes stories. And Blassingame's pun was even worse than the one he quoted in his letter.

What were the dials set at? Think about it. If I said, "IJK, Jim Harbell," what would be his logical comeback?

"LMN, Terry Watson."

Elementary, Watson.

THE MAN WHO READ
G.K. CHESTERTON

"With Father O'Toole on the youth-group outing and Mrs. Surmin having a day off, there's just the two of us to keep the rectory running properly, Charles." Monsignor Francis Gogherty lowered himself gingerly into the chair at the head of the long dining table, made the sign of the cross, and murmured a short benediction. "I hope you don't mind cold ham and deviled eggs," he went on. "That's what Mrs. Surmin left in the icebox for us."

At the far end of the table, Father Charles Kenney smiled at his pastor's use of the word "icebox." At the age of seventy-two, Monsignor Gogherty was not about to let some newfangled invention like a refrigerator change his speech patterns.

"I note that you're wearing not only your collar but also your suit coat at table, Charles," the monsignor continued. "A commendable practice. But since, in spite of my urging, both you and Father O'Toole usually adopt a somewhat less formal mode of dress, I suspect something's on your mind, and you're trying to butter me up before discussing it with me. Out with it, lad. What is it?"

Father Kenney ran his fingers through his close-cropped hair. Lad, indeed! His forty-second birthday was just a month away. But, to the monsignor, anyone not old enough to collect Social Security was a mere child.

"It's about Tim Harrington," Father Kenney began haltingly. "I've been reading up on the case in today's paper. And I don't believe we have the right to refuse — "

"Oh?" Monsignor Gogherty's eyebrows shot up. "So it's now a case, is it? May I suggest, Charles, that you stick to Holy Writ and keep your nose out of those penny-dreadful detective stories you've become so fond of."

"Sir, I hardly think you can classify Gilbert K. Chesterton as an author of penny-dreadfuls," replied Father Kenney. "Why, his critical essays alone would earn him a place in literary history, to say nothing of his works on St. Francis and St. Thomas Aquinas. And then — "

"Then there's that priest who goes around playing detective," interrupted Monsignor Gogherty. "The one your room's littered with stories about. Father Black, isn't it?"

"Father Brown, Monsignor."

"Brown, Black, what's the difference? We all have a place in this world, Charles, and that of the priest is not messing about trying to do the work of the police."

"But, sir, the beauty of the Father Brown stories is in the insights the priest has about the other characters. In 'The Hammer of God,' you actually feel a certain amount of pity for the murderer. Then there's 'The Man in the Passage,' in which several people reveal new facets of their personalities after witnessing the same — "

"Charles, I've had enough of Father Brown. I take it, though, that there's some connection in your mind between him and the Harrington suicide."

Father Kenney allowed himself a soft chuckle. "Yes, I suppose so. You see, I know — knew — Tim Harrington quite well. We served on several committees together, and I've been to his house for meals. He has a fine wife and two delightful little girls. And — well, he just couldn't have committed suicide. It wasn't in his character."

"Charles, I read the papers, too, you know. Especially when the news has to do with one of St. Bartholomew's parishioners. And the evidence in the Harrington case is quite clear. Suicide, pure and simple."

"But evidence can be — "

"Evidence is evidence!" Monsignor Gogherty thundered. "I'm sorry, Charles. Forgive me for raising my voice. But it was all in the newspaper. Yesterday morning, Timothy Harrington entered his office on the top floor of the Professional Building at nine o'clock. The elevator operator remembers the time. About thirty minutes later, a shot was heard. The building guard investigated and, when nobody answered his knocking, finally let himself into Harrington's office with a master key. He found Harrington lying on the floor, shot through the head. There were powder burns about the wound and a smoking gun in his hand. What do you need to convince you, lad? Motion pictures of the actual shooting?"

"Speaking of pictures, Monsignor, there's the one found under the body," said Father Kenney. "Tim Harrington would never — "

"That picture is the crux of the whole matter," said the older man. "Obviously, the paper couldn't print the picture, but their description left no doubt as to what kind of a thing it was. Lewd, filthy."

"Hard-core pornography, no doubt about it. But that's my point. Tim Harrington would never traffic in anything like that."

"But it was there in his office. He must have been looking at it. I suggest to you that, in spite of what you think, he was peddling that trash to innocent people. Corrupting clean minds for money. And perhaps his conscience finally troubled him to the extent that he could no longer tolerate life itself. Or, more likely, he received notification that someone was threatening to expose him. In either case, suicide would be fully explained."

"Then you still intend to — "

" — deny Timothy Harrington the last rites of the Church? Of course that's what I intend. The issue is quite clear. Oh, I realize that a more liberal person might take the position that suicide is ipso facto proof of mental disorder. But then what becomes of personal responsibility? No, lad, St. Bartholomew's will not be a party to a funeral mass or the burial of a suicide, not while I'm the pastor."

"But, Monsignor, consider his family. Aren't they going through enough without adding to their trouble?"

"I feel sorry for the family, of course. But not enough to disregard Church doctrine. The one who should have considered the family was Timothy Harrington — before he killed himself."

"Sir, I must protest. You have no right to condemn Tim Harrington in the eyes of the Church. You have no right to hurt his wife and daughters by — "

Monsignor Gogherty's fist struck the table with a blow that rattled the glasses and silverware. "As the pastor of St. Bartholomew's, I have every right!" he shouted. "Some day, Charles, with luck, you'll have a parish of your own. In the meantime, I will make the decisions in this one."

There was a long silence, broken only by the ticking of the clock in the corner of the room. Father Kenney realized he had been wrong to be drawn into open argument with his pastor. And yet he also knew, through years of working with Timothy Harrington, that the man had earned and now deserved a Christian burial. If only he could convince Monsignor Gogherty. Or, even better, if he could —

"Monsignor," he said softly, "please forgive my harsh words."

"Eh? Well — oh, I suppose so," was the growled reply.

"But I wonder what will happen when Bishop Dalton gets

word of your decision," Father Kenney went on smoothly.

"The bishop? Why, he'll approve, of course. Why wouldn't he?"

"Remember, sir, that only last year Tim Harrington was appointed to that special diocesan committee by Bishop Dalton himself. Now, how's the bishop going to feel when he learns that you refused Harrington a proper burial without any investigation whatsoever?"

Monsignor Gogherty considered the question gravely. It would hardly do for him to be overruled by the bishop. And then another thought struck him. He looked oddly at Father Kenney.

"That's what this whole thing's been getting around to, isn't it, lad?" he asked.

"What do you mean, sir?"

"Oh, don't play the innocent with me. You want to pretend you're that Father Brown chap, the priest who plays detective. Isn't that it?"

This last remark brought Father Kenney up short. Was he interested only in the fate of the late Tim Harrington, or did he really have the urge to emulate Chesterton's little priest and solve a crime? The idea that he might be motivated even in part by the latter reason was totally unworthy of a man of God. And yet Father Kenney was honest enough to admit that he didn't know the answer to the pastor's question.

"Well, you may have a point, lad," Monsignor Gogherty went on, "whatever your reasons. So I'll allow you your investigation, although I doubt you'll turn up anything the police haven't already found. But I'll not accept any nonsense about insanity. I'll reverse my decision only if you find convincing proof that Harrington didn't kill himself."

"Thank you, sir," Father Kenney replied. "When can I get started?"

"Tomorrow's your free day. You can devote your full time to it. I'll expect your report at the evening meal."

"You mean I have only one day?"

"I do. Later this week, you have those weddings, and then there's novena. And I'll expect you to serve your regular time on duty. So tomorrow's as long as I can spare you. And one more thing, lad."

"Yes, Monsignor?"

"That wide-brimmed hat he wore suited Father Brown very well. On you, though, it would look foolish. Don't forget, Charles, that you're an actual priest, not a character in a detective story."

The fact that Father Kenney had been the official chaplain for the village's police force for the past six years opened a lot of doors when he began his investigation the following morning. Patrolman Dom Virgilio, who often took up collections at Father Kenney's masses, quickly ushered him into the squad room, where he was introduced to Detective John Unsell, who was in charge of the Harrington case. Unsell, a heavy-set man with a mop of unruly blond hair, looked up grimly from the report he was typing. It was obvious that Unsell had no desire to talk to the priest and was only doing it as a favor to Virgilio.

"You got most of the facts we have, just by reading the paper," Unsell began, when Father Kenney had given his reason for calling. "Harrington got to his law office at nine. Forty minutes after that, he was discovered shot through the head, and he had a pistol in his hand, a .38. It was his own gun, by the way, and he had a permit to keep it in his office. The bullet went completely through his skull and punctured the glass in the window in the east wall of the office. That's about it. What could we say, except that he'd committed suicide?"

"So the bullet was never recovered?"

"Look, Father Kenney, at five stories the Professional Building is the tallest one around. That bullet went over the roofs and out of the business district. It's probably lodged in a tree somewhere."

"But the hole in the window? Are you sure — ?"

Unsell stubbed out a cigarette in the ashtray and immediately lit another. "Give us credit for knowing our stuff, padre," he said. "When a bullet hits a pane of glass, it doesn't blow the whole pane out. It just punches a neat little hole. And the lab crew was able to tell us that the hole was in keeping with a slightly misshapen .38 slug having passed through — from the inside out."

Father Kenney's face fell. The police certainly hadn't taken the apparent suicide at face value. What could his investigation possibly turn up that hadn't already been considered?

"You said the body was discovered at nine-forty," he said. "But the papers place the time of the shot at nine-thirty. What about that?"

Unsell thrust his newly lit cigarette into a paper container with dregs of cold coffee in the bottom and listened to the hiss. "You're really grasping at straws, aren't you, Father?" he said, trying to keep the annoyance out of his voice. He went on as if he were explaining something to a backward child. "The shot was heard at nine-thirty. But nobody knew where it came from at the time. The guard and a couple of custodians had to check every office in the building. It took them ten minutes to get to the top floor. Okay?"

"And the picture, the one found under the body?" There was a note of desperation in Father Kenney's voice.

"The picture was a slide — you know, one of those transparent things in a little cardboard frame. The subject? Let's just say it's the sort of thing weirdos peddle in dark alleyways. It showed a man and a woman who were — well, it wasn't the kind of thing I'd want my kids to look at." Unsell turned back to his report.

"Please, I know you're busy," said Father Kenney, "but this is very important to me. These transparent slides, don't they require a projector of some kind?"

"It's not absolutely necessary, but the fact is Harrington had one. It was set up on his desk. A real complicated machine — remote control and all that. There was also a screen at the far end of the room."

At last Father Kenney thought he was getting somewhere. "Doesn't it seem a little unusual, Detective Unsell," he said shyly, "that a lawyer would have a slide projector and screen in his office?" He waited expectantly for the answer.

"No."

"I beg your pardon?"

"No, it doesn't seem unusual. Harrington often took pictures to help him with his law cases. Almost everyone in the building knew he had a projector and screen. Of course, none of them knew he was using it to show dirty pictures." He turned again to his typewriter and began laboriously pecking at the keys. "That's all I can tell you, Father," he growled. "Look, you'll have to excuse me. This report's overdue."

Father Kenney got slowly to his feet. That was the end of it. The police had all the facts. All he had was a deep conviction that Tim Harrington would never, under any circumstances, have taken his own life. But knowledge of a man's character wasn't evidence.

Father Kenney looked forward with dread to the evening meal at the rectory and the gibes he'd hear from Monsignor Gogherty. He was certain the monsignor would bring up Father Brown again.

But even Father Brown couldn't do more in the circumstances.

Or could he?

"Yes!" The priest shouted the word into the stagnant air of the squad room, freezing in their places three detectives, a uniformed patrolman, and a suspected pickpocket who'd been brought in for questioning. Unsell, his index finger poised over the typewriter, looked up at Father Kenney in astonishment.

"Yes what, Father?" he asked.

"Yes, there is another answer to Tim Harrington's death besides suicide," was the crisp reply. "And I intend to find it if it takes all day. Mr. Unsell, I would like to see the office where he died."

"Oh, come on, padre. That office is sealed. Nobody can go in there without an official okay."

"Look, Unsell," snapped the priest. "You're new around here — at least, I've never seen you before. But I've been police chaplain for the past six years. I've done everything the job requires, from giving talks at the Benevolent Association dinners to saying masses for men killed or wounded in the line of duty. Now I'm asking for one little favor. And by all that's holy, I'm going to get it — or you guys can get yourselves a new chaplain!"

Unsell looked the priest up and down. "Father Kenney," he began, in a voice menacingly soft, "I don't have to — "

He was interrupted by Detective Raymond Case tapping him on the shoulder.

"He'll do it, Johnny," said Case. "He'll quit, just like he says. You don't know Father Chuck when he gets this sore."

"What do I care? I'm a Methodist."

"Yeah, but most of the guys here go to St. Bartholomew's. And you gotta work with us, remember?"

"But the room's officially sealed. Besides, this report — "

"So unseal the room. You're in charge of the case. And I'll finish your report myself. Okay?"

"Aaaah." Unsell started to say more, looked at Father Kenney, and thought better of it. Grabbing his hat, he stalked to the door, followed by the now-smiling priest. "Let's go, padre," he grumbled.

Timothy Harrington's office, one of the largest in the Professional Building, remained as nearly as possible in the same condition it had been in two days earlier, when his body had been discovered. There was even a chalked outline on the dark brown rug to show where he had lain in death.

"Try not to touch anything," warned Unsell. "The lab boys have dusted the place for prints, but they may want to come back and do some more looking."

Father Kenney placed his hands firmly in his pockets and glanced around. The east wall of the office was dominated by a wide window, flanked by maroon velvet drapes that hung from a brass rod and were tied back with thick ropes that gleamed as if made of gold. On the large desk in front of the window sat a slide projector, pointed at a screen at the far end of the room. Two of the other walls were lined with shelves of books, and on the fourth were hung several diplomas and award plaques. A small door on this same wall led to a tiny lavatory and a storage closet.

"Well, Mr. Great Detective," said Unsell with heavy sarcasm, "this is it. We found about six zillion latent prints in here, most of which we're trying to run down. Seems like Harrington had just about everybody in town for a client at one time or another. So come up with a clue, will you? Show me you can do my job better'n I can."

Father Kenney walked around the desk and peered at the window. The upper pane had a small hole in it, just above the horizontal dividing strip. Three cracks radiated from the hole to the edge of the glass. The priest rubbed his thumb and forefinger against the tied-back drapes and then touched the hole gingerly.

"Hey, leave that alone!" barked Unsell. "You might knock out a chip of glass or something. How do I know that hole won't turn out to be important at the inquest?"

The hand was rapidly pulled back. "Mr. Unsell," said Father Kenney softly, "about those pictures. Did Harrington develop his own?"

"Nope. He had 'em done at Benton's Photo Shop, just down the street. Matter of fact, Benton was sending some new ones over the same morning Harrington shot himself. Only the deliveryman had to return 'em, because, by the time he got here, the police had the office closed off. Why do you ask?"

"Well, I just thought that, since the one picture was important to the case, the others might be, too."

"Maybe they were to Harrington, but not to us. Twenty slides of an automobile accident in a liability case he was handling, that's all. Besides, that one picture we found under the body wasn't developed at Benton's."

"Oh? How do you know?"

"The cardboard frame. Benton has a little ad for his shop on everything he processes. The one we found had a plain white frame."

"I see." Father Kenney's shoulders sagged. "And you haven't touched anything in here?"

"The body was removed after it had been photographed. The smooth surfaces were dusted for fingerprints. When we went through Harrington's papers, looking for a motive for suicide, we were careful to put everything back, just the way we found it. So can I take you home now and get back to work?"

Slowly, Father Kenney nodded. He had failed, no mistake about that. The police had covered everything he could think of. He walked out of the office ahead of Unsell, considering how lucky Father Brown had been that his author had strewn clues about for the fictional priest to find and interpret. G.K. Chesterton should be working on this case, he thought wryly.

They left the building and strode to Unsell's car at the curb. Unsell motioned the priest inside, closed the door after him, then got in behind the wheel. Groping in his pocket for the keys, Unsell was unaware of Father Kenney's preoccupation with the morning sun glinting off the hood and front fenders of the car.

"Mr. Unsell," said the priest softly, as the key slid into the ignition, "what kind of day was it when Harrington died?"

"Huh?"

"The weather. What was it like?"

"Fine. Just like today. Sunny, not a cloud in the sky. Why?" The starter whirred.

"Stop!" cried Father Kenney suddenly. "Turn it off. I've got to go back to that office."

Unsell gave a deep sigh. "You were just up there," he almost moaned.

"Yes, but I didn't know what I was looking for. Now I do."

"But — "

"Listen, in ten more minutes I'll know positively if Harrington committed suicide. Isn't that what you've spent the last two days trying to find out?"

"Yeah, yeah. Fine, come on. But I'm only doing this because I want to stay on speaking terms with the other guys I work with."

The Harrington office was just as they had left it. Unsell looked at Father Kenney, who turned to him, eyes shining with excitement.

"Stand over there, near where Harrington's body was found," said the priest. "That's it. The time now, Mr. Unsell, is just a few minutes before ten — for all practical purposes

the same time at which, two days ago, Tim Harrington sup-
posedly shot himself."

"So?" the detective asked resignedly.

"So pretend for a minute that you're Harrington. You're
preparing to show some slides. What would be the first thing
you'd do?"

"Well ... I guess I'd get out the projector and screen. I'd
probably set them up just about the way they are."

"Okay, fine. What next?"

"Probably I'd plug in the projector and start showing the
pictures. Look, Father, I know you believe that Harrington
couldn't have killed himself, but, according to the evidence
—"

"Unsell, you've been cursed with a lack of imagination,"
said Father Kenney. "Don't you see? He couldn't possibly
show the pictures!"

"Why not?"

"The window, man! Look at the window!"

Unsell turned, shading his eyes. "We're too high up to see
much," he said. "Besides, the sun's shining right in my eyes."
After a pause, the detective began to nod his head. "That's
what you're getting at, isn't it? The sun?"

"Of course. This room faces east. So the morning sun
would be shining into the room through that window, making it impossible to project slides with any degree of clarity."

"Yeah," murmured Unsell. "You've got something there.
Harrington would have had to pull the drapes, that's for
sure. But they were open when we got here. And nobody in
the building said anything about touching them. But maybe
Harrington opened them himself — before he shot himself."

"Maybe," said Father Kenney, walking to the window.
"Let's pull the drapes." He released the gold tie-back ropes
and pulled the thick draperies across the window. The room
was immediately plunged into an eerie gloom.

"Now it occurs to me," Father Kenney went on, "that, if
Harrington were contemplating suicide after seeing the picture, he'd do it in this atmosphere, rather than having the
sun beating in on him."

"You're just guessing, padre. That's not proof."

"True, Mr. Unsell. By the way, do you have a pocket flashlight?"

"Sure, on my keychain. Here."

There was a clinking of keys as the flashlight was passed
to Father Kenney. He pressed the switch, and a circle of light
the size of a silver dollar gleamed on the maroon cloth. Be-

hind him, the priest could hear Unsell's breathing.

Taking a ballpoint pen from his pocket, Father Kenney probed delicately at the drapery material. Suddenly the pen penetrated the cloth.

"There's a hole in the drapes, right at this spot," he said. "Just opposite the hole in the glass."

"It must have been made by the same bullet that killed Harrington," said Unsell. "But, if the drapes were closed when he was shot, then who — ?"

"Exactly the question I'm going to ask if I hear one more word about Tim Harrington's 'suicide,'" said Father Kenney, throwing open the drapes so that sunlight again flooded the room. "Who opened the drapes after Harrington was lying dead on the floor?"

"It had to be whoever shot him," said Unsell. "Unless the guard who found the body lied to us, which I doubt. But who could it have been, Father?"

"As I've often been reminded lately, that's your job, not mine," answered the priest. "But I might offer a logical line of inquiry. Let's assume that whoever made the deliveries of the slides from Benton's Photo Shop was the same person who's been responsible for peddling those pornographic pictures. On the day Harrington was shot, this person had two deliveries to make — the pictures of the auto accident to Mr. Harrington and a packet of the other pictures to someone else. He came to Harrington's office first. Suppose he gave Harrington the wrong package?"

"Yeah, I see." Unsell was now excited. "And Harrington put the pictures in his projector while the deliveryman was still there. When Harrington saw what the pictures were, he threatened the man with exposure — probably he took out the pistol to make sure the guy didn't leave the office."

Father Kenney nodded. "There could have been a struggle, in which Harrington was shot through the head. Our unknown person used the few minutes he had before the guard got here to put the gun in Harrington's hand and pick up the pictures. He probably threw back the drapes so he could see if any pictures had dropped on the floor. But he missed the one under Harrington's body."

Suddenly, Father Kenney held up an admonishing finger. "We've been talking as if we knew how the murder took place," he said. "Actually, we haven't a shred of proof."

"We'll find proof," said Unsell.

"I wish you luck," said the priest. "I'll pray for your success, but that's all the help you'll be getting from me. My job was finished the moment you admitted that Tim Harrington's death wasn't a suicide. But if you don't mind, I'd rather you didn't inform Monsignor Gogherty of that fact. I'd like to tell him myself."

That evening, at dinner in the St. Bartholomew's rectory, Father Kenney was seated at one side of the large table at the end of which was Monsignor Gogherty. Across from Father Kenney sat the young curate, Father O'Toole, oblivious of his pastor's disdain for the grimy sweatshirt he was wearing. Monsignor Gogherty murmured a benediction of which Father Kenney caught only the last few words: "Bless this day's endeavors and make them fruitful."

Crossing himself, Father Kenney uttered a fervent "Amen."

"Now," said Monsignor Gogherty, seating himself, "while we wait for Mrs. Surmin to bring out food, I have a question for Father Brown here." He smiled archly. "Forgive me, I mean for Father Kenney, our budding detective. What say you, lad? Give us the results – if any – of your investigation."

Father Kenney's reply was interrupted by the entrance of Mrs. Surmin. "You'll have to wait a bit for the stew," she said. "I've been on the telephone. It was for you, Father Kenney – somebody named Unsell. You're to call him back."

"Did he say anything else?" asked Father Kenney.

"Just that he's been investigating some deliveryman. He said to tell you the man's name is Colin Patten, and his sister's the girl in some photograph – he said you'd know which one. There was something about the case looking better all the time. Then Mr. Unsell said that Timothy Harrington's murder – he laid a lot of stress on that word murder – would probably be solved within a week."

"Thank you," said Father Kenney. He turned back to Monsignor Gogherty, whose mouth had opened in amazement at Mrs. Surmin's last remark.

"Now then, sir," said Father Kenney, "what was that you were asking about Father Brown and me?"

THE MAN WHO READ
DASHIELL HAMMETT

"Prichard? I know you're in here somewhere. Probably with your nose stuck in another of those mystery thrillers. Well, come out at once. I need you."

Mr. Deacon's nasal whisper was strangely muffled amid the closely set shelves of books that made up the fiction room of the Caldwell Public Library. Clarence Prichard, his aged joints creaking almost audibly, rose stiffly from the little stool on which he had been sitting. With a sigh of regret, he closed the book he had been reading and slipped it into its place. The urbane conversations between Nick and Nora Charles would have to remain frozen in print till he could get back to them.

"Oh, there you are, Prichard." Mr. Deacon, the head librarian, rounded the corner of a passageway between the shelves and caught sight of the old man. "I wish you'd keep the front desk informed of your whereabouts. We aren't the size of the big-city libraries, but it's sometimes devilishly hard to find a stack boy when we need one."

Boy? Prichard snorted audibly. His sixty-fifth birthday and enforced retirement from his bookkeeping job had both occurred five years before. The long illness that preceded his wife's death had wiped out his savings, and the government check he received each month was insufficient for his needs. The offer of a job replacing library books in their proper places had seemed like a godsend, and, boring as it was, it did allow him time to read his beloved mystery stories. So if Mr. Deacon insisted on the term "stack boy," that was all right. Besides, what other term was there? Stack septuagenarian?

He did envy Deacon's well-tailored clothes and his position of responsibility, of course. To deal with the public, to be of real assistance to the library's patrons, to be addressed as "Mr. Prichard" — that would be something. But it was only a dream. Mr. Deacon was trained in every facet of the library's operation, while Prichard's familiarity with mystery stories, encyclopedic as it was, was not in demand.

"Prichard, I've heard rumors that you're uncommonly

knowledgeable about mystery stories. Is that true?"

Prichard could hardly believe his ears. It was almost as if Mr. Deacon had been reading his mind.

"Yes, sir," he answered. "I've read all of 'em in the library here, and I've got a lot more in my room. But I don't let it interfere with my job, Mr. Deacon, and that's a fact."

Deacon shook his head and honored Prichard with a rare smile. "I'm not concerned with your work in the stacks right now," he said.

"Then what — ?"

"Prichard, I" — the words came out reluctantly — "I need you. It's not part of your regular work, but you seem to be the only one on our staff who reads detective fiction regularly, and I hope you won't consider it an imposition if — "

"You're not imposing, Mr. Deacon. I'll be glad to help in any way I can."

"Very well. There are two men waiting in the research room. One of them — the short one in the black suit — is a Mr. Farragut. I've never seen him before. But the other is Andrew King. Do you recognize that name, Prichard?"

"Oh, sure. He's the president of the library board, isn't he?"

Deacon nodded ominously. "They insist on talking with a mystery reader. I could hardly admit to Mr. King that nobody on the staff qualifies. So, willy-nilly, it's up to you, Prichard. Go. And make the Caldwell Public Library proud of you."

Deacon's gesture of dismissal would have been worthy of King Henry sending his troops into battle at Agincourt.

On reaching the research room, Prichard immediately recognized Mr. Farragut from Deacon's description. He was a little balding man with wire-rimmed spectacles, wearing a wrinkled black suit that gave him the appearance of a seedy undertaker. The other man, heavyset and sporting a checked jacket of blinding red and green, had to be Mr. King.

There was a round of handshaking as Prichard introduced himself.

"Sit down, Mr. Prichard."

Mr. Prichard! The title sounded strange when attached to his own name. The old man fairly glowed with satisfaction.

"Deacon told us you know your mysteries," King began. "Are you familiar with the works of Dashiell Hammett?"

"Yes, sir. Read everything he ever wrote. *Red Harvest*, *The Dain Curse*, all of 'em."

"I was thinking in particular of *The Maltese Falcon*."

"Sure. One of the greatest. But if you want it, you'll have to apply through our county loan service. This library doesn't have a copy."

"It does now," wheezed Farragut with a nasty chuckle.

"I don't get you."

"No reason why you should." Farragut's smile threatened to split his face in two. "Get to the point, Andrew."

"All right, Edmund," said King with a sigh. He turned to Prichard. "Mr. Farragut and I have been friends for a good many years. During his lifetime, he has amassed a collection of detective-story first editions, many of them quite rare and valuable. And he has expressed a willingness to donate the entire collection — well over five hundred volumes — to our library."

"Maybe so and maybe no," chuckled Farragut. "First, Andrew, you and your library have to prove yourselves worthy."

Prichard shook his head uncomprehendingly.

"The test," added Farragut. "Tell him about the test, Andrew."

"Yes, of course." King leaned toward Prichard. "Both Edmund and I are mystery fans. Like yourself. But we've tended to specialize. I prefer the tough thriller — the so-called *Black Mask* type of story. Sam Spade, Philip Marlowe, Lew Archer, even Mike Hammer. The rugged lone-wolf types who live just barely within the law and sometimes outside it. They're really the only truly interesting characters in mystery fiction. And the greatest of these, of course, is Hammett's Sam Spade."

"Rubbish," snapped Farragut. "Give me your English country house with rich old Aunt Matilda garroted by her own scarf and skewered to the divan with the antique sword from over the mantel. Enter the Great Detective — Holmes, Poirot, Fell, whoever. A sifting of clues, a questioning of suspects, a bit of logical analysis interrupted only by a bountiful meal and perhaps another killing or two, and the murderer is brought to justice. That is, if he doesn't have the decency to commit suicide to protect the family's good name. All nice and civilized. Why, Andrew, those ham-fisted, trench-coated thugs you read about couldn't detect their way out of a phone booth."

"Not so, Edmund! They deal with real people, not the clay figurines who populate the stories you're so fond of. Furthermore — "

"Gentlemen," whispered Prichard, a finger to his lips. "I'm afraid you're getting a bit loud."

"Quite so," said Farragut softly. "At any rate, I've decided on a little test for Mr. Andrew King. I want to see if his idiotic stories have taught him anything about the deductive process. So I've set him a little problem. If he solves it, my collection goes to the library. If not, I'll take it someplace else, where fine detective stories are really appreciated."

"But where do I fit in?" asked Prichard.

"Sherlock Holmes had his Watson, Poirot his Hastings, and so on. Even in those shocking Hammett stories the private eyes have friends on the police force who provide access to official reports and open otherwise closed doors. Therefore, I agreed that Andrew could have one member of the library staff assist him in his search."

"Search?" asked Prichard. "What search?"

"That's the test we've been talking about," answered Farragut. "Basically, it amounts to this. I have concealed, somewhere in this library, one of the first editions from my collection. In deference to Andrew's abominable taste in mysteries, the volume I selected was Hammett's *The Maltese Falcon*." He drew a large watch from his coat pocket. "It's now three o'clock. Find the book in one hour, and I'll give all my first editions to the library. Otherwise...."

Farragut shrugged and spread his hands wide.

For a long moment, Prichard and King stared at one another. "But this is hardly fair, Edmund," said King finally. "I mean, you can't expect us to start rummaging through all the shelves and cabinets and packing boxes in a single hour. It's impossible."

"A point well taken," murmured Farragut. "But the book is on a shelf — where books would be expected to be."

"Umm." King rubbed his nose with a fist. "The criminal-hiding-in-the-crowd ploy, eh? The old leaf-in-the-forest ploy?" He turned to Prichard. "Well, what about it? Do we have time to scan all the shelves in a single hour?"

"Maybe, just barely," replied Prichard. "You're sure the book is in plain sight, Mr. Farragut?"

"I didn't say that. I said it's on one of the shelves."

"Well, you can't expect us to pull every book down to see if there's something behind it. I mean, it would take days just to put everything back."

"That won't be necessary. It's at the front of its shelf. Besides, you're not allowed to grasp books at random. You may look at the spines all you wish, but the very first book you pull from its place will be considered your final selection. Right or wrong, you get only one chance."

There was a long silence. King gnawed at his knuckles. Prichard suspected, quite correctly, that the man was not so worried over the prospect of losing the collection of books as he was annoyed at the possibility of being bested by Farragut.

"See here," King said finally. "This really isn't fair, Edmund. I mean, all detectives have some time to gather clues. That's what this test of yours is lacking — clues. We're expected to go rummaging around the building without having any opportunity to discover when you might have come in here to conceal the book or" — his voice trailed off lamely — "or anything."

"I was wondering when you'd get to that," answered Farragut. "Clues." He reached into his coat pocket and pulled out a white envelope. "Here are your clues. All neatly wrapped."

He threw onto the table a letter-size white envelope. Scrawled on its back was a series of numbers: 3.14.

Prichard examined the numbers. "Excuse me," he said, getting to his feet. He walked quickly to a corner of the research room. There he paused for a moment, then went out through the door.

A little over ten minutes later, he returned, shaking his head morosely.

"Where in blazes have you been?" asked King. "Now we only have about forty-five minutes."

"I figured that number might represent the Dewey system of book cataloguing," said Prichard, catching his breath. "But it didn't. We've got no books numbered 3.14. The nearest I could come in the file cards was a pamphlet listing government agencies. But then I thought the decimal might have been a red herring, so I tried 314."

"And — " said King expectantly.

"Nothing. Just one book on educational statistics."

"Ten minutes for that?"

Prichard shook his head. "I had another thought. That number — 3.14 — is what they call pi in mathematics."

"Pie?"

"Yes, sir. It has something to do with circles. So I checked the sections in the catalogue on pure and applied sciences, mathematics in particular. Quite a few cards to look through. Then, thinking it might be the other kind of pie, I looked through all our cards on cookbooks."

"You didn't take any book off the shelves, did you?" asked Farragut sharply.

"No, sir."

"Good tries, all of them, though," said King. "I'm impressed — Deacon didn't make a mistake assigning you to me. That pi business would have escaped me completely. Well, we still have nearly three-quarters of an hour, till four o'clock sharp. And two other clues."

He reached into the envelope, removed a small white card, and flipped it to Prichard. One side was black. The other side had two words neatly printed in pencil: *double dozen*.

While Prichard examined the card, King handed him a second one. It was similar to the first, except that its message read: *Maltese falcon*.

Prichard tried to recall every book he'd ever heard of with either "double" or "dozen" in its title.

While King went to the card catalogue to check those two words, Prichard ran down all references to either Malta or falconry. Thirty minutes later, with nothing to show for their labors, they returned to the table, where Farragut was waiting — and grinning.

"You're perspiring, Andrew," he said with a chuckle. "Is it the physical exertion, or just nervousness at the idea of losing to me?"

"Edmund, you've been smirking at me like that for nearly fifty years. But this time I'll win, I swear it."

"Only fifteen minutes to go."

"Yes, well." King turned to Prichard, his face drooping. "What about it?" he asked. "Can you make anything out of these so-called clues?"

"I — I think the mistake we've been making is to take the three clues one at a time," said Prichard. "They must all hang together in some way. Two false clues and only one real one would be downright unfair."

"All right." King arranged the cards and their envelope in front of him. "Pi," he said. "Then *double dozen*. And finally *Maltese falcon*. I don't know what to make of them."

"Give up, Andrew?" asked Farragut.

"Oh, I suppose we might as well — "

"Wait a minute, please." Prichard reached across the table and slid the clue cards and envelope closer. "These don't have to stay in the same order, you know." He arranged the cards and envelope in various ways, each time shaking his head.

"You know, I like Mr. Prichard's style better than yours, Andrew," said Farragut. "He keeps going. What would your hardboiled detectives think if they saw you giving up so easily? Just remember, Mr. Prichard: things aren't always what they seem."

Prichard, who had only been half listening, suddenly looked up and stared at Farragut, then swiveled toward King.

"How much more time?" he asked.

"About seven minutes. Why?"

Prichard pointed at the envelope. "Three point one four," he said. "That's pi. Now what's a double dozen?"

"Twenty-four," replied King. "So what?"

"I think I see a little light at the end of the tunnel," said Prichard. "Mr. Farragut just said that things aren't always what they seem. He thought he was being clever and sneaking something past us, but it was a new clue. Isn't that right, Mr. Farragut?"

For the first time, the little man in black didn't seem so sure of himself.

"We've got three clues," Prichard went on, "each saying a thing one way that could be said another. Three point one four is pi. And a double dozen is twenty-four. Now who's to say the other card doesn't do the same thing?"

"*Maltese falcon*," muttered King. "It's a book, that's all."

"No, Mr. King," said Prichard, his voice rising in excitement. "Look, the word *falcon* doesn't start with a capital letter. So either Mr. Farragut made a mistake — which I doubt — or he wasn't thinking about the book but the bird itself."

"That sounds reasonable," said King. "Keep talking."

"It seems to me that Mr. Farragut must have read *The Maltese Falcon* at some time, even if he didn't like it too well. I mean, he had it in his collection, didn't he?"

"I've read it," Farragut admitted grudgingly.

"Yes, so the *Maltese falcon* card must be connected with the story in some way. Now, I've been giving a little thought to the falcon — small f — in Hammett's book. That falcon was supposed to be a gold statue covered with jewels that Kasper Gutman and Joel Cairo wanted Sam Spade to help them find. According to Gutman, the fat man, the Knights of Rhodes had the statue made and sent to the Spanish king as a kind of reward for allowing them to live on Malta some time in the fifteen hundreds. But while it was being taken to the king, the bird was captured by pirates. It got passed from one person to another for a couple of hundred years, and during that time it was dunked in black paint to disguise what it was really worth."

"The man's uncanny," said Farragut to King.

"Because of the black covering," Prichard went on, "Spade and several other characters gave the statue a kind of nickname."

"Sure," said King. "The black bird."

Again Prichard shuffled the cards and envelope. Finally

satisfied, he took a pencil from his pocket and scribbled on the envelope, then on each of the cards in turn. Then he rose from his chair.

"C'mon," he said. "I know where to find the book."

Two minutes later, they came to the bottom of the stairs that led to the basement. "But this is the children's section," said King. "Farragut wouldn't hide one of Hammett's books here. It would stand out like a sore thumb."

"Oh?" Prichard nodded at Farragut. "Take a look at his face and tell me I'm wrong. He looks as worried as a basset hound with fallen arches."

Prichard moved among the shelves, peering intently at the books. "*The Maltese Falcon* is on a shelf, according to him," he said to King. "But he wouldn't admit that it's in plain sight. Therefore, there must be a wrapper or dust jacket on it, from another book."

He ran his fingers along a line of books, all but one of which had no jackets, and finally pointed to the exception, a book with a blue-paper covering. The spine of the jacket had a picture of Humpty Dumpty. Carefully, he leaned over to examine the top of the book.

"It seems a little small for its jacket," said Prichard. "You'd almost think the two weren't made to fit together." He reached out, grasped the book, and jerked it free of the shelf.

"There, Mr. Farragut," he said. "That's the book you hid."

On the wall, the clock clicked loudly, and the minute hand pointed straight up. Four o'clock.

King took the book and, with trembling hands, slid it out of its ill-fitting paper jacket covered with nursery-rhyme characters. He leafed through the pages and then looked wide-eyed at Prichard. "This is it!" he whispered in awed tones. "A first edition of *The Maltese Falcon*." He turned to Farragut.

"I've won, Edmund." King's voice trembled with excitement. "Your collection belongs to the library. At last I've gotten the best of you."

"Oh, I suppose so," replied Farragut testily. "But I still stick to my opinion of your choice of detective stories. After all, it was Mr. Prichard here who did all the detective work."

"It really wasn't — " Prichard began.

"No, it's true, Mr. Prichard," said King. "And I'm eternally grateful. But would you mind telling me how you figured it out? Why here in the children's section, of all places?"

"It was in the three clues," smiled Prichard. "Three point one four equals pi. And *Maltese falcon* is black bird. And *double dozen* is twenty-four."

He took the cards and envelope from his pocket and arranged them on a table. King read them aloud as Prichard had rewritten them.

"Four and twenty ... black bird ... pi."

"Not quite," said Prichard. "Remember, pi was written on the envelope. And the cards were in the envelope."

"All right, then, four and twenty ... black bird ... in pi. Of course! The old nursery rhyme: 'Sing a song of sixpence, a pocket full of rye, four-and-twenty blackbirds baked in a pie!'"

Prichard pantomimed withdrawing the book from the false jacket and took up the chant: "'When the pie was opened, the birds began to sing.'" He pointed to the book in Andrew King's hand and concluded the poem: "'Now wasn't that a dainty dish to set before the king?'"

Andrew King applauded heartily. Farragut remained stolidly silent.

"Naturally, when I spotted this book jacket I figured I'd found what we were looking for," added Prichard. "Especially when I saw that the book didn't fit the jacket."

"*Sing a Song of Sixpence, and Other Childhood Poems*," read King from the paper jacket. "Of course, this had to be it — the only nursery-rhyme book with a jacket. A superb bit of deduction, Mr. Prichard."

"Andrew," said Farragut drily, "I'm attaching another condition to your acquisition of my mystery collection."

"No fair, Edmund." King waved an admonishing finger.

"No, I think you'll like this one. A collection as valuable as mine needs someone to take care of it. And I insist that you appoint Mr. Prichard here. At a whacking good increase in salary, of course. A man of his talents ought to be put to better use than just shoving books onto shelves. And who knows? Maybe he can even get you interested in the truly great detective-story writers. Doyle, Christie, Sayers — "

" — Hammett, Chandler, Macdonald," countered King.

As the litany of names droned on, Prichard silently backed out of the room. Hardboiled stories or the classical "great detective" variety? Which were better? He didn't care to argue the point.

He liked 'em all.

THE MAN WHO READ GEORGES SIMENON

With a hiss of air from its brakes, the gigantic tractor-trailer rig with LINTEN VAN LINES emblazoned across each side in brilliant orange came to a stop at the edge of the narrow road. The driver was a hulk of a man whose lumpy, battered face resembled a culturally deprived beanbag. He took a last drag on his cigarette, then threw the butt out the window.

"I think this is the place, Barney," he said. "Only I don't see no house. Just that fancy sign with Bannering's name on it on the post next to the driveway."

His companion, short and wiry, closed the book he had been reading. He brushed a lock of flaming red hair back into place and regarded the driver through watery blue eyes.

"You ain't gonna see no houses along this stretch, Harold," he said. "This here's rich-people country. And rich people build their houses back from the road, so's they don't have to watch the traffic go by. Just go on up the driveway there and lemme get back to my reading."

There was a grinding of gears as Harold shifted into low. "Barney," he said, revving the motor, "how come you're always readin' them books when you ain't driving? I mean, the guys on the other runs talk about girls and sports and things, but all you do when I'm at the wheel is read them dumb books."

Barney looked at the cover of his book as if seeing it for the first time. "This book ain't dumb," he replied. "It's about one very smart cookie. A detective. Maigret's his moniker."

"Maigret, huh? That's a funny name, 'specially for a detective."

"He's a Frenchman, stupid. And he's really got brains. 'Course I feel sorry for him in some of the stories. His feet are always hurting, or he gets wet from standing in the rain. Not like some of these detectives in books who act like they're Superman. But he sure does know what makes people tick. He solves a lot of his crimes more by knowing how people act than by putting a lot of clues together."

"A lot of his crimes?" Harold glanced at Barney. "How many books are there about this guy?"

"I dunno. I read a couple dozen of 'em already. I figure if you do your share of the driving I ought to be finished with this one by the time we dump this load and make the trip back to Jersey. It's real good. *Maigret's Boyhood Friend*, it's called. Y'know, Maigret's the only detective I heard of who ever was a kid. All the rest of 'em — "

"There's the house," Harold interrupted. "Looks like a castle through the trees, don't it?"

"Yeah. I wonder what you gotta do to get the bread to buy a place like that." Barney closed the book and put it on the sleeping compartment behind the seat.

Harold parked the rig expertly, so its rear doors were next to the marble steps of the house. "I'll go see if this Lightfoot Larry guy we're supposed to meet is around," said Barney, opening the door and climbing down. "If not, we're gonna have to take the load back, because he's got the only key to the padlock on the trailer doors."

He went up the steps and pressed the doorbell. He could hear the chimes ringing inside. Moments later, the door was opened by a man with an athlete's wide shoulders and narrow hips. The man wore a green corduroy jacket with large pockets and tight brown trousers; the legs of the trousers were tucked into oversize bright-red cowboy boots onto which had been stitched pieces of colored leather — irregular shapes of yellow and orange, turquoise green, electric blue — to form a brilliant design.

Expensive, thought Barney. Just like everything else about this place.

"You gotta be Lightfoot Larry Schofield," Barney said. "Mr. Bannering said I'd recognize you from the cowboy boots."

"That's me," said the man. "I just got here a little while ago myself. The bus was late, and then I couldn't find a taxi from town. Had to walk the whole way — almost two miles."

"Things are tough all over," shrugged Barney. He looked curiously at Schofield's left jacket pocket. "You packin' a rod?" he asked.

"Of course I am. That truck of yours contains the entire Maurice Bannering art collection. When Mr. Bannering bought this place, he asked me to come on ahead to see that his collection got here safely and that nothing happened to it. Suppose someone broke in here after the objects were delivered? My orders are to protect these things until Mr.

Bannering arrives, and that's what I intend to do."

"Okay, Schofield, okay," said Barney, holding up his hands in a gesture of peace. "Keep your shirt on. We're bonded drivers, and this load is insured to the hilt. We're just making a delivery. We don't plan on stealin' nothing. Now how about coming out and unlocking the rig for us?"

Schofield reached into a pocket and brought out a key, which he tossed to Barney. "Do it yourselves. You were hired to do the unloading. And wipe your shoes before you come inside. The whole house has just had very expensive carpeting laid down, and I don't want to see your dirty footprints on it when you're finished."

Barney returned to the rig and motioned Harold to get out. "That Schofield's a real charmer," he said, unsnapping the heavy padlock on the rear doors. "Wipe your shoes, he says, like I ain't never carted nothing into nobody's house before. Ah, maybe he's just nervous because he's responsible for all them high-priced pictures and statues and junk we brought."

On his first trip into the house, Harold carried a flat object, which had been carefully crated. As he entered, the crate banged loudly against the side of the doorway.

"You imbecile!" Schofield yelled. "Unpack it at once, so I can see if you've damaged it."

Harold brought a hammer from the toolbox under the seat and, with a screeching of nails and rustling of excelsior, released the object from its wooden case. "It ain't even scratched," he said. "Besides, it's just a picture. Not very good, at that. A line here and a blotch of color there. My kid paints better pictures than that."

"That, my good man, is a genuine Miró," replied Schofield. "If it had been harmed, you'd have spent the rest of your life paying for it. Now please be more careful. The jade pieces in particular are very fragile."

The next item, a large painting, was brought in without incident, Barney and Harold carrying it between them.

"Put the larger things in there," said Schofield, pointing toward a room off the magnificent entrance hall. "The painter has been working in there, so don't kick over any of his cans."

Mumbling unprintables under his breath, Barney led Harold into the indicated room. They set the crate gently on the floor and flexed aching fingers.

"Heavy," said Harold.

"Yeah." Barney considered the room's opposite wall, in front of which lay a wild disarray of drop cloths, paint cans, and stained rags. "Hey, look. Don't that seem funny to you?"

"Nah, I kind of like yellow."

"No, I mean the way the painter's doin' it. He quit right in the middle of the wall."

Schofield appeared in the doorway. "You two are being paid to unload a truck," he said. "Not to comment on the décor."

"I was Mr. Bannering, I'd get somebody else to do this room," said Barney. "Any painter worth his salt quits at a corner or an edge somewhere. Like this, when he starts up again you'll have a lap mark where the new paint dries over the stuff already on the wall."

"That's none of your concern. Just get back to unloading the truck."

"Okay. But when Mr. Bannering gets here, you tell him Barney Joplin says he's bein' gypped on the paint job."

As they left the room, Harold padded across the thick carpeting with exaggerated steps, like a child feeling sand underfoot for the first time. "Geez, it's like walkin' on sponges," he said with a broad smile. "How much you figure it cost to have the whole house done this way, Barney?"

"You couldn't afford it," came the answer. "This is rich-people carpet. C'mon, let's get back to work."

For the next two hours, the men unloaded the truck, with Schofield standing just inside the doorway with a clipboard full of papers, checking each crate as it went past him. Finally, the trailer — as large as a small house — was empty.

"I'll sign the delivery slip now," said Schofield to a perspiring Barney. "Then you two can be on your way."

"Now just a second," said Barney. "Maybe you don't know it, but me and Harold have been working damn hard to get this stuff in here. And you weren't much help, just hanging around inside with a wad of papers all the time. Would it break your heart to give us a beer and let us sit in a soft chair for a few minutes and grab a rest?" He looked about the room, which was empty except for the crates from the truck. "I'd even settle for a lie-down on that nice soft rug, seein' as the furniture ain't arrived yet."

"Well, I — " Schofield paused, then shrugged. "I can't do anything about the beer," he said at last. "There's none in the house. However, there's some old furniture in the den that the previous owner left. You can rest there, I suppose. But I'll have to keep an eye on you."

"Fine. C'mon, Harold. The beer can wait till we get back on the road."

Schofield led them to the den, where Harold flopped down on an old leather couch and Barney took an easy chair, stretching his feet with a groan of contentment. Schofield himself sat bolt upright in an upholstered chair large enough to have been a throne. Barney kicked a footstool toward him, but Schofield ignored it.

"What kind of training you need before somebody like Bannering hires you to guard his stuff?" asked Barney.

"Let's just say I could kill you with my bare hands with no effort at all," answered Schofield. "And if your partner tried anything, he'd be dead with a bullet between the eyes before he got his feet off the couch and onto the floor."

"Yeah, Mr. Bannering told us you weren't a guy to mess around with," said Barney. "Well, we ain't gonna try and steal any of his precious pictures and stuff. So relax, Mr. Schofield. Put your feet up, and let's get a closer look at them famous cowboy boots of yours."

Schofield shook his head, keeping his feet planted firmly on the floor.

"Barney, maybe we oughta get goin'," said Harold. "We want to make Jersey by tomorrow night, we can't sit around here too much longer."

"Just a little while more," said Barney. "Y'know, I'm beginnin' to feel just the way Maigret does in the stories."

"Maigret? And who might that be?" asked Schofield.

"He's an inspector with the Paris police," answered Barney. "This guy named Georges Simenon writes books about him. I started readin' them because — well, they were about France and all. The Bronx ain't too exotic a place to come from, if you know what I mean."

"But you said you was beginning to feel like him," said Harold. "What do you mean?"

"Well, Maigret ain't always so sure that what seems to have happened in a crime is what really did happen. All you gotta do is read *Maigret Hesitates* or *Maigret's Mistake* to see that. And I got a hunch we'd be making a bad mistake if we left this house right now."

"Don't worry," said Schofield. "I'm quite capable of guarding this place until Mr. Bannering and his staff arrive."

"I bet you are. Man, I wish you'd relax, Mr. Schofield. You ain't shifted position since we sat down here."

"I'll be happy to see you to the door at any time you say. Or do you insist on continuing with this Maigret business?"

"Yeah, I think I will," said Barney, crossing his legs. He reached into a cardboard box beside his chair and removed a glass paperweight in which a glittering stone was embedded. "I ever tell you I used to pitch on a baseball team, Mr. Schofield? Oh, it was only semi-pro, but I was good, real good. Fact is, I think I could bounce this thing off your noggin before you made the first move toward that gun in your jacket pocket. Harold, go over and take that thing away from him before it goes off and hurts somebody."

Harold gave Barney an odd glance but hauled himself up from the sofa, then walked to Schofield's chair. He half expected Schofield to strike out at him, but the man remained still, his eyes flashing angrily. Gingerly, Harold removed the .38 revolver from his pocket.

"Okay, Harold, now sit down and keep that thing aimed at him. I don't think Mr. Schofield here is as good at fighting as he says he is, but let's not take no chances. I wouldn't get out of that chair if I was you, Mr. Schofield. Harold is very nervous around guns, and there's no tellin' what he'll do if you was to get him excited."

"I have no intention of moving," said Schofield. "If you're going to steal the pictures, go ahead. Although why you didn't just drive off when you had them in the truck, I –"

"Come off it, Schofield. We ain't gonna steal nothing. We was just talkin' about Inspector Maigret, remember?"

"Well, what about him?"

"I was sayin' to Harold earlier, Maigret don't spend all his time goin' around scraping clues into little envelopes, the way Sherlock Holmes and them other detectives do. He understands people and the way they think and feel. That's the way he solves his crimes. Like now, Mr. Schofield, the sweat's pouring off you like a fountain. So I know you're scared. See what I mean? You know, in *Maigret and the Burglar's Wife* there's a part where – "

"Cut to the chase, sir. You'd be scared too, with a pistol pointed at you. And if you're not after the paintings, would you mind telling me what all this talk about crimes and detectives is about?"

"Sure. Two days ago, Maurice Bannering talked to us personally before he shipped them pictures and things. He told us we'd be met here by a man he called Lightfoot Larry Schofield. Said we'd know him at a glance because he'd be wearing these wild-looking cowboy boots. Said they were kind of his trademark."

"Well, that's me. So what?"

"The thing is, he never showed us no photo of Lightfoot Larry or nothin'. All we had to go on was the boots."

"Look, give me a few days, and I'll send you a hundred photographs. All autographed."

"If I'm right in what I'm thinking, you'd be signing the wrong name even if you was to make good on the pictures. Y'see, I dunno who you are. But the one person I think you're not is Lightfoot Larry Schofield."

Harold almost dropped the pistol. "Barney," he said, "you gone nuts or something?"

"I don't think so, Harold. What about his name, Lightfoot Larry? Your feet are about as big as a couple of rowboats, Mr. Schofield or whoever you are. You don't look like no lightfoot to me."

"The name refers to my boots, not my feet. Bright leather — therefore Lightfoot."

"That's pretty clever," said Barney. "I never thought of that. But then there's the paint job in the other room."

"What about it?"

"Like I said, no real painter who knew his business would stop in the middle of a wall that way. But let's say it wasn't a painter, but somebody who wanted to get into this house while the real Lightfoot Larry was here. One man alone couldn't force his way in. Schofield, from what Mr. Bannering said, would have broke him in two. But if a 'painter' showed up at the door, complete with buckets and drop cloths — at a house the owner hadn't even moved into yet — Schofield would let him in without a suspicion in the world. The man would have to start painting, of course, to make his disguise look real. But he'd stop painting soon as he saw a chance to hit Schofield over the head when he wasn't looking.

"Now, if things happened that way, it wouldn't be too hard for the 'painter' to tie up the real Schofield and stash him in a closet somewhere. Then he could put on Schofield's clothes, and when us dumb drivers showed up with the paintings, he could see 'em all delivered and then, when the truck was gone, he'd have all the time in the world to get them out of here."

"I find your theory absolutely ridiculous," came the reply. "So now, to prove myself innocent, I suppose you want me either to let you search the whole house for the man I'm supposed to be impersonating or else allow you to hold me at gunpoint for a couple of days, until Mr. Bannering arrives from halfway across the country to identify me. No way, Mr. Barney Joplin. You tell your friend there to give me back my gun and get the hell out of here. Otherwise, I'm going to call the police right now and have a good laugh as they cart you off to the loony bin."

Barney shook his head. "I'm probably way out of line treating you this way, Mr. Schofield. And if I'm wrong about what I said, I wouldn't blame you for being plenty sore. But me and Maigret, we're great ones for wondering why people act in a certain way. Like right now, I'm wondering why you don't move around much. You don't cross your legs or put your feet up on a stool or nothin'. You just sit there like there was a poker up your back, even though that easy chair just begs to be snuggled in. And you was acting that way before Harold took your gun, so he ain't the reason. It must be somethin' else, huh?"

"Why, I — "

"Y'see, it seems to me that, if you was to cook up this little scheme, the one item belonging to the real Lightfoot Larry Schofield you couldn't wear would be his boots. There ain't too many men around with feet as big as yours. You'd have to buy a pair just like his, with all that fancy stitching, to make your plan work. It wouldn't have been hard to smuggle 'em in with the painting equipment and put 'em on after you slugged the real Schofield.

"But if the boots was brand-new — bought for this occasion — the only place you'd have walked in 'em would be on the carpets inside this house. You didn't even go outside to help us open the truck. So the boots would still have shiny leather on the bottoms. On the other hand, if you're really Schofield, and you walked a couple of miles out here from town like you said, the soles would be all scuffed up.

"So there you are, Mr. Schofield or whoever. I think you've kept the bottoms of those boots flat on the carpet so we couldn't get a look at 'em and see how shiny they are. If you'd put your feet up on the stool or even crossed your legs, you'd've given your whole game away. So we ain't got to wait for Mr. Bannering to see if you're the real McCoy or not. Just put your feet up on the footstool there while we take a gander at the soles of your boots. If they're scuffed, we'll be on our way. But if they're shiny, you got a lot of explainin' to do."

Barney shoved the footstool in front of the seated man. "Up with the feet," he said. "Harold, he makes one false move, shoot him anywhere you think it'll do the most good."

Slowly, first one boot and then the other were raised and settled on the footstool.

Harold could almost see his own reflection in the gleaming boot soles.

you shoot him anywhere you think it'll do the most good."

Slowly, first one boot and then the other were raised and settled on the footstool.

Harold could almost see his own reflection in the gleaming boot soles.

Several hours and many telephone calls later, the police had identified the fake Schofield as Willie Needleman, a former employee of Bannerman's who had been dismissed for dipping into the petty cash. They found the real Schofield trussed up in a closet on the second floor. Two policemen were left to guard the art treasures until Bannerman could make his own arrangements for protecting them. And the tractor-trailer rig was cruising back toward New Jersey with Harold at the wheel.

From time to time he glanced at Barney, who was again reading Maigret's adventures with rapt concentration. But now Barney was making motions with his free hand which, to say the least, were puzzling.

In spite of the fact that Barney was bareheaded and had nothing in his mouth, he seemed to be adjusting a hat and curving his fingers around the bowl of a pipe.

THE GIRL WHO READ
JOHN CREASEY

Stiffly, Emil Pratt hitched himself out of his car and plodded up the side steps to his house. His mind was groggy, and his feet ached with every step he took. These double tours of duty were getting to be too much for him. He'd ask the captain for some kind of desk job once the Dawkins case was closed.

If it ever was closed.

He opened the side door and entered the kitchen. Warmth, and the smell of frying chicken. With a little sigh, he sagged into a chair.

"Oh, Emil, you look exhausted," said his wife Dorothy, who was standing at the stove. "Supper will be on the table soon, honey. Marilee, come take your father's coat and hang it up."

"In a minute, Mom," said a voice from the living room.

"Please, Marilee. You can finish your book after supper."

"Okay, Mom. Whatever you say." Fifteen-year-old Marilee Pratt shuffled into the kitchen. She wore one of her father's old white shirts, tucked into faded blue jeans, on one knee of which was a large patch with the words: *If at first you do succeed, try hard to hide your astonishment.* On her feet were furry white slippers, which looked to her father like a couple of dead rabbits. With one hand, she was holding a book open in front of her face; in the other hand was an apple, which disappeared behind the book from time to time, with appropriate munching sounds.

Emil shucked off his coat and draped it over one of his daughter's arms. "Want me to take your gun, too?" asked Marilee, nodding at the holster on Emil's belt.

"Naw, I just want to eat and then get some shuteye," said Emil. "I gotta be back first thing in the morning."

"You've hardly been home all week, Emil." Dorothy Pratt's eyes mirrored her concern for her husband. "How long can you go on like this?"

"Until we break the Dawkins case," Emil answered. "And it isn't only us at the precinct, honey. Homicide's been working just as hard today, explaining things to some guy from the British Consulate. Hell, why couldn't Fred Dawkins at least have been a US citizen?"

"Supper's ready, Marilee!" called Dorothy. "Come on, don't keep your father waiting."

Again Marilee entered the kitchen, still holding the book. "Let's make a deal," said Dorothy. "If you don't spend suppertime reading, you won't have to help with the dishes."

"Gee, Mom, I'm right at the good part! Besides, I won't have time to help with the dishes, anyway. I've got to finish the book for an assignment at school. We have to read something in which the setting is important and do a paper on the city where the story takes place."

"And you left it until the last minute as usual, I suppose?" said Emil with a smile.

"Well," said Marilee slowly, "it was due this morning. But I got a one-day extension from Mr. Budwick. You two go ahead and talk. I'll listen while I'm reading."

"Who can argue with logic like that?" laughed her father.

"But you're so seldom here for meals lately, Emil," said Dorothy.

"Oh, let her read. I'm too tired to care, anyway." He peered at the book's jacket. "*Gideon's Staff*," he read slowly, "by J.J. Marric. Is it something about the Bible, darlin'?"

"No, Daddy, it's about a detective named George Gideon — G.G. to his friends. He's commander of Scotland Yard's Criminal Investigation Department in London. He does all kinds of real neat things. Right now, he's investigating four murders — including two policemen — and a man who's going to blow himself up with nitroglycerin. It's a lot more exciting than real-life detective work, I bet."

"Oh?" Emil's expression registered mock surprise. "And what does that make me?"

Tears sprang to Marilee's eyes. "Daddy, I — I didn't — "

"It's all right," said Emil soothingly. "A lot of what we do at the precinct isn't very exciting. But your author — Marric — sounds European. What's he doing writing about London?"

"Oh, Marric's just a pen name. His real name's John Creasey, and he's written tons of books. So he uses a lot of different names." She paused, and her lower lip began to quiver. "I really didn't mean it, about what you do at work," she went on. "It's just that — well, when people find out my father's a detective, they want to hear something exciting about you. But you spend so much time just asking questions and making out reports."

"Well, I'm working on a case now that your friends might find pretty exciting," said Emil. "It's a murder. You've probably read about it in the papers. Fred Dawkins."

"Murder?" Marilee Pratt looked enraptured. "Tell us about it, Daddy. Please?"

"Don't you have that assignment to do?"

"Oh, I've already read up on the background — London, I mean."

"Marilee, your father's tired," said Dorothy.

"That's all right," said Emil indulgently. "But I wish I had your man Gideon working on this one, darlin'. You see, Fred Dawkins was a British subject. Born in London, practically across the street from the Bank of England."

"Then he's a real Cockney," said Marilee.

"Huh?"

"St. Mary-le-Bow Church is in that part of the city," the girl said. "So this man Dawkins was born within hearing of the Bow Bells. And that's what makes a real Cockney."

"It does, eh? Where'd you find that out?"

"It's for the assignment. The one about Commander Gideon. I've done a lot of studying about London. But go on, Daddy. Tell about the murder."

"Well, a few weeks ago, Dawkins apparently won some kind of a football pool in England and came into a lot of money. About twelve hundred pounds, whatever that comes to."

"Around three thousand dollars," said Marilee.

"Uh huh. So, being single with no family, he decided to take a trip to the States. First stop, New York City. He got a room at the Parkleigh Hotel, right in the center of town. Then he did a damfool thing."

"Emil, such language in front of your daughter," said Dorothy.

"That's okay, Mom. Go on, Daddy. What was the damfool thing Mr. Dawkins did?"

"He got all his prize money converted into cash — American dollars."

"Why did he do that?" asked Dorothy.

"Seems he didn't trust banks. Never had enough money to have an account before he won the pool. And, once he got to New York, he had a yen to see all his winnings in cash."

"How'd you find that out?" asked Marilee. "I mean, if Dawkins was murdered — "

"The bellhop who serviced Dawkins' room told us. A little old guy named Paul Kipps — he comes from England, too.

The two of 'em struck up quite an acquaintance, as soon as Dawkins found out Kipps was a countryman and could get him a bottle of real English stout whenever he wanted one. The first day there, Dawkins told Kipps practically his whole life history."

For a moment, Emil was silent, chewing a forkful of salad. "Poor Kipps," he continued finally. "He's the one who found Dawkins' body. Beside the bed, with a knife in it. When I first saw Kipps, I thought he was going to start crying. Of course I don't know which he missed most, Dawkins himself or the big tips he handed out."

"Oh, Emil," said Dorothy, "I don't like all this talk about murder while we're eating."

"Go on, Daddy," said Marilee. "Please."

"Well, I took the call from the officer on the beat after Kipps reported finding the body. Both Kipps and the officer met me out front when I got to the Parkleigh."

"I'll bet there was a lot of excitement," said Marilee.

"You don't know New York hotels," smiled Emil. "They don't want any bad publicity. Kipps had kept his cool, so the other guests didn't know about the body. The officer took one look into the room and called me. But aside from the three of us — and the hotel manager, of course — it was business as usual at the Parkleigh. The whole thing was hushed up. A little too hushed up, as it turned out."

"What do you mean by that, Daddy?"

"When I went into the room, the body looked dead enough. But when I got down close, I could see that Dawkins was still breathing."

"You mean he was alive?" gulped Dorothy. "With a knife in him?"

"He was," nodded Emil. "Apparently Kipps took one look inside — it was night, remember, and only a single light was on — and assumed Dawkins was dead. The officer should have checked, but the fact is he didn't. Some people don't like to get too near corpses, even cops."

Dorothy, her face a bit green, cast her eyes upward. Marilee motioned impatiently for her father to continue.

"Anyway, Dawkins was still alive when I got to him. Next to him was an empty briefcase with a broken lock. I figure that's where he kept his money before his killer took it."

"Did he say anything?" asked Marilee.

"Yeah. He opened his eyes, real slow. He saw me bending over him. Then he said something that sounded like *fishin'*."

"Fishin', Daddy?"

"Yep. After that, he gulped and got out a few more words. *'Twas Ol' Fishin' as done me in*. At least, that's what it sounded like to me. But the effort of talking must have been too much for him. Blood began spilling out of his mouth, and he went limp. I yelled to the officer to get a doctor, but Dawkins died right there in my arms."

"A dying message!" exclaimed Marilee, clapping her hands enthusiastically.

"Yeah, it was a dying message, all right. One that's had me climbing the walls, ever since I heard it."

"What do you mean by that?"

"When there's been a murder, a lot of people have to be around to start the investigation. The medical examiner, laboratory technicians, homicide detectives, and so on. They were as quiet as they could be, but they still woke up just about everybody on that floor of the hotel. Since people were coming out into the hall, anyway, I used the time to ask them some questions. It seems Dawkins had gotten friendly with three other men who were staying at the hotel. As a matter of fact, the four of 'em had been in a poker game in Dawkins' room earlier that same evening."

"And you think one of them killed him?" asked Marilee.

"Has to be. They were the only ones who'd been in the room and knew he had all that money."

"Then if you can just connect one of them with fishin' — "

"It's not that easy, darlin'. The first of the three I talked to was a Rudolph Steinman. About seventy, thick glasses, almost completely bald. He was in town to visit the Cloisters. He's got a thing about medieval tapestries."

"I don't see how he could — "

"Steinman's a professor of physics up in Canada somewhere. During World War II, he was one of the brains behind the Manhattan Project — the atomic bomb thing. I'm sure he'd have told Dawkins about it."

"Nuclear fission," said Marilee softly. "Daddy, that's it. Dawkins didn't say *fishin'* — he said *fission*. Steinman did it!"

"Yeah?" Emil sank his teeth into a chicken leg. "That's what I thought at first. But Steinman told me about Dawkins' other two friends. One of 'em was John Langworthy. Sixty-two years old, nuts about opera. He spends most of his time in New York up at Lincoln Center. Runs a factory in St. Paul. And what do you think he manufactures? Yeah, fishing rods and reels."

"But that doesn't have anything to do with atomic fission," said Marilee.

"The way Dawkins was mumbling," Emil said, "I figure he might have been saying either *fishin'* or *fission*. He might have called Langworthy Ol' Fishin' — or something like it — because of the stuff he manufactures."

Marilee nodded. "But, Daddy, that's only two men. If you're sure one of them killed Dawkins, can't you have them both investigated?"

"It's not quite that easy. If we need a certain number of men to investigate one person, it takes twice as many for two. And when we add a third — "

"Emil," said his wife, "don't you think you should finish your supper and go up to bed? I'm not sure all this talk about murder is good for Marilee."

"Oh, Mother," the girl said, "I'm fine. Come on, Daddy, tell about the third man."

"A schoolteacher from New Jersey. Doing some kind of research. Most days he hangs out at the Public Library at 42nd Street and Fifth Avenue."

"Well, at least you can't suspect him," said Marilee.

"No? His name's Bass. Leland Bass. And a bass is a fish. So it's possible Dawkins called him Ol' Fishin'. You see, there's my problem. If we knew which one of the three to zero in on, we'd find the evidence soon enough. But we've had to spread our available manpower too thin, tracking down the backgrounds and movements of all three. I'm sure we'll get the killer eventually. But, in the meantime, the British government is after us for action. Langworthy's family is raising the roof because he didn't come back home when he was supposed to, and Bass is afraid that, with all the bad publicity, he might lose his job. Steinman's about the only one who's taking the investigation at all well." Emil pointed tiredly at his daughter's book. "Wish I had your Commander Gideon's help on this case."

"Do you suspect any one of them more than the others?" Marilee asked.

"At first, we were pretty sure it was Bass, the teacher. Both Steinman and Langworthy are fairly wealthy men. Three thousand dollars is a lot of money, but not enough to make either of them kill for it."

"You said at first," said Marilee. "That sounds like you're not so sure any more it's Bass."

Emil nodded glumly. "We found out Bass writes books on the side. No bestsellers, but, with his teacher's salary, he's not hurting for money. Besides, Steinman and Langworthy both agree that Dawkins probably wouldn't have called Bass

Ol' Fishin'. He had another nickname for the teacher, though heaven knows where he got it."

"What nickname?" asked Dorothy, looking better now that there was less talk of dead bodies.

Grinning broadly, her husband shook his head as if puzzled by the foibles of the world. "Bonnie," he chuckled.

"Bonnie?"

"Yep. Isn't that the craziest — "

"Oh!"

Emil and Dorothy both turned to stare at their daughter. Marilee was sitting bolt upright in her chair. Both hands were clapped over her mouth, and her eyes were big and round.

"Are you all right, darlin'?" asked Emil. "Did something go down the wrong way?"

Slowly, Marilee shook her head.

"What is it, then?"

"Daddy, I think I know who killed Mr. Dawkins."

Emil gave a roar of laughter. "So you think you're better than all of New York's Finest, do you?" he hooted.

"Not me, Daddy. Commander Gideon."

"Huh?"

"No, that's not what I mean. But you remember I told you I had to do some research on London for the paper I'm writing about *Gideon's Staff?*"

"Uh huh."

"Daddy, did you know that, in the nineteenth century, London pickpockets made up a kind of slang so the police wouldn't understand them?"

"No. But this isn't the nineteenth century. And we're not talking about London, either."

"Sure, but remember I said Mr. Dawkins was a Cockney? Well, lots of Cockneys still use that old slang. It works by rhymes. Like apples and pears means stairs. Mince pie is eye. And sky rocket is — "

"Pocket?" asked Emil.

"That's the idea, Daddy. So, if I said I'm taking a ball of chalk up the frog and toad, it means I'm taking a walk up the road. See?"

"Marilee," said Dorothy, "I don't think your father's interested in a lecture on — "

"Wait a minute," said Emil, waving his wife into silence. "Go on, Marilee."

"Finally, the Cockneys got so used to the slang they could make it shorter. So I'm taking a ball up the frog would still mean a walk up the road."

"And what's that got to do with the case I'm working on?"

"Oh, Daddy, Mr. Dawkins was a Cockney, and he called Mr. Bass Bonnie. What would that be in rhyming slang?"

"I haven't the slightest idea."

"Bonnie lass, that's what. Mr. Dawkins' name for the teacher was Bonnie, because bonnie lass rhymes with Bass."

"Okay," said Emil. "And what's the connection between that and what Dawkins told me — Ol' Fishin'?"

"Daddy, your suspect has to be old, right?"

"I suppose so. But that applies to all three of them."

"Yes, but he also has to be someone who'd been in Dawkins' hotel room and had seen the money. Someone who might have needed that money enough to kill for it."

"Thanks a lot. All three men were in the room that evening. And needing the money eliminates everyone."

"No, it doesn't." Marilee's eyes glittered with excitement. "You heard Mr. Dawkins say Ol' Fishin', but he might have been saying something else."

"What's that?"

Marilee paused dramatically. "Ol' fish an' — "

For a moment, Emil Pratt wrinkled his brow thoughtfully. Then suddenly he stared at Marilee. He sprang from his chair, rounded the table, and hugged his daughter in his huge arms. "You're wonderful!" he cried. "Your research paper is wonderful! Even your Commander Gideon is wonderful!"

Dorothy Pratt, who had failed to make heads or tails of the conversation between her daughter and her husband, began picking up the dishes from the table and piling them in the sink. "My family are all wonderful," she said positively. "But I still don't get it."

"Dawkins wasn't talking about fission or fishin'." Emil was shouting and laughing at the same time. "He was using rhyming slang. And he was giving me the nickname he'd pinned on his murderer. A term dear to the heart of every Cockney."

"Oh?" said Dorothy, looking puzzled. "What?"

"Chips! Fish and chips! Don't you see, honey? It wasn't any of the three guests who stabbed Dawkins. It was that little old bellhop who told us he discovered Dawkins' body: Paul Kipps!"

THE MEN WHO READ ISAAC ASIMOV

"I called you here today to see if we could agree among ourselves on a sequence of five numbers." Paul Haskill, the local history teacher, got to his feet, his chair scraping against the bare floorboards of the Merry Tinker Tavern. "But before formally presenting our guest, I think I should explain to him that the sole purpose of our little group is to emulate as far as possible an assemblage of men who exist only in the imagination and writings of Dr. Isaac Asimov."

Edgar Varsey, who'd come to Holcomb Mills to write a story for his newspaper, the *Times-Herald*, looked up quizzically at Haskill. His pencil was poised over the notebook in which he had been jotting impressions of the tavern and its occupants.

"Who?" the reporter asked.

"Asimov. That scientist fella who does all the writing." The voice of Jasper Zimmerman, a linesman for the Holcomb Mills Telephone Company, reminded Varsey of the chattering of a squirrel. There was nothing squirrel-like, however, about the other two men at the table. Gabriel Doone, the blacksmith, was huge, with muscles that bunched and rippled under his sweat-stained work shirt. And portly Sidney Warwick was the image of small-town respectability, as befitted his position as president of the Holcomb Mills National Bank.

"A lot of Asimov's material is about science," said Haskill. "Several of his books are standard references over at our school."

"He's written about history, too," Zimmerman put in.

"And mathematics." Numbers, especially as they related to money, were never far from the thoughts of banker Warwick.

"He writes good stories," rumbled Doone. "With rockets and robots and all kinds of exciting things. Better'n television."

Poetry, mythology, the Bible ... the men tossed subjects at the astounded Varsey like verbal baseballs being peppered around a conversational infield until the reporter shook his head in dismay. "You mean one man has turned out all that?"

Haskill nodded. "Asimov's output is incredible."

"Not so," Zimmerman grinned. "All anyone would need is the ability to use both hands and both feet to keep four typewriters goin' at the same time."

"The Black Widowers, however, are of special interest to us." Haskill indicated Doone, Warwick, Zimmerman, and himself.

"The Black what?" asked Varsey.

"In addition to his other works," Haskill explained, "Dr. Asimov has written a series of detective short stories. They concern a club called the Black Widowers — a group of men, most of whom have out-of-the-ordinary occupations, who meet monthly. At each meeting, an invited guest is asked to pose a problem. The Black Widowers then attempt to solve it through a discussion that is carried on while postprandial drinks are served."

He turned toward the bar at the far end of the room. "And, speaking of drinks, the sun's over the yardarm and I could use one. Anybody else?"

There was a chorus of assent from around the table.

"Findlay!" Haskill shouted. "A round for us here. Bourbon is traditional, Mr. Varsey. Okay with you?"

The reporter nodded. "Tell me more about the Black Widowers and you four," he said.

"It's five, including Findlay," said Haskill. "While talking here one day we found that we all shared an interest in the Black Widower stories. So we decided to meet from time to time, to solve problems just as they do."

"And how many problems have you solved?" asked Varsey.

The table was enveloped in sudden silence. Finally, Doone cleared his throat. "You're the first, Mr. Varsey."

"Not much happens in a village like Holcomb Mills," added Warwick.

"We daydream a lot," Zimmerman mumbled.

The drinks arrived, carried by an astonishingly agile old man dressed in black, who put Varsey in mind of a cricket. "This is Findlay," said Warwick, "the proprietor of the Merry Tinker and a charter member of our little group. He seldom offers an opinion, but, when he does, he makes incredibly good sense."

"Verra fine o' ye tae say that, Mr. Warwick," said the elfin Findlay, in accents reminiscent of plaid kilts, bagpipes, and heather. He passed out the drinks with spasmodic jerks of his hands, then returned to his place behind the bar.

Paul Haskill sipped from his glass and then rubbed his hands together expectantly. "Now, then, Mr. Varsey. The problem. Pose it for us, if you please."

Varsey pocketed his notebook and got to his feet. "I guess you already know most of the background," he began.

"Go over it anyway," urged Zimmerman. "From the beginning. If we're going to be like the Black Widowers, we've got to do things right."

Varsey shrugged good-naturedly. "Okay, here goes. Just up the street here in Holcomb Mills, one of the biggest revolutions in retail selling in the country is happening: the Value Today department store. That's the story I want to get for my newspaper."

"If Value Today gets any bigger," grumbled Doone, "there won't be a parking space in town during business hours."

"Davey Lotus — formerly David Lotocetto — owns the store," the reporter went on. "He was born and grew up right here in Holcomb Mills. As a kid, he raised more hell than most, and everybody predicted he'd come to a bad end. But then, at the age of twenty-two, he got into a high-stakes poker game."

"I remember it well," sighed Warwick. "He walked away with nearly three thousand dollars — a good part of it my money."

"Yes, but, much to the surprise of the townspeople, Lotus didn't fritter away his winnings. Instead, he rented an old building that had once been the Grange Hall. Within a month, he'd painted VALUE TODAY across the front of it, installed a couple of display windows, and stocked it with merchandise, most of it obtained on credit. He sold items not usually found in a small town: the latest fashions, quality sporting goods, exotic perfumes, and such. Essentially, Lotus had created a huge department store, much too large for a village of this size.

"People laughed at him, expecting him to go bankrupt within a year. But Lotus had the last laugh. Soon customers were coming from all over the county, then the state, because of a sales gimmick he developed."

"He let folks dicker with the clerks over prices," chirped Zimmerman. "It was fun. And, for a while, we figured we was puttin' one over on ol' Davey. But he was too smart for that."

"Yes, he was," agreed Varsey. "Every item in the store had its price clearly marked. But after the price came a series of letters — for example, '$7.00 — VUY.' Most people thought it was just a shipping code or something. Then, after several months, a clerk let the cat out of the bag what those letters meant. But by that time, Lotus was well on his way to becoming a millionaire."

"The letters was really numbers," said Doone.

"Exactly. Davey Lotus used the letters of his own name, and assigned to each of them a number. D was one, A was two, V was three, and so on, right up to the final letter, S, which was zero. So '$7.00 — VUY' meant that the article cost Lotus $3.95, and between $3.95 and $7.00 the clerk was entitled to do a little bargaining. Lotus never claimed the idea was original, but he turned it into a bundle of money.

"Eventually, of course, people caught on. The resulting national publicity didn't do Value Today any harm, either — and by then Lotus was on to his next selling gimmick: a rare gold coin placed in plain sight somewhere inside the store. For weeks, people hunted, until at last it was found, glued to a display bottle of perfume, where it looked like part of the fancy label. Meanwhile, with all those people coming into the store, the cash registers were ringing merrily.

"Senior-citizen beauty contests, games, raffles — Lotus constantly promoted Value Today, and the store continued to thrive. But now he's come up with the greatest sales campaign of all."

"The safe," nodded Haskill.

"Yes," said Varsey. "An old safe that Lotus discovered in the basement of the building. The thing has a combination dial with one hundred numbers on it. Lotus set the combination and placed the safe in one of his display windows. Then he invited one and all to try and dial the correct five-number combination. The person who opens the safe door gets the thousand-dollar bill that Lotus has locked inside."

"Huh," grunted Warwick. "With a hundred numbers on the dial, the possible variations are almost endless."

"Apparently, the people lined up to try their luck don't agree with you," said Varsey. "They come in to open the safe, of course. But they're buying, gentlemen. They're also buying."

"That's the problem, then?" asked Zimmerman. "You want us to see if we can figure out the correct combination?"

"I do. My paper sent me down here to do a feature story on Lotus. One of the first people I contacted was Mr. Haskill, here. As a history teacher — as well as the village's unofficial historian — I knew he'd have all the background information."

"I also suggested that, if our group could figure out the safe's combination, it would add reader interest," said Haskill.

"A moment, please," interrupted Warwick, the banker. "We're getting into difficulties here. When the Black Widowers confront a problem, there are clues, hints, inferences that can be made. But here we're presented with nothing but a dial with a hundred numbers on it, from which we're to pick five. Unfair, Mr. Varsey."

"Not as unfair as you think," replied Varsey. "I ran into Lotus out in front of his store and mentioned that very problem."

"What did he say?" asked Doone, the blacksmith.

"He insists the numbers aren't random at all. There are clues."

"Clues?" Zimmerman sat up straighter. "Where?"

The reporter made an expansive wave of his hand. "Lotus pointed at those display windows of his. 'Right there,' he told me. I took pictures of both of them. Here, have a look."

From his pocket, the reporter produced two color photographs. "Here's the left window," he said, holding up one photo. "You can see the safe — the name Mapes etched in the door is apparently the name of the manufacturer — and the line of people. Down in front of the safe are some fake bills and coins to stress the money angle."

He held up the second photograph. "And here's the other window. You'll note the huge telephone dial with the five silk scarves draped vertically through its holes. Above it is a sign that reads, 'From White to Bright, It's a Call to Fashion.'"

"What's that over on the other side of the window?" asked Warwick.

"A series of posters on sale in the stationery department. 'Great Moments in American History.' The Revolutionary War is represented by that painting of the three marching men. Then there's Woodrow Wilson, a prospector panning for gold, Charles Lindbergh, and, finally, Babe Ruth."

Varsey placed both photographs on the table. "Well, there you have it, gentlemen. What is there in one or both of these pictures that would indicate the correct combination?"

Doone and Warwick took the picture of the safe and examined it closely. Zimmerman and Haskill showed equal interest in the scarves and posters.

Findlay was almost ignored as he brought a second round of drinks. At length, Varsey broke the silence.

"Any ideas?"

There was a murmur of assent. The four men sat back in

their chairs, each smiling confidently.

"You first, Gabriel," suggested Haskill.

The blacksmith rose ponderously. "A fine piece of metalwork, that safe." He looked about as if daring someone to contradict him.

"We all yield to your knowledge of the subject, Gabriel," said Warwick. "But get on with your theory."

"The people who made that old safe were proud of their work," Doone continued. "Carved the company name right into the steel of the door. Not just painted on or a paper label like today's products. Mapes ... a good name. An honest name."

"We agree, we agree," nodded Zimmerman, the phone-company linesman. "But what's the point you're havin' so much trouble makin'?"

"Davey Lotus has the safe in his window. Why wouldn't he have the clue to the combination right on the safe itself? Right there on the door? The combination has five numbers. The name Mapes has five letters."

"But how — ?" Warwick began.

"Let him go on, Sidney," interrupted Haskill. "I see what he's driving at."

"If we find where each of the five letters comes in the alphabet, we'll have five numbers." Doone consulted a greasy bit of paper on which he'd scribbled some notes. "Like M is the thirteenth letter. A is the first. See what I mean?"

Varsey took out his notebook and looked up expectantly at Doone. "So your idea of the combination is — ?"

He quickly wrote down the blacksmith's answer:

$$13 - 1 - 16 - 5 - 19$$

"Who's next?" the reporter asked.

"I'll go, if I may," said Warwick. "Like Gabriel, I too was interested in the window containing the safe. But, unlike him, I wasn't taken by the safe itself as much as the display of money."

"I'll bet you talk banking in your sleep, Sidney," said Zimmerman.

Warwick ignored the gibe. "The display of money includes both bills and coins. But why coins, since the money inside is said to be a thousand-dollar bill? Could there be some hidden meaning to the coins? Certainly not in the way they're displayed, just dumped in a pile." He paused dramatically.

Zimmerman groaned. "Sidney, you can say fewer things

using more words than anybody else I know."

"Scoff if you will, Jasper. But when I saw those coins, it immediately struck me that America has exactly five coins that make up fractions of a dollar: the penny, the nickel, the dime, the quarter, and the half dollar. Five coins, gentlemen – one for each number of the combination, and each with a specific numerical value. It's quite obvious that my solution is the correct one."

Edgar Varsey put Warwick's solution directly under Doone's:

$$1 - 5 - 10 - 25 - 50$$

Then, after a moment's hesitation:

$$50 - 25 - 10 - 5 - 1$$

"Mr. Zimmerman?" he said when he'd finished. "Do you agree with either Mr. Doone or Mr. Warwick?"

"It ain't just their ideas I don't agree with," said Zimmerman. "I don't even think they was lookin' at the right window. There's only one place in either window where numbers actually appear. And that's on the big telephone dial with the scarves hangin' from it."

"And you accused me of always thinking about my work," chided Warwick. "I'll just bet you were itching to string a new wire from that huge dial."

"You'll be sorry you said that when my numbers open the safe," Zimmerman commented.

"What numbers, Jasper?" asked Haskill.

"Look, the scarves are stuck through the five holes at the top of the dial – the numbers one through five. And they hang vertically, so each scarf covers a second numbered hole below. The one connects with the zero, the two with the nine, and so on. Furthermore, the right-hand scarf is white. The further left, the more colorful the scarf – until the last one, which covers the five and six – is red."

"Yeah, we can see that in the picture. But so what, Jasper?" queried Doone.

"The sign, Gabriel. The sign: 'From White to Bright.' That's how the numbers go. The white scarf covers the one and zero, making ten. That's the first number of the combination, and – "

Varsey made the next entry in his notebook:

$$10 - 29 - 38 - 47 - 56$$

"I guess now it's your turn, Paul." Varsey nodded in Haskill's direction.

"Like the rest of you, I may have let my work get in the way of my detecting," said the teacher. "I chose the same window Jasper did. But I was interested in those five posters on American history. And, you know, it wasn't hard to assign a specific number to each of them."

"Oh?" Warwick asked. "How?"

"Take the first one, the painting. It's called 'The Spirit of '76'. Next, Woodrow Wilson. His Fourteen Points — his war aims — are known to any high-school student. Or at least they should be."

Varsey chuckled at the teacher's sternness. "Continue," he urged him.

"The prospector mining for gold?" Haskill went on. "A Forty-Niner, of course — the year of the California Gold Rush." He hummed a few bars of "Clementine," and his listeners nodded their agreement. "And then Lindbergh, the Lone Eagle, the first man to fly solo across the Atlantic Ocean. What could he represent except the number one?

"Finally, Babe Ruth. And, even though it was finally broken, who can ever forget his record number of home runs?"

"Sixty!" chimed in Warwick and Zimmerman together.

"So there you have it, Edgar. Put my numbers in that book of yours with the rest of 'em."

Varsey did just that:

$$76 - 14 - 49 - 1 - 60$$

"Come on," said the reporter, draining his glass and getting to his feet. "Let's go down and get on that line to try the safe. We'll soon know which of you has the right answer."

Two hours later, the little group was back at their table in the taproom of the Merry Tinker. Full glasses mirrored despondent faces.

None of the suggested combinations had coaxed the safe's door to open.

"And we wanted to be like the Black Widowers," moaned Zimmerman. "I'm glad that Asimov fella ain't here at this meeting. I'd have to hide my face."

"A failure," said Warwick. "A complete fiasco."

"A bunch of dunderheads trying to be detectives," Doone

murmured. "That's us."

"Hey, let's not be too hard on ourselves." Paul Haskill managed a weak smile. "At least we tried. That should get us a mention in your newspaper, huh, Edgar?"

Varsey shook his head. "The public wants to read about winners," he said. "Not losers." He pushed back his chair. "Well, it's been fun. But I've got to be getting back to — "

"Wait a bit, wait a bit," came a reedy voice from beside him. Varsey turned and found himself looking at the seamed face of Findlay, the barman and proprietor of the Merry Tinker.

"I could nae let ye go till ye've heard from all of us," said Findlay. "Could I now, Mr. Varsey?"

"But everybody had a turn."

"I didn't. Ye see, trouble with these fellers is, they've nae read the Black Widowers yarns thorough enough."

"Come again, Findlay?" said the reporter.

"They clean forgot, sir, that while most of the Black Widowers sit at table for the meal, there's one who's up and about the entire time."

"Henry the waiter," breathed Haskill. "Of course."

"Aye," said Findlay, "Henry. And while the others blather on at great length — just as you gentlemen have done — it's Henry as gets down to findin' the solutions. That waiter has an odd and refreshingly original way of lookin' at problems. Somethin' I've been accused of meself."

"Wait a minute." Varsey eyed Findlay closely. "Are you saying you saw something in one of those windows that none of the rest of us saw?"

"Nae, not a bit of it." Findlay shook his head firmly. "Ye see, them windows ye've been examinin' with such care have naught tae do with the clue Davey Lotus was givin' out about the combination."

"But they have to! Lotus told me — " the reporter began.

"Sit down, Henry — ah, Findlay," interrupted Haskill, dragging up a chair from the next table. "Are you telling us you've got the solution? What are the numbers? How did you get them? What do you — ?"

"Easy, Mr. Haskill. Now, first, I'll remind ye all of one set of numbers ye've apparently overlooked. I'm speakin', of course, of the ones Davey Lotus assigned tae his name when he first opened his Value Today store. That story's still well known."

"Yeah, yeah," said Zimmerman impatiently. "D is one, A is two, right up to S is zero. And even if we paired 'em — twelve, thirty-four, fifty-six, and so on — that idea was tried the first day Lotus put the safe in the window."

"And Lotus said the clue was in the windows" — Varsey pounded the table positively — "when we talked in front of the store."

"Did he now?" replied Findlay. "Did he say that in so many words? I did nae get that impression when you first spoke of the conversation."

Varsey wrinkled his brow thoughtfully. "No," he replied slowly. "When I asked him where the clues were, he just said, 'Right there.' But he pointed to the windows."

"Are ye certain sure?" asked Findlay. "Or did he just wave, like?" The little barman made a vague gesture with his hand toward the corner of the room. "As ye did yerself, when ye spoke of it earlier?"

"Well — yes, that was about the way he did it," admitted the reporter. "But, except for the windows, there's nothing special about that old building he could have been pointing to."

"With deepest respect," countered Findlay, "I submit there is something, Mr. Varsey. Ye could hardly uv missed it, standin' where the two o' ye was."

"Look, Findlay," said Warwick, "are you saying we've been studying those damned windows when Lotus was actually pointing to something else? What was it?"

"It was letters — ten uv 'em, tae be exact. At least a foot high. And they spell out the name of Davey Lotus' store: VALUE TODAY."

"You — you mean the store sign was the clue, Findlay? But how?"

"Don't it strike ye odd, sir, that every one o' them ten letters in Value Today is found somewhere in Davey Lotus' own name? Quite a coincidence, ain't it? Only I don't really think it is one. I think Davey had this little scheme in mind from the time he found the safe and opened the store. He named the place accordingly."

"Value Today," mused Haskill, while the others buzzed excitedly. "Ten letters. Now if we break them down into two-letter groups — "

"Exactly, Mr. Haskill," grinned Findlay. "Take VA, for example. Now we assign numbers tae them letters, based on the way Davey first used his name to code prices. VA, therefore, becomes thirty-two."

"And LU is sixty-nine, because L is the sixth letter in Davey's name, and U the ninth," added Varsey.

"Now ye have it, sirs." Findlay reached across the table and pulled a piece of paper from Varsey's notebook. "Unless I'm far off the mark, these numbers'll open that safe."

He began to write with a stub of pencil:

$$32 - 69 - 48 - 71 - 25$$

Warwick leaped to his feet. "Come on! Let's go down there and give it a whirl!"

The words were scarcely out of his mouth when there was the sound of a door opening, then slamming shut. A thin, lively woman darted into the room, looking around sharply. She spotted Findlay and hurried over to him. "I got it, Findlay! I got it!" she cried excitedly. "See?"

She reached into the depths of her ample purse and withdrew a rectangle of green paper. It bore a portrait of President Grover Cleveland, as well as the figure "1000" in all four corners.

"Gentlemen," said Findlay, "I'd like ye tae meet Dorrie, my wife. I sent her on ahead tae test me theory."

He peered slyly at the little group at the table. "I did nae think ye'd mind, since yer own interest was purely in the problem itself, not the money involved."

The others looked at one another ruefully, shaking their heads.

"There is one thing ye could do fer me, though, Mr. Haskill."

"Anything, Findlay," said the teacher.

"Could ye find me the address uv the gude Dr. Asimov? I'd like tae write him a letter an' ask him tae extend tae each an' every one o' the Black Widowers me personal thanks."

PART II

THE MR. STRANG STORIES

MR. STRANG GIVES A LECTURE

Detective Paul Roberts walked along the third-floor hall-way of Aldershot High School, glancing at each door as he passed it. As a county detective, he'd been in the school be-fore, checking on students who were in trouble, but this was the first time he'd gone beyond the principal's office and up to the classrooms.

The building was quiet, now that the Friday dismissal bell had rung, and only some crumpled homework papers and a locker door hanging open gave evidence that, a few minutes earlier, seventeen hundred teenagers had charged toward the exit doors and a weekend of freedom like lemmings re-turning to the sea.

Although the hallway in which Detective Roberts found himself was a relatively modern addition to the building, the ubiquitous smell of chalk dust and floor wax brought back memories of his own school days at P.S. 189. He looked fur-tively about, half expecting one of his old teachers to stick her head out of a doorway and tell him to tuck his shirttail in.

He stopped in front of Room 319. A plastic sign on the door read SCIENCE and, below that, MR. STRANG. With a chuckle, Roberts noted that someone had scrawled *is a fink* after the name.

Roberts, who spent much of his off-duty time organizing the Aldershot Police Boys Club, had heard of Mr. Strang. To some boys, he was a holy terror, and they considered the student lucky who could get through all four years of high school without ever being assigned to one of Mr. Strang's classes. Other students spoke of the teacher in the reverent tones usually reserved for discussions concerning hot rods or the newest dance craze. Roberts had yet to find the youth who was neutral on the subject. But everyone admitted that Aldershot High School without Mr. Strang was as unimagi-nable as a boy who didn't want his driver's license on the morning of his sixteenth birthday.

The county detective opened the door and stepped inside. The room — with its demonstration stand, sink, and Bunsen burner — was about what he had expected. The movable desks and chairs were in neat rows, and along the shelves by the windows were hamster cages and aquariums filled with green scum.

"Be with you in a minute."

Roberts glanced around the room, trying to find where the voice had come from. Finally, he looked behind the door through which he had just entered. The man standing there had his back to Roberts. He wore an old lab coat that hung limply from narrow shoulders, and the hair on the back of his head was getting thin.

The man was working on some project that required a complicated tangle of glass tubing. Roberts saw him raise a test tube containing brown powder, measure the powder with his eye, then pour it into a cone of filter paper. Finally, he set the cone in a glass funnel and poured a clear liquid over it. Roberts was reminded of an old movie, in which Dr. Jekyll was about to be transformed into Mr. Hyde.

Then the man turned around and peered at Roberts, pushing black-rimmed glasses up onto a forehead made even more impressive by a receding hairline. "I'm sorry," he said. "I thought you were one of my students. You're a parent?"

"Yeah, I've got a little girl, three years old," said the detective, before he realized why the question had been asked. He took his badge and identification out of a hip pocket. "Detective Bureau," he continued tersely. "Official business. I'm looking for a Mr. Strang — Mr. Leonard Strang?"

The man reached out a slender hand and grasped the flask, which now contained a brown liquid that had dripped through the filter paper. He put the flask to his lips and took a long swallow. "I'm Mr. Strang," he said.

Roberts found it difficult to associate this thin, soft-spoken man with the terrible and wonderful Mr. Strang he had heard so much about. He began to wonder if the brown liquid did, after all, have some effect on Mr. Strang's personality.

Mr. Strang held out the flask to the detective. "Can I offer you some coffee?" he asked.

Roberts shook his head, feeling relieved somehow to know what the teacher was drinking.

"Then perhaps you'll tell me," Mr. Strang continued, "what your business with me is. My principal, Mr. Guthrey, warned me against driving across the grass in front of the school, but isn't calling in a detective a little extreme?"

Roberts looked at the teacher, who was waiting for an

answer with an expression of curiosity on his face. The detective suddenly and illogically began to feel like a small boy in short pants who had just committed an infraction of the school rules. It would not have surprised him at all if Mr. Strang had ordered him to remain after school.

"Do you know a kid named Julius Malesco?" Roberts asked gruffly, trying to regain control of himself.

"Yes, I have him in one of my classes. We call him Beanie here at school."

"What can you tell me about him?"

"Off the record?"

"Off the record."

Mr. Strang carefully removed his glasses from his forehead. He breathed on the lenses and then polished them on his necktie. Roberts could almost see the teacher arranging his mental notes in proper order. One hand was carefully inserted into a jacket pocket, while the other made jabbing motions with the glasses. Although these gestures were new to the detective, thousands of students from hundreds of classes knew what they meant. Mr. Strang was about to begin A Lecture.

"Beanie Malesco," Mr. Strang began musingly. "Beanie Malesco is what I'd call a happy imbecile. He's well down in the bottom quarter of his class, and he seems not only content but pleased with that subterranean scholastic position. He does, however, seem to have an interest in cars that is abnormally strong, even for a boy of his age. He wears his hair much too long for my taste, and he belongs to a gang called the Gear Grinders. I've taken a rather personal dislike to the boy's intentionally grubby appearance, but — as far as I know — he's never been in any real trouble."

With a flick of his hand, Mr. Strang replaced the glasses on his nose and removed the other hand from his pocket. The Lecture was over. "Why do you ask?"

"Because there was an armed robbery in a diner downtown late yesterday, and he's our chief suspect, that's why."

"I see. But what's that got to do with me?"

"Well, Mr. Strang" — Roberts swayed from one foot to the other, as if he'd been caught cheating on an examination — "it kind of looks like you're the owner of the getaway car."

Roberts almost chuckled at the amazed expression on Mr. Strang's face. That set the old boy back, he thought. He kept looking at the teacher and could barely refrain from laughing. Those old-fashioned glasses, the stooped shoulders, the nervous interlacing of the hands —

"*Amphineura!*" shouted Mr. Strang suddenly.

"Look," said Roberts, "don't get — "

"*Scaphopoda!*" snapped the teacher. "*Gastropoda! Pelecypoda! Cephalopoda!*"

"Mr. Strang, there might be some kids still in the building. You ought to watch your language."

Mr. Strang let out a long sigh. "Forgive me," he said. "But it's Friday, and I've had a long and tiring week. Right now, my only desire is to get myself into a restful horizontal position. But it seems I'm about to have a rather eventful weekend. At any rate, I doubt my students would be offended by my recitation of the classes of the Phylum Mollusca."

"Huh?"

"A system of identifying animals in a scientific manner. There are certain similarities to the Bertillon system of human classification."

"Oh," said Roberts vaguely.

"What do I do now?" asked Mr. Strang. "Call a lawyer? Would it help if I told you that Beanie took my car to Lundeen's Service Station yesterday to grease it and put in antifreeze? He works there after school, and he said he'd give my car special attention."

"We know that, Mr. Strang. Harvey Lundeen told us. We're not accusing you of anything. Malesco just used your car for the holdup, that's all."

"You know, Roberts, armed robbery doesn't seem to me to be in Beanie's line. Oh, I could see him stealing something, if the owner weren't present, but not holding a man at gunpoint. I assume that, when you said 'armed robbery,' you were referring to a gun?"

"Yeah, he had a gun. A revolver."

"No, that doesn't sound at all like Beanie. It's not that he's particularly honest — he's just cowardly. I wonder if I could see the boy?"

"Not a chance, Mr. Strang. He's been assigned a lawyer, who's keeping all visitors away from him. Besides, we're taking no chances on hurting the case because of some twisty legal angle when it finally comes up for trial."

"Trial? Won't Beanie be considered a juvenile offender?"

"Not any more. He turned eighteen last week."

"I see. But would it at least be possible for me to go down to Lundeen's to get my car? Surely I have the right to reclaim my own property?"

"I guess that'll be okay. We're done checking it out."

Mr. Strang shrugged off his lab coat and took his hat from

a hook behind the door. The casual observer might have assumed that Mr. Strang's battered felt hat had been frequently flung to the ground and stamped on during its owner's outbursts of frustration. The casual observer would have been entirely correct in that assumption.

A black-and-white police car was pulled up in front of the gas pumps when they arrived at the service station. Behind it, like a baby elephant following its mother, stood Mr. Strang's dusty purple compact automobile. A large CLOSED sign hung on the station's front door.

As the detective and the teacher walked across the asphalt apron, a man came out of the station's small office and waved to Roberts. He was wearing a sports jacket of large red-and-white checks, and his necktie bore a hand-painted picture of a green palm tree. On his feet were sport shoes that, while run down at the heels, were heavily coated with a new layer of white polish. Roberts introduced the man to Mr. Strang as Harvey Lundeen, owner of the station.

"With all this excitement, I'm takin' me a holiday," said Lundeen, grinning happily. "Any business I lose today, I'll make up with all the publicity I'll get out of this."

Mr. Strang fought back a desire to shade his eyes from the brilliant glare of Lundeen's attire. "Just to satisfy the curiosity of a customer, Mr. Lundeen," he said, "I wonder if you'd tell me just what happened last night."

"There ain't much I can tell you first-hand," said Lundeen. "I went home about six. I locked the tow truck and another car being repaired in the service shop and took the keys with me. There wasn't enough room for your car inside, so it stayed out here. I left young Malesco to pump gas until nine. He couldn't get into the service shop, but there wasn't any reason for him to go in there, anyway. I guess that's why he took your car when he drove off."

"He drove off?" asked Mr. Strang. "Where?"

"To Gruderman's Diner," interrupted Roberts. "It's not very far from here. That's the place that was robbed."

Mr. Strang nodded. "I'm familiar with it," he said. "Since my car was involved, could I hear about the robbery itself?"

"Sure," said the detective. "Alvin Gruderman was the only one working there last night. He says that, about nine-thirty, he was just getting ready to close up when this purple compact car pulled into the driveway that leads back to the parking lot behind the diner. That driveway's real narrow, what with the diner on one side and a high cement wall on the other, and Al was afraid the guy was going to try and park there all night.

"So Al came out to tell him to move, because there wasn't enough room for anyone else to get by him. But when he got up beside the car, the man in it pulled a gun and forced Al back into the diner. Al remembers the man left the car with the motor running, so he must have been planning a fast getaway. He cleaned out the cash register, hit Al on the head with the gun, backed his car out, and took off. Al was out for almost half an hour."

"What led you to Beanie Malesco?" asked the science teacher. "Did Gruderman recognize him?"

"No, the man was masked. But he was wearing a leather jacket."

"So?"

"There was lettering on the back of it. It said 'The Gear Grinders.'"

"That wasn't very smart of the criminal, was it?"

"Well, you said yourself Malesco isn't very bright. Anyway, we checked out all the members of the Gear Grinders and found out that Malesco worked here yesterday from right after school until nine o'clock. But he didn't get home until nearly one. Tried to tell us he took in a movie. We drove out here and looked around."

"That's gratitude for you," Lundeen growled. "I give the kid a job, figure maybe it's a break for him, at least he can earn some pocket money. And he's not here two weeks before he steals a customer's car and pulls this job. Show Mr. Strang what you found on the front seat, Roberts."

The detective gave Mr. Strang a pale-yellow rectangular piece of paper. It was a check for fifteen dollars, made out to Alvin Gruderman.

"We even talked to the man who wrote this," said Roberts. "He gave it to Gruderman about seven o'clock last night — Al often cashes small checks for his customers."

Mr. Strang returned the check to Roberts. "Is it all right if I look over my car for damages?" he asked.

Roberts nodded, and Mr. Strang walked over to the purple car. As he stood contemplating a dirty front fender, he pulled from his pocket a massive briar pipe and a pouch of tobacco. Ramming tobacco into the bowl, he applied a match and sent clouds of foul smoke into the clear autumn air. Lundeen, who was downwind of the teacher, compared the smell to that of a burning tire, but Mr. Strang was too deep in thought to hear the comment.

He crawled in and around the car, examining the area under the seats and sighting along the body for any sign of a new dent. When he looked under the hood, his pipe still in his teeth, Roberts saw the huge volume of smoke pouring forth and wondered if the engine had caught on fire.

Finally, after a glance at the instruments on the dashboard and a slamming of both doors, Mr. Strang returned to where Roberts and Lundeen were talking to a bulky uniformed policeman who had come from inside the station office.

"Excuse me," said Mr. Strang, "but could you tell me how far Gruderman's Diner is from here?"

"About a mile, I'd say," Lundeen answered.

"Pardon my making sounds like a science teacher," replied Mr. Strang, "but I'd like it a little more precise than that. Could you possibly give me the exact distance?"

Roberts shrugged. "Bell," he said, turning to the policeman, "take another drive down to Gruderman's and back. Check the mileage — to the tenth of a mile. And bring Al Gruderman back with you. I want to talk to him again."

Bell got into the police car and zoomed out onto the street in the direction of the diner. "I'm going inside," said Lundeen, heading for the office. "Call me if you need me."

Mr. Strang turned to the detective. "How much was stolen?" he asked.

"A little under five hundred dollars."

"Have you found any of it?"

"Nothing except that check — which Malesco couldn't cash, anyway. Don't worry, he won't get a chance to spend any of the money."

"Of course he won't. Because he didn't commit the robbery."

"What?"

Mr. Strang spread his hands and shrugged, as if he were clearing up a simple point of general science for a not-too-bright student. "I said Beanie Malesco is innocent. At least, the evidence would tend to indicate that he is. Besides, I know the boy too well to believe he'd be capable of clubbing a man with a gun."

Roberts angrily drove his right fist into the palm of his left hand. He had had enough of this — this schoolteacher! — who continually made him feel like an incompetent boy of twelve. Why couldn't he stick to his ivory tower, anyway? It was only with an effort that Roberts kept himself from shouting.

"Look, Mr. Strang, I've been pretty patient with you, bringing you down here, sending my man to check the mileage and all. But, frankly, you're beginning to bug me. You teachers get a kid in school, give him a few tests, see him in class once a day, and all of a sudden you can tell whether or not he's a criminal. You — you think you know him. Phooey! I've got enough evidence on Malesco to — "

Mr. Strang just stared at the detective, as if he were only a minor problem in classroom discipline. "What evidence?" he asked, enunciating carefully. "A man with a gun commits a robbery. And you pick up Beanie, because the robber was wearing a leather jacket with 'The Gear Grinders' on it. Give me a can of white paint, and I could provide myself with a jacket like that in a few minutes, and you know it.

"Besides, why would Beanie wear an incriminating jacket? He watches enough crime shows on TV to know better than that. If he wanted to get arrested, he could just as easily have left a calling card with his name and address on it."

As Roberts started to reply, the police car pulled up in front of the gas pumps and Bell got out, accompanied by a small man with a bandaged head whom he introduced to Mr. Strang as Alvin Gruderman, owner of the diner. Gruderman mumbled a greeting and then shuffled off to the office, where he could sit down.

"Eight-tenths of a mile," said Bell. "That's how far it is to the diner."

"Interesting," said Mr. Strang. He motioned Roberts to the purple car and opened the driver's door, pointing at the frame. "Recognize that?" he asked.

"Sure," said Roberts. The detective turned to Bell, who was trying to peer over his shoulder. "It's one of those stickers they put on a car after they grease it. It shows the mileage at the time of the lube job."

"Seventy-six thousand, two hundred and forty-one," read Bell, "and one-tenth."

"What are you getting at, Mr. Strang?" asked Roberts.

"Look at the odometer."

"Uh huh. Seventy-six thousand, two hundred and forty-one and nine-tenths. The car was driven eight-tenths of a mile after the grease job. Exactly the distance to the diner."

Mr. Strang slapped the palm of one hand against his forehead. "I'll bet you were a real joy to your arithmetic teacher," he said. "Never mind the New Math — you can't even cope with the old kind. Don't those numbers suggest something to you?"

It was Bell who answered the question with one of his

own. "If the car traveled eight-tenths of a mile to the diner," he said slowly, "then how did it get back here?"

Roberts felt as if someone had slammed him across the back of the knees with a baseball bat. He sadly admitted to himself that he had overlooked the lubrication sticker and the odometer in his examination of the car, and he thanked the gods who watch over detectives that he hadn't yet filed a report.

Mr. Strang was grinning from ear to ear. "If Beanie drove to the diner and back, there'd be another eight-tenths of a mile on the odometer," he said. "The owner of the diner said that my car pulled up into the narrow driveway. That accounts for the eight-tenths of a mile. It's a simple question of distance."

"Maybe the odometer isn't working properly," hazarded Roberts. "Or maybe Malesco turned it back somehow." Then he saw Bell, who had helped him check the car, shaking his head.

"Do you still want to bet on Beanie's guilt?" asked Mr. Strang.

Roberts' face turned a shade that almost matched the color of Mr. Strang's car. "Bell!" he shouted. "Why didn't you – ?"

There was another shout from the door of the station office, and the owner, Lundeen, came running across the asphalt, his tie fluttering over his shoulder like the brilliant banner on a knight's lance.

"Mr. Roberts!" he called. "I just found this in the station. I'm afraid this really cooks Malesco's goose."

He handed the detective a slip of paper. Roberts looked at it carefully. Then he smiled. Not only would the paper clinch the case against Malesco, but it would also quiet the babbling of the schoolteacher. "I'll just bet this is in Malesco's handwriting," he said. "And, if it is, that just about makes me right and you wrong, Mr. Strang. What do you think?"

He thrust the slip into Mr. Strang's hand. The almost illegible handwriting on one side testified eloquently to Beanie Malesco's authorship. The brief scrawl read:

al – in mr s car

"You see?" said the detective triumphantly. "Everybody calls Alvin Gruderman Al, even the kids. The way I see it, this note proves that Malesco went to Al's diner in your car."

Mr. Strang read the note several times. The clouds of thick smoke still issuing from his pipe and the faraway look in his eyes indicated that the teacher was concentrating deeply. He turned the note upside down, and he peered at the reverse side of the paper.

Then the science teacher began to laugh.

"What's so funny, Mr. Strang?" asked Bell. "You flipped or something?"

"How many times," Mr. Strang chortled, his thin body shaking with merriment, "have I asked to be delivered from the functional illiterates I have in my classes? And now Beanie Malesco is going to be proved innocent, just because he can't write decently! You say you just found this, Lundeen?"

"Well, it was actually Al Gruderman who found it. We were inside, rehashing the robbery, and he sort of absent-mindedly lifted up a road map from my desk. My memo pad was underneath, and this was written on the top sheet."

"I hope today will be a lesson to you, Roberts," said Mr. Strang, "not to equate the word 'teacher' with 'numbskull.' I told you Beanie was innocent, and I'm going to prove he is. Officer Bell, would you ask Mr. Gruderman to come out here, please?"

Bell went to the office and beckoned to the owner of the diner.

"Mr. Gruderman," said Mr. Strang, when they had returned, "tell me about that driveway into your parking lot. Is it as narrow as the detective described it to me?"

"Sure is," said Gruderman. "It's got a high cement wall on one side and the diner itself on the other. Last year, a car got stuck in there, and nobody could get in or out for twenty minutes."

"And you're absolutely sure you saw the robber drive up in my car?"

"Mr. Strang," Roberts interrupted, "Al has already gone over that. It was your car that Malesco took — there's no possible question about it."

Mr. Strang merely nodded at the interruption and addressed another question to Gruderman. "When my car stopped — with the motor running — it completely blocked your driveway. Is that right?"

"Yep. There wasn't more than three feet of clearance on either side of the car, maybe not that much."

"Thank you," said Mr. Strang. He glanced quickly at Roberts, Bell, Lundeen, and Gruderman, as if to see that everyone was in place before The Lecture started. "I would like you all to give me your complete and undivided attention," he said. "Class is now in session, and I don't want you to miss a word."

Once again, Mr. Strang's black-rimmed glasses were polished on his necktie, and one hand was carefully inserted into a jacket pocket.

"Beanie Malesco," began Mr. Strang, waving his glasses like a king's scepter, "is hard put to spell his own name correctly. Therefore, to hide his lack of ability, he abbreviates as often as possible, as the note indicates. Unfortunately, he isn't aware that some words don't have abbreviated forms. Being a free spirit, he abbreviates them anyway. And, being lazy, he omits the periods.

"Now, when I gave Beanie my car to bring down here, I asked him to lubricate it and put in antifreeze. But none of the expensive stuff for me — a simple schoolteacher can't afford it.

"It's my opinion that he brought the car here and drained the radiator, but then became too busy to fill it again. So he wrote a note to remind himself to do it later. What I suspect happened was that, before he got around to filling the radiator, Lundeen closed the doors of the repair shop, locking all the cans of antifreeze inside.

"That's the significance of the note, Roberts. Even Beanie wouldn't leave written plans for a robbery where they were sure to be found. His note, 'al – in mr s car,' was merely a reminder to put alcohol in Mr. Strang's car."

"But we pulled Malesco in this morning, before he came down here," said Roberts. "That means your radiator ought to still be empty."

"The evidence certainly points in that direction. Suppose we put your hypothesis to the test. Would you please do the honors, Officer Bell?"

Bell trotted over to Mr. Strang's car, a sheepish expression on his face, and lifted the hood. He unscrewed the radiator cap and flashed his light inside. Then he bent down and looked under the car.

"Dry as a bone," he said finally.

"It seems that, in your eagerness to convict Beanie, you overlooked several pieces of evidence in my car," said Mr. Strang to the county detective.

"But your car couldn't have traveled that far with a dry radiator," said Roberts. "Isn't that right, Lundeen?"

"Yeah, the pistons would have expanded with the heat and jammed in the cylinders." Lundeen looked down in annoyance at a spot of grease that marred the gleam of his freshly polished white shoes.

"Exactly," said Mr. Strang. "My car was driven almost a mile to the diner. Then, according to Mr. Gruderman, the criminal left the motor running while he went inside, rifled the cash register, and knocked Gruderman out. What's the logical conclusion?"

"Why, the heat must have jammed up the motor while it was right there in my driveway," said Gruderman, fingering the bandage on his head.

"Go to the head of the class," said Mr. Strang.

"Then how did the car get back here?" asked the detective.

"I'm more interested in why than how," replied Mr. Strang.

"What do you mean?" demanded Roberts.

"Consider for a moment all the things we're forced to believe if we assume that Beanie is guilty. Would Beanie Malesco be stupid enough to wear his Gear Grinders jacket after taking the trouble to put on a mask? Would he be stupid enough to overlook a check that would prove my car was used in the robbery?"

"Are you telling us that Malesco was framed?" asked Roberts.

"Answer your own question," said Mr. Strang. "If the car was left in Gruderman's driveway, Beanie could always claim it was stolen. But no, the robber took great pains to make sure it was returned to the station. What possible motive could there be for that, except to lead the police directly to Beanie?"

"But how did the robber get the car back here from the diner?" snapped Roberts. "And why didn't the added distance register on the odometer? Did the guy carry it on his back?"

"No, but – curiously enough – you're getting warm," Mr. Strang smiled.

"Well, he couldn't get another car to push him, that's a cinch: no other car could have gotten past him in that driveway. And I can't see anybody shoving a car for almost a mile with his shoulder. What the guy really needed was a tow truck."

"Eureka! At last a little common sense is beginning to reveal itself."

"Huh?"

"You've hit it, Roberts. The robber backed a tow truck up to the rear of the car – he couldn't get around to the front, since it was parked head-in within the narrow driveway. He lifted the rear wheels off the ground and towed the car back to the station. That's why the added distance didn't register on the odometer: since that instrument is connected to the rear wheels, it wouldn't register while those wheels were in the air."

"And just where did this character get a tow truck?" asked Bell.

"Gruderman was knocked out for almost half an hour, remember? That would give a man enough time to run back here and get the tow truck from the repair shop."

"Hey, wait a minute!" Roberts bellowed. "The only person who could have gotten to that tow truck was – "

" – was the same man who would have had plenty of opportunity to examine Beanie's jacket and make himself a copy," said Mr. Strang. "Especially since he obviously had access to white shoe polish for painting on the letters. The man who did all he could to frame Beanie under the guise of giving him a job. The man – the only man – who could have opened the shop where the tow truck was kept, since, as the owner, he was the only person with a key."

As Mr. Strang slipped his glasses back on, indicating that The Lecture was finished, there was a brief scuffling sound, which ended abruptly as Bell's fist scored a bull's-eye on the center button of a brightly colored sports jacket.

"Lundeen," said Mr. Strang, gazing down at the figure lying on the asphalt, "will you go along quietly, or shall I have the pleasure of watching Officer Bell jump up and down on your supine body?"

As Roberts got into the police car with Bell to take Lundeen away, the county detective turned to the thin, stooped teacher. "Malesco will be glad to hear he's been cleared," he said. "Maybe he'll even get a haircut out of gratitude.

"By the way," he continued, "after all your car's been through, you'll probably be wanting another one. I've got a brother who's in the used-car business, and – "

"Sell my car? Never!" exclaimed Mr. Strang. "Where would I find another vehicle that was only ever driven by a little old schoolteacher?

MR. STRANG PERFORMS AN EXPERIMENT

Mr. Strang stood behind the demonstration table, a satanic smile on his face, and held aloft a human skull in his hand. "Hugo, here," he said, pointing to the fleshless jaws, "was probably a rather young man. You will note that his teeth are in excellent condition — he undoubtedly brushed after every meal and saw his dentist twice a year."

Although one or two of the girls were turning a bit green, the twenty-eight students in Mr. Strang's biology class laughed dutifully. Mr. Strang smiled appreciatively in return. The thin science teacher had enough of the ham actor in him to play to an audience — even a captive one — when the occasion presented itself.

The bell rang, ending the period. The students shifted restlessly but did not rise from their seats. They had learned early in the semester that, in Mr. Strang's classes, there was only one signal for dismissal.

Mr. Strang took a long last look at the skull and murmured, "Alas, poor Yorick!" — while twenty-eight pairs of eyes stared fixedly at the black-rimmed glasses on the demonstration table.

Mr. Strang picked up his glasses and put them in his jacket pocket.

There was a scraping of chairs and a few minor skirmishes at the rear of the classroom as most of the students tried to squeeze through the doorway at the same time. The man who was standing just outside the room, about to enter, was swept aside by the mass of teenaged humanity.

Finally, the doorway cleared, and the man entered Mr. Strang's room. Mr. Strang looked up, smiled, and placed the skull in a plastic bag on the table. "Come in, Russ," he said, "and I'll make you a cup of coffee. I've got a free period, and my brew is better than that mud they make down in the Faculty Room."

Mr. Strang busied himself heating water over a Bunsen burner and arranging filter paper in a glass funnel. He spooned coffee into the filter-paper cone and poured boiling water over it, watching the brown liquid flow down the stem of the funnel and into the flask below it. Only when each had been provided with a beakerful of steaming coffee did Mr. Strang ask a question.

"What's bothering you, Russ?"

"It's — it's awful, Mr. Strang. I've got to talk to somebody. This just can't be happening to me. But how did you know about it? Did someone tell you?"

"*Coelenterata!*" muttered Mr. Strang, making Phylum IV of animal classification sound like a wizard's magic word. "Russell Donato, do you take me for an idiot? You walk in here pale as a ghost, with your hands shaking as if you have the St. Vitus' dance. And then, while you wonder how I know you're worried, you keep gnawing at that thumbnail as if you want to leave nothing but a mashed stump. Now, let's not beat around the bush. What's the trouble?"

"I've just come from Mr. Guthrey's office," said the younger man. "I've been suspended."

"Suspended? What do you mean?"

"Mr. Guthrey just handed me a thirty-day suspension. I can't teach — here or anywhere else — for the next month. Maybe ever, for all I know."

Mr. Strang's jaw dropped. Although it was only the beginning of his second year at Aldershot High School, Russell Donato had the makings of an excellent chemistry teacher. He knew his field, he was a hard worker, and he had quickly learned to deal with his students without overstepping the thin line between friendliness and familiarity. The students not only liked him, they respected him — and, to Mr. Strang, the second was far more important than the first. For Aldershot High School to lose him would be, in Mr. Strang's eyes, little short of a crime. He ran thin fingers through his rapidly disappearing hair.

"Why, Russ?" he asked.

"Because of Sheila Palinger," answered Donato.

"Who?"

"Sheila Palinger. She's a sophomore in my seventh-period study hall. She told Mr. Guthrey that I — well, she was in my room and — how do you say a thing like this, Mr. Strang?"

"She accused you of molesting her? Is that what you mean?"

"Yes. And now I've been suspended while the Board of Education investigates."

Mr. Strang toyed for several seconds with a glass rod on the table. "Did you do it, Russ?" he asked finally.

Donato turned suddenly. His face showed hurt and anger. "Of course not," he snapped. "What do you think I am?"

"That's what the Board of Education has thirty days to find out," said Mr. Strang. "Do you want to tell me what happened?"

Donato shrugged. "There's not much to tell," he said. "I was working late in my classroom yesterday, correcting some examination papers I wanted to give back this morning. About four o'clock, Sheila Palinger walked in and asked me if I'd help her with some footnotes for an English term paper. I suggested she see her English teacher, but she said he'd gone home, and she needed the information right away."

"Does Sheila take chemistry?"

"No, she's more interested in art. Anyway, I'm not too sure about footnoting myself, but I hauled out an old book I have on formatting written reports and found what she wanted. She wasn't in my room for more than five minutes."

"But surely Mr. Guthrey knows that not much could have happened in only five minutes."

"Mr. Strang, you ought to hear the story Sheila told him. According to her, she spent almost half an hour in my room after school yesterday. And she sounded pretty convincing, believe me. She said things about the way the room looked that even I couldn't remember. But when I checked this morning, she was absolutely perfect — one hundred per cent. What was on my desk, the exact way the seats were arranged, everything."

Mr. Strang looked thoughtfully at the skull in its transparent bag. "Russ," he said finally, "I wouldn't worry too much about this. An accusation has been made, and you can't expect them to ignore it. But the principal and the Board aren't against you. Let me see what I can find out from Mr. Guthrey."

"But can they do this, Mr. Strang? Can they kick me out on the word of one kid?"

"If it comes to a showdown, Russ, I'm afraid they can. You haven't got tenure yet, and, until you get it, the Board of Education can suspend you or even fire you just because they don't like the style of shoes you wear or the color of your socks. But don't get too worked up until I see Mr. Guthrey. Tell me one thing: is there any reason Sheila Palinger would want to make trouble for you?"

Donato shook his head. "None I can think of," he said. "Oh,

she's kind of a pain in the neck in study hall. Keeps coming up with idiotic questions about her work, hangs around my desk most of the period — things like that. But she's never made any real trouble. I just can't understand it."

"Well, don't be in too big a hurry to leave school today. I may want to talk to you again later. But right now, I want to hear what Mr. Guthrey has to say."

As he went down the stairs toward the main office, Mr. Strang found it hard to keep a worried expression from his face. In the outer office, he passed the Lost and Found box and noticed that a chemistry textbook topped the pile of misplaced articles. He walked through the door marked Marvin W. Guthrey without knocking, an action that was not likely to endear him to the principal of Aldershot High School, and sat stiffly in a chair in front of Guthrey's enormous desk.

Behind the desk, Guthrey — a small man with a head of wavy snow-white hair of which he was inordinately proud — was talking on the telephone. His eyebrows shot up in surprise at the sight of the science teacher.

"I'll call you back on this, Fred," he said into the phone, "or maybe we can talk about it just before the Board meeting. In the meantime, I'll try to find out what I can at this end." The principal hung up the phone. "Now, then, Mr. Strang," he said, turning in his swivel chair, "what's the meaning of this? I'm not in the habit of having — "

"I'm here about Russ Donato," interrupted Mr. Strang.

"I suppose Donato has told you what the trouble is," said Guthrey, "so there's nothing more for me to add. Fred Landerhoff — he's on the Board of Education, you know — has been on the phone all morning. He just finished his fourth call to me when you walked in. He's the one who ordered me to suspend Donato."

"So what happens now, Mr. Guthrey? How do you go about finding out whether Donato is innocent or guilty?"

Guthrey let out a long breath. "I wish I knew, Mr. Strang," he said. "A situation like this is hard on everybody. As soon as word leaks out, I'm going to get a hundred calls asking why I hired Donato in the first place. Of course, if there's no proof of guilt, we'll keep him on — at least until the end of the school year. By that time, the good citizens of Aldershot will probably have made it so hot for him that he'll have to leave."

"Shades of Alice in Wonderland," muttered Mr. Strang.

"I beg your pardon?"

"I was just thinking of Alice's trial, where the Red Queen

says, 'Sentence first, verdict afterwards.' The analogy seems to apply."

"Unfortunately, that's true. Words like 'perversion' and 'sex maniac' are going to be tossed around pretty carelessly. Donato will have a rough time finding another teaching job, if we have to let him go. Oh, if he leaves, I'll write him a good recommendation, of course."

"*Protozoa, Mesozoa, Porifera,*" growled Mr. Strang. His face turned an angry red. "Make up your mind. If he attacked the girl or did anything at all improper, he's not fit to be in a classroom — any classroom. But give him a chance to defend himself. Don't hang the man on the unsupported testimony of a child."

Guthrey stuck out his chin belligerently. "Mr. Strang," he rumbled, "you burst in here without permission to question me about Donato. Taking into consideration your friendship with him, as well as your years of service to the school, I overlooked this breach of the rules and decided to discuss the matter with you. But I do not intend to — to — "

Guthrey raised his hand dramatically and then let it fall slowly to the desk. "Oh, hell, Leonard," he said, looking sadly at the science teacher. "They've got me over a barrel. You know there isn't a chance in a thousand of getting any evidence. It's just Donato's word against Sheila's. And you won't find a parent in a thousand who thinks his child — his flesh and blood — would lie about a thing like this. The kids know it, and there are some — only a very few, fortunately — who are just waiting for the chance to take advantage of it."

Marvin Guthrey looked forlornly at Mr. Strang and seemed tiny and lost in his huge swivel chair. For the first time in many years, the science teacher could find it in his heart to feel sorry for his principal.

There was a thick silence, broken only by the ticking of the clock on the wall. Then Mr. Strang banged his fist loudly on Guthrey's desk.

"No!" he shouted.

"What is it, Mr. Strang?" asked Guthrey.

"Are we going to let a man's reputation — his whole future — be ruined? Are we going to let the good name of this school be dragged through the mud, with every teacher afraid to be pleasant and helpful with his students because of the possible consequences? Are we all going to cringe every time some asinine accusation is made? No! No! No!"

He pounded the desk three times to punctuate his last words.

Guthrey stared at the teacher as if he'd lost his senses. "But what can you do, Mr. Strang?" he asked, a worried look on his face.

"There must be some indication somewhere of what really happened yesterday, and we're going to find it. If Russ Donato is guilty, at least we'll have cleaned our own house. And if he's innocent — which I'm sure is the case — we'll serve notice that nobody can make such a bald accusation and get away with it. Mr. Guthrey, can you get someone to take over my classes for the next couple of periods? Anybody in the department ought to be able to describe that skull as well as I can."

"What are you going to do?"

"We," said Mr. Strang, indicating Guthrey and himself, "are going to have a little talk with Sheila Palinger. She's still in the building, isn't she?"

Guthrey smiled wryly. "You must have passed Sheila and her mother when you came through the outer office," he said. "They were camped at my door when I got in this morning. I spent over an hour listening to them go on and on about Donato, and my secretary says they want to see me again as soon as I'm free. Between those two and Fred Landerhoff, I haven't had time to take a deep breath yet today." He spread his hands helplessly. "I don't know what I can tell them that they haven't already heard."

"You won't have to say a word, Mr. Guthrey," the teacher replied. "But if that girl's as big a liar as I think she is, I'd just as soon have a witness to what's said here over the next few minutes."

Mr. Guthrey buzzed his secretary, and, a few minutes later, Sheila Palinger entered the office. She was wearing a simple cotton dress — and a tragic expression that would have done credit to an actress playing Camille. Behind her came her mother, a look of self-pity on her face.

After the introductions had been made, Mr. Strang turned to the girl. "Sheila," he began, "according to Mr. Guthrey, you've made a rather serious charge against Mr. Donato. I wonder if you'd tell me about it."

"Sheila already told him everything," interrupted Mrs. Palinger, indicating Guthrey with a jerk of her thumb, "and I gave Fred Landerhoff the whole story on the telephone last night. Fred's a good friend of mine. I can't see any sense in repeating it and further disturbing the child. I just want to find out what you're going to do about that — that teacher."

"No, Mother," said Sheila. "I'll tell them. I want to cooperate in any way I can. I feel I owe it to my classmates and to the school."

Mr. Strang had all he could do to keep from shouting, "Academy Award!"

"What is it you want to know?" Sheila asked.

"Just tell us in your own words what happened, Sheila," said Mr. Strang in a kindly voice. "Right from the beginning."

"Well," Sheila began, her voice becoming low and confidential, "it was about five minutes to four yesterday. School had been out for almost an hour, and the halls were completely empty. I had some questions about an English assignment, and Mr. Donato was the only one I could find in the building, so I went to his room. He was there — alone."

"So nobody saw you go into the room?" asked Mr. Strang.

"Nobody," answered Sheila. "When I was inside, Mr. Donato asked me to sit down. He walked over to the windows and pulled down the shades. I didn't know why at the time.

"While I was waiting, I noticed a pile of examination papers on his desk. He had corrected about half of them. The paper on the top had a mark of eighty. He also had a chemistry book propped open to page seventy-three."

Mr. Strang's eyes widened. The girl seemed to have total recall concerning all the details of the meeting. "Did you happen to notice the color of Mr. Donato's necktie?" he asked sarcastically.

"Oh, yes. It was blue, with little red squares on it. Each square had a white dot in the center. I thought it went well with his gray suit."

Mr. Strang couldn't even remember the color of the tie he was wearing today. He looked down to check. Brown, with green acid stains.

"Mr. Donato came over to my desk with a book," Sheila continued. "I remember thinking how dim the room was with the shades down and the lights out. But I could still see that gold college ring he wears, and I thought it was funny that the ring should shine in such a soft light.

"As he leaned over my desk to help me, he pointed to the book with one hand. But he kept brushing my hair very lightly with the fingers of the other hand."

And, since he was leaning over the desk, he probably fell flat on his face, thought Mr. Strang, since he couldn't use either hand to prop himself up. But the science teacher remained silent.

"Pretty soon," the girl went on, "he closed the book and just stared into my eyes. I began to get a little frightened. But

I didn't dare say anything. After all, he is a teacher. Then he said — he said — "

"What did he say?" Mr. Strang asked gently.

"He began telling me how — how lovely he thought I was — and how it meant so much to him to be alone with me. Then he began to touch me. He — he — oh!" She buried her face in her hands.

Guthrey cleared his throat loudly. "And what did you do, Sheila?"

"I didn't know what to do, Mr. Guthrey. I remember getting up and backing away from him, toward the door. Then I ran out."

"Did you remember to take your books?" asked Mr. Strang.

"I must have. That part isn't too clear."

"You seem to remember every little detail of what went on in that room before — er — anything happened."

Mrs. Palinger burst into the conversation. "There's nothing wrong with that, is there? She's had a severe emotional upset. And now you two are almost acting like you don't believe her."

Mr. Strang ignored the interruption. "Sheila," he said, "how long were you in Mr. Donato's room?"

"It must have been at least half an hour."

"Mr. Donato said you were there no longer than five minutes."

"He's lying!" cried the girl. "Why, he even had time to do his old experiment before he started talking to me."

"Experiment?" said Mr. Strang. "I don't recall Mr. Donato saying anything about an experiment when he talked to me. What experiment was it, Sheila?"

"How should I know? I don't take chemistry. But, anyway, he did it while I was there. That ought to prove I was in the room for more than five minutes."

"But there was no sign this morning of any experiment having been done," said Guthrey.

"Hmph," snorted Mrs. Palinger. "He probably cleaned it up before anybody saw it. Just what you'd expect of a snake like that."

"Do you remember anything about the experiment, Sheila?" asked Mr. Strang.

"Well, he had an iron stand on the table, and under it was one of those burners — "

"A Bunsen burner?"

"I guess so. There was this big glass thing like a bottle on the stand, and some tubes and — oh, I don't know. It's hard to explain. It was like what you see in the mad-scientist movies. But I could draw you a picture of how it looked."

"Splendid," said Mr. Strang. He gave Sheila a pencil and a piece of paper from Guthrey's desk. The girl busied herself with them, and in a few minutes she showed the results to Mr. Strang.

If Sheila Palinger knew nothing about chemistry, she was an excellent artist. The picture showed a ring stand over a Bunsen burner. On the stand was a large flask with a rubber stopper in it. A glass tube and a funnel were stuck through holes in the stopper. At one side of the flask were two bottles. Although the labels on the bottles were visible, their small size in the drawing had made it necessary for Sheila to omit the printing on them. But the extreme realism of the sketch made it certain that Sheila had seen the experiment somewhere. Guthrey looked worriedly at Mr. Strang.

"Sheila," said the teacher. "About those two bottles. What was in them?"

"Let me think. Oh, yes, one of them had Hickle on the label."

"Hickle?"

"Yes. And the other one was full of a black powder called Fess."

"I never heard of Hickle and Fess," said Guthrey. "Mean anything to you, Mr. Strang?"

Mr. Strang's eyebrows narrowed in a frown. He reached into a pocket and dragged out a battered briar pipe and a pouch of tobacco. Ramming tobacco into the bowl of the pipe, he lit it and sent clouds of smoke billowing into the small office. Guthrey and Mrs. Palinger wrinkled their noses disapprovingly, but Mr. Strang ignored them. He leaned back in his chair and closed his eyes.

Several minutes passed, and Guthrey was just about to inquire if Mr. Strang was feeling all right when a smile spread over the face of the science teacher. He chuckled softly, and then not so softly. Soon he was emitting gales of laughter, while his slender body shook with mirth.

"Hickle and Fess!" he gasped, when he could catch his breath. "Sounds like a vaudeville team, doesn't it, Mr. Guthrey?"

"Let me in on it, Leonard," replied Guthrey. "What's so funny?"

Instead of answering, Mr. Strang took the drawing and made some rapid marks on the back of it with his pen. "Is this what you saw on the labels, Sheila?" he asked, showing her the paper.

"Yes, that's it."

Mr. Strang turned the paper so that Guthrey and Mrs. Palinger could see it. Printed on the paper in red ink were two chemical symbols, HCl and FeS.

"Hickle, or HCl," explained the teacher, "is the chemical symbol for hydrochloric acid. And Fess is FeS, or ferrous sulfide. Sheila made words out of the chemical symbols."

"That doesn't prove anything against her," said Mrs. Palinger. "She couldn't be expected to know any of that — she told you she doesn't take chemistry."

"No, she doesn't," Mr. Strang agreed. "Now then, Sheila, what did Mr. Donato do with the Hickle and Fess?"

"He mixed them together in the big bottle."

"It's called a flask, Sheila. What happened then? In the experiment, I mean."

"Mr. Donato put it over the flame. But I don't remember anything else about it. That was when he started to — you know."

"I see," said Mr. Strang. "Well, you've been very helpful, Sheila, and I think I have a pretty good idea of what really happened. I wonder, though, if it would be possible for you to come back to school this evening — with your mother, of course — just to tie up a few loose ends. Say about eight o'clock?"

Mother and daughter looked at each other and shrugged. "Eight o'clock will be all right," said Mrs. Palinger finally. "Just so long as Mr. Donato is dismissed from this school. The very idea of letting a man like that teach our children!"

"I assure you, Mrs. Palinger, that the entire truth of the situation will be brought to light this evening. And you mentioned Mr. Landerhoff on the Board of Education. Would you mind bringing him along? We'll be meeting in Mr. Donato's room."

"If it'll help get rid of that — that monster, I'll see that Fred Landerhoff's there," replied Mrs. Palinger. She stood up and patted her daughter's head lovingly.

"Until tonight, then," smiled Mr. Strang, holding the office door open.

When the Palingers had left, Guthrey leaned across his desk and scowled at Mr. Strang. "I hope you know what you're doing," he rumbled. "Parents, kids, a member of the Board — what's on your mind, Leonard?"

"You forgot one other person I'm inviting to the meeting," said the teacher.

"Who's that?"

"My principal. See you tonight at eight, Mr. Guthrey."

The meeting in Mr. Donato's science room that evening resembled a meeting between the legendary Hatfields and McCoys at the height of their feud. In one corner of the room sat Russ Donato. He was looking daggers at Sheila Palinger and her mother, who were sitting as far removed from the accused teacher as the walls of the room permitted.

In the center of the room, Marvin Guthrey whispered nervously to Board member Landerhoff. From behind the demonstration table, Mr. Strang grinned at his strange assortment of "students" like some diabolic gnome, while he busily arranged the materials of the experiment Sheila Palinger had described earlier.

When he had completed his preparations, Mr. Strang rapped for order. An uneasy quiet descended on the room. "I believe you all know each other," he said, "so introductions will be unnecessary."

Fred Landerhoff raised his hand. Although he was there representing the Aldershot Board of Education, the sight of the thin science teacher in the front of the room made him feel like a schoolboy who didn't have his lesson prepared.

"This is highly irregular, Mr. Strang," he said. "I'd like to make it quite clear that I'm here at Mrs. Palinger's request. While I'm naturally interested in getting to the bottom of this incident, I'm here to see that – "

"We're all here to see that justice is done, Mr. Landerhoff," interrupted Mr. Strang, "and, although the circumstances of this meeting are unusual, it's my opinion that recent events warrant it. I would like it noted, however, that the idea for the meeting was mine. Mr. Guthrey had no part in it."

The nervous principal let out a sigh.

"Today," Mr. Strang continued, "Mr. Donato was accused of – shall we say – making improper advances yesterday toward Miss Palinger here. The school administration followed the only course of action open to it. Mr. Donato was suspended, pending an investigation."

Mr. Strang removed his glasses and polished them on his necktie. Holding the glasses between the thumb and forefinger of his right hand, he examined them closely. Then he put his other hand into his jacket pocket and leaned across the table, shaking the glasses at the group in front of him. He was ready to teach his "class."

"The difficulty in a situation like this," he began, "is the

lack of evidence. Nobody witnessed the alleged incident —
for all intents and purposes, the building was empty. And, if
there is no evidence, Mr. Donato can neither be proved innocent or guilty.

"But consider the effect of the accusation itself. Should
the parents of this community be asked to entrust their children to a man who is guilty of the charge made against Mr.
Donato? Absolutely not. On the other hand, if the accusation
is false, what of Mr. Donato's reputation? The man will have
been damned without proof.

"No, the whole situation is intolerable. And, for that reason, I began to look for something what would confirm Mr.
Donato's guilt or innocence. I believe I've found it."

Mr. Strang reached into a drawer of the demonstration table and pulled out Sheila's sketch of the experiment. "When I
saw this drawing," he went on, "I couldn't help noticing the
striking resemblance to a picture in the chemistry textbook
used in Mr. Donato's classes. Look."

He took a book titled *Elements of Chemistry* from the
drawer and opened it to a previously marked page. The page
showed a photograph of an experiment in progress. Holding
Sheila's drawing next to the photograph, he continued.

"Notice the position of the bottles in the drawing and in
the photograph," he said. "Look at the shadow cast by the
ring stand. It goes off at the same angle as the one in Sheila's
sketch. There are other points of similarity to which I might
draw your attention, such as the fact that all of the objects in
the photograph are in the same relative places as they are in
the drawing, but I think you see my point. It is possible that
Sheila drew this picture, not from life, but from this textbook
photo."

"Why on Earth would my daughter do a thing like that?"
demanded Mrs. Palinger angrily.

"Simply in order to 'prove' that she had spent half an hour
in this room, rather than the five minutes claimed by Mr.
Donato."

Fred Landerhoff peered closely at the book and the drawing. "Possible, Mr. Strang," he said, "but hardly conclusive. It
could be a coincidence."

"True," said the teacher. "But let's go a step further. According to the description of the experiment in the book, one
of the bottles in the photograph contains hydrochloric acid
— notice the HCl label — and the other is filled with ferrous
sulfide, chemical formula FeS."

"My daughter told you all that this morning," cried Mrs.

Palinger. "How do you know she didn't see that very experiment being done by Mr. Donato, right here in this room?"

"As a matter of fact," replied Mr. Strang, "I'm proceeding on the assumption that she did see it here, rather than in the book. And, in order to clear up any confusion as to what really happened yesterday, I'd like to re-enact the events just as Sheila described them — including the experiment."

"No!" cried Sheila. "I won't let that man — "

"I will play the part of Mr. Donato," said Mr. Strang gently. "You have nothing to fear from me, Sheila. Now, according to the way the experiment is described in the book, we first dump in some — er — Fess." He removed the stopper from the flask and poured in a black powder from a bottle labeled FeS.

"Now for the hydrochloric acid." Mr. Strang replaced the stopper and poured a generous amount of liquid from the acid bottle through the funnel. "And, finally, the flask goes on the stand over the flame." He lit the Bunsen burner.

"Now what?" asked Landerhoff.

"I pull down the shades," said Mr. Strang. "You did say they were down, didn't you, Sheila?"

"Yes, that's right."

The flask on the front table bubbled gently. Mr. Guthrey wrinkled his nose and peered furtively at Landerhoff.

"Now, Sheila," smiled Mr. Strang, when the shades had been pulled down, "pretend that I'm Mr. Donato. What happened next?" The teacher noticed that Donato was chuckling to himself, while Mrs. Palinger had taken a perfumed handkerchief from her purse and placed it over her nose.

"Why — " Sheila began to shift restlessly in her seat. Her eyes were on the bubbling flask in the front of the room. "Why, Mr. Donato came over to the desk — "

"Like this?" Mr. Strang walked slowly up beside Sheila. Those in the rear of the room started coughing loudly. Fred Landerhoff fanned the air in front of his face with a small notebook.

"Yes, sir," replied Sheila. "Then he touched my hair with his hand."

The chemicals in the flask were bubbling more violently now.

"And then?"

"He put his face down into my hair. He said it smelled like — like — "

"Rotten eggs!" cried a voice.

"What's that?" said Mr. Strang. "I'm afraid you're out of

order, Mr. Landerhoff."

"Maybe so, but that kid's out of her mind if she wants me to believe somebody made love to her in a room where there was a stink like this! It smells like all the rotten eggs in the world! Mr. Strang, I'm willing to agree that Donato's not guilty of anything. Just let me out of this room before I suffocate. What is that stuff, anyway?"

Without waiting for an answer, he dashed to the door, flinging desks aside in his hurry to escape the overpowering stench. He was followed in rapid succession by the Palingers, Guthrey, and Donato.

Mr. Strang remained behind only long enough to pour the bubbling mixture from the flask into the sink and throw open all the windows of the room. Then he, too, dashed into the hallway and took deep breaths of comparatively fresh air.

Later, in Guthrey's office, Landerhoff repeated his question. "I've asked Sheila and her mother to wait outside," he said. "Now what was that stuff, Mr. Strang?"

"Hydrogen sulfide," said the teacher. "It's a gas formed when hydrochloric acid is combined with ferrous sulfide and heated. As you noticed in the classroom, it's the same gas that gives rotten eggs their characteristic odor. I admit to using a bit more of the chemicals than is ordinarily used, but I think my point was made. One good whiff of that gas is enough to dispel all thought of *l'amour*."

"When did you first catch on that Sheila was lying?" asked Landerhoff.

"As soon as I realized the experiment she was describing was the manufacture of hydrogen sulfide. She said that Russ began the experiment shortly after she entered the room. But I knew she couldn't have lasted in there for thirty minutes with a smell like that.

"Of course, when I saw the picture she drew, I knew she'd gotten it from the textbook — I've taught enough chemistry to know that book by heart. She'd have been better off if she hadn't been such a good artist. Fortunately for Mr. Donato, she didn't know the devastating effect that hydrogen sulfide has on the olfactory nerves."

"But why didn't Donato recognize the experiment?"

"She never mentioned it in his hearing. It was only after Mr. Guthrey had sent Donato out of the office that Sheila realized time might be an issue. She spotted the chemistry text in the Lost and Found box while she and her mother were waiting in the outer office. It was just too bad for her that she happened to open the book to that particular experiment."

"But why would Sheila do a thing like this?" asked Donato.

"Maybe it was a way of getting into the limelight among her friends. Or it could be as simple as her coming home late and blaming you, so she wouldn't be punished. Also, you're a fairly handsome young man, Russ. Perhaps it was a case of puppy love, and she carried her daydreaming too far. Perhaps Sheila herself doesn't know the real reason."

"What happens now, Fred?" Guthrey asked Landerhoff.

"Well, Mr. Donato will be reinstated, of course, with our apologies, and I think I can convince Mrs. Palinger that Sheila should have a psychiatric examination. But what I'm wondering is what will happen if a similar situation comes up in the future."

"That's up to you, Mr. Landerhoff," said Mr. Strang. "You have a duty as a member of the Board of Education, not only to the children of the district but also to the men and women who teach them. Given an accusation without proof, who will you believe — the child or the teacher?"

Landerhoff looked from Mr. Strang to Donato and back again. He couldn't give an answer to Mr. Strang's question. He just didn't know.

Mr. Strang smiled. The look of doubt in Landerhoff's eyes was enough for him. A reasonable doubt.

That was enough.

MR. STRANG TAKES A FIELD TRIP

The yellow bus with Aldershot High School painted on its side in large black letters came to a creaking halt in front of the Central City Natural History Museum. As the driver opened the door, the twenty-seven teenagers inside shifted excitedly in their seats. Mr. Strang, his battered felt hat perched squarely on the middle of his head to hide a bald spot that was increasing in size at an alarming rate, stood up and hobbled stiffly down the steps of the bus, followed by his biology students, who milled about in what looked like utter confusion.

Silently, the short slender teacher raised one hand over his head. The shrill yelps of the girls and the raucous comments of the boys stopped abruptly. The students formed themselves into two straight lines that would have done credit to a Marine drill instructor. With a quick nod, Mr. Strang led his class into the building.

"Ouch!"

Mr. Strang turned just in time to see the boy at the head of one line clutch at the seat of his pants, a distressed look on his face.

The teacher glared at the second boy in line and held out his hand. "The pin, Mr. Grier," he said wryly. "Give me the pin, if you please."

Smirking, Bradley Grier handed Mr. Strang the long map pin with which he had jabbed his fellow student.

"I'd hoped that for just this one day you would forego the practical jokes, Bradley," said the teacher. "We go on few enough field trips without having you ruin them with your childish attempts at humor. You and I can discuss your little prank later, but right now the doors of the museum are about to open. We'll be among the first ones inside, and I hope the place won't be a shambles when we leave."

Inside the museum, Mr. Strang ushered his class to the foot of a long curving stairway leading upward. "We'll go straight up to the top floor to the Hall of Mammals and work our way down from there," he announced. "Any questions?"

Seeing no raised hands, the teacher started up the steps.

The students broke ranks, pausing from time to time to look at the stuffed animals placed on each landing.

"Git your hands off that before I report you!"

Mr. Strang turned to see Bradley Grier, his arms wrapped around an enormous grizzly bear that seemed to be embracing him lovingly in return. The boy was looking guiltily at a small man in a leather workman's apron who eyed the group belligerently.

"I been from top to bottom of this building today collecting exhibits for cleaning," snarled the man. "They've had everything on 'em from shoe polish to bubble gum. I just finished brushing down that bear not more'n two hours ago, and there's about twenty more animals in the basement to do. So look but don't touch!"

Mr. Strang found himself wishing that Bradley had chosen today for one of his numerous absences from school.

The members of the class reached the top floor and found themselves facing two large arched doorways. Bronze letters over the left doorway read INDIANS OF THE WESTERN HEMISPHERE; to the right was the entrance to THE HALL OF MAMMALS. A smaller sheet-metal door at the extreme right end of the hallways bore a cardboard sign saying EMPLOYEES ONLY, and Mr. Strang wondered how long it would be before one of the students pulled the ancient gag of asking to see the stuffed employees.

The Hall of Mammals was devoted almost entirely to unusual types of furred animals. Just inside the doorway, a duck-billed platypus lay curled around its egg on top of a glass case filled with small creatures neatly classified as being either CARNIVOROUS or HERBIVOROUS. Beyond this was the skeleton of a burro supported by hidden braces, and a vampire bat hung from the ceiling, its enormous wings outstretched. Even the mighty sperm whale was represented in the middle of a grouping of aquatic mammals by a single tooth almost twelve inches in length.

While his students dashed from one zoological oddity to another, Mr. Strang stood in front of a large niche in one wall. At one side of the niche, an opossum and an Australian koala, mounted on polished wooden pedestals high enough to bring them to eye level, were separated from a Tasmanian devil on a similar stand by an empty space about four feet wide. The devil, which resembled a small long-tailed bear, had lips curled back to reveal sharp teeth, and Mr. Strang was glad the little monster wasn't alive.

"Mean-looking thing, isn't he?"

The teacher turned to face a tall cadaverous man who wore the gray blazer of a museum attendant. "My name's Talbot," said the man in a soft voice, extending his hand, "and you must be Mr. Strang. We were told to expect your class. I'm assigned to the Hall of Mammals, so if you have any questions please feel free to ask."

Mr. Strang shook Mr. Talbot's hand and then glanced to one side in time to see Bradley Grier, accompanied by another student, disappear through a doorway at the rear.

"Where does that lead?" asked the teacher warily, gesturing toward the rear door.

"Just into the next room — the Indian exhibit," replied Talbot. "Don't worry about the boys. Our Mr. Albemarle has charge of that area. He'll look after them."

"It's not the boys I'm worried about. It's — "

Mr. Strang was abruptly interrupted by the roar of a man's voice from the next room. The cry was one of mingled outrage and disbelief. "It's gone!"

As the shout echoed off the museum's marble walls, the babbling of the students stopped abruptly, creating an eerie silence. There was a sound of footsteps tapping across a hard surface, and then a man appeared in the rear doorway.

The man, who wore a blazer similar to Talbot's, stood there a moment, an angry expression on his face. Finally he spotted Mr. Strang and pointed an accusing finger in the teacher's direction.

"One of your kids stole my mask," said the man, striding purposefully toward Mr. Strang, "and I want it back. Where is it?"

The teacher stared at the man in amazed silence. It was Talbot who finally spoke up. "Mr. Albemarle," he said stiffly, "this is Mr. Strang. He's here on a field trip with his class, and he hasn't been out of my sight since he got to this floor. Now what's this all about?"

"Maybe the teacher hasn't been out of your sight, but you can't say the same for the kids," said Albemarle. "Two of them came through the door back there and were looking at the Indian exhibits. I went to see if I could help them, and that's when I saw the mask was missing."

"What mask?" asked Mr. Strang.

"Come on and I'll show you," said Albemarle. "When are you teachers going to learn how to look after your classes while they're in the museum? That's your job, isn't it — to keep them from stealing and wrecking everything in sight?"

Restraining an impulse to plant a foot in Albemarle's ample backside, Mr. Strang followed the attendant into the next room. As he walked through the doorway, two boys standing next to one wall launched themselves at the teacher and began chattering loudly.

"We didn't do nothin', Mr. Strang!"

"Look, sir, if this man would just tell us what's missing – "

Mr. Strang considered the youth who was standing beside Bradley Grier. "Why, Mr. Pellman," said the teacher with a mocking smile, "imagine meeting you here. Did you and Bradley decide to take a little stroll, or were you planning to escape from the rest of the class?"

"This isn't funny, Mr. Strang," moaned Steven Pellman. "Bradley and me – I – well, anyway, we just wanted to see what was in here. And we hadn't been in this room more than a minute when that museum guard grabbed us and started yelling about how we stole something. I still don't know what he's talking about."

"I'll show you what I'm talking about," growled Albemarle, and he motioned for Mr. Strang to follow him.

The room containing the Indian exhibits was divided neatly down the middle by a velvet rope. On one side were displays of North American Indians, featuring cases full of flint arrowheads and other artifacts, and a full-sized canoe and tepee. On the other were the Central and South American Indian exhibits. Albemarle led the teacher across the room and pointed to a spot on one wall behind a high rack of pottery.

Set in a circular pattern on the wall were a group of the most grotesque masks that Mr. Strang had ever seen. Made of wood, stone, and other materials, their bulging eyes, thick rounded mouths, and oddly colored chins and cheeks made a display that was both fascinating and frightening.

On the wall in the center of the circle was a dark wooden plaque about eighteen inches square. But whatever had been mounted on the plaque was now gone.

"It was an ancient Inca burial mask," said Albemarle. "Pre-Columbian, and solid gold, too. That thing was worth a fortune, and one of these two took it. Probably both of them had a hand in it."

"If one of my students took it, I'll get it back for you," said Mr. Strang.

"What do you mean, if? They're the only ones who have been in here this morning." Albemarle pointed to the large arched doorway at the other end of the room. "I haven't been more than ten feet from that entrance since I came to work," he said. "Nobody could have come through there without my seeing them. The only other way in here is from the Hall of Mammals next door. And your kids are the only ones who have been on this floor so far today. Most people start their looking downstairs. We don't get much of a crowd up here until noon."

"And of my class only these two — Grier and Pellman — came into this room. Is that right?"

"That's right."

"Any possibility that they could have taken the mask out of here — say, into the Hall of Mammals?"

"None at all. I had my eyes on them from the moment they came in. Oh, they could have gotten the mask off the wall without my seeing them — that shelf of pottery hides the place where the mask was hanging from the front doorway. But they didn't go back next door. I'm sure of that."

Mr. Strang turned to the two students. "You've heard what the man said, boys," he murmured, "and I think you'll agree the joke's gone far enough. Now, where did you put it?"

Bradley Grier and Steve Pellman were pictures of outraged innocence. Mr. Strang noticed that the rest of his students were now gathering in the rear doorway.

"Keep them in the next room, please, Mr. Talbot," called Mr. Strang. He turned back to the two boys standing at the wall. "If you don't tell me where that infernal thing is," he went on, "I'm going to have to treat this not as a joke but as an attempt to steal museum property. So, for the last time, where is the mask?"

Steve Pellman took a step forward. "Honest, Mr. Strang," he began, "we didn't take anything. Sure, we looked at that board on the wall. Brad asked me what I thought was mounted on it. Before I could answer, this man grabbed the both of us."

"Mr. String, or whatever your name is," said Albemarle, "that mask was one of the most valuable articles in this museum. Why, the gold alone must be worth a fortune, to say nothing of its archeological value. If it doesn't turn up, I'm just going to have to call the police."

The police!

Mr. Strang pictured himself trying to explain to his principal how he took a class on a field trip and got involved with the police. "Wait a minute," he said placatingly. "How big is this mask?"

"Why, it's — well, the size of a mask. Made to fit over a man's face. And thick. The gold is — "

"Then it's not exactly the sort of thing one could slip into a pocket and walk off with, is it?" asked the teacher.

"No, I guess not – not unless you had oversized pockets. Even then, there would be quite a bulge."

"Then you'll agree that neither of the boys has it on his person?"

"Why, yes, I suppose so," replied Albemarle, looking closely at the students in their tight-fitting clothing.

"And you admit they didn't leave this room?"

Albemarle nodded.

"Then the mask has to be somewhere in the room. I suggest that you and I search for it. And you might tell Mr. Talbot to keep any other visitors off this floor until we're finished."

Mr. Strang considered his theory to be flawless. But the fact remained that, half an hour later, he and Albemarle were covered with dust, the exhibit of INDIANS OF THE WESTERN HEMISPHERE had been thoroughly searched – and the mask was still missing.

"It's impossible," said Albemarle, rubbing his hands against his now grimy blazer. "Nobody has it, it isn't here – what could have happened to it?"

Mr. Strang rubbed his hand across his forehead, leaving streaks of dirt over one eye. He set his jaw grimly. "I may have been mistaken about the mask's still being in this room," he said, "but we know for sure the boys haven't been off this floor. I'm going to take my class out to the top of the stairs. Mr. Talbot can stay with them. You and I are going to go over this entire floor with a fine-tooth comb. And when we've found the mask – which we're certain to do – we'll come back in here and wring the necks of both these boys."

"But, Mr. Strang," began Bradley Grier.

"Shut up," replied the red-faced teacher, in a most unprofessional burst of anger. "Right now, I want to be left alone with my thoughts – which at present concern slow lingering torture for you and Steve Pellman."

The class was led out to the landing at the top of the stairs. After glancing at each student in turn and examining two of the girls' larger handbags, Albemarle announced that he was satisfied that nobody had the mask in his possession. At that, leaving Talbot with the students, he and Mr. Strang went into the Hall of Mammals.

"What about these stuffed animals?" asked Mr. Strang, picking up the koala from its stand and shaking it. "Is there any way one of them could be cut open and –"

"Not a chance," said Albemarle. "The skins are mounted over fiberglass shells. Nothing short of an ax would go through them. Even then, there'd be a sound like a bass drum. Listen." The attendant struck his knuckles against a raccoon mounted on the branch of a tree. There was a hollow, booming sound. "It would be impossible to do it without somebody hearing or seeing," he concluded.

"Then our search shouldn't take long," said the teacher.

It didn't. In less than half an hour, the room had been carefully searched, the mask was still missing, and Mr. Strang was considering the possibility that black magic was involved.

"*Priapulida!*" muttered the teacher. "The mask has to be on this floor, doesn't it? I mean, you saw it here earlier, didn't you?"

"That's right. I inspect all my exhibits when I come to work. That mask was in its place at least an hour before the museum opened."

"Then it has to be here — but it isn't," said Mr. Strang, walking out of the Hall of Mammals. He glanced at the metal door at the end of the hall. "There's a place we haven't searched. What's in there?"

"An elevator shaft," said Albemarle.

"Oh? Then maybe — "

"Maybe somebody pitched the mask into the shaft? Forget it, Mr. Strang. That door can only be opened from the other side — so nobody will fall down the shaft by accident."

Mr. Strang had to remind himself sternly that teachers must not break down in front of their students.

Tired, dusty, and bedraggled, the teacher walked out to the head of the stairs, where Steve Pellman and Bradley Grier were standing near Talbot. Mr. Strang looked at the boys, a forlorn expression on his face.

"Where?" he asked simply.

"Honest, Mr. Strang," Steve began, "we didn't — "

"Forget it, Steve," interrupted Bradley. "He's got it all figured out that we did it, no matter how much we deny it. He can't think of anything except that we took it. I guess that's what the great Mr. Strang calls keeping an open mind."

The other students held their collective breath as Mr. Strang glared at Bradley. They were waiting for the verbal explosion that the boy's insolence would undoubtedly trigger. The teacher clenched his fists, and his eyes flashed.

Then the anger died, the thin shoulders slumped wearily, and a low chuckle came from the teacher.

"You're absolutely right, Bradley," he said softly, "although you might have put it a bit more delicately. My procedure up to now has been most unfair and highly unscientific. I'm afraid I've allowed your reputation to influence my thinking. Still, the mask is missing. Do you have any suggestions?"

"Mr. Strang," replied Bradley, a note of relief in his voice, "you've always told us there's no problem that can't be solved if enough thought is given to it. It seems to me — excuse me, sir — that now's a good time for you to either, er, put up or shut up."

"Hmmm." Deep in thought, the teacher walked slowly to the entrance to the Hall of Mammals. He paused and scratched his head. Peering through the doorway, he could see the opossum and the koala perched innocently on their stands.

And then he remembered something Albemarle had told him.

"Outrageous," he murmured to himself, "and yet there's no other possible — "

"What are you mumbling about?" asked Albemarle. "I'm going to have to call the police and report — "

"Just a minute, please," said Mr. Strang, waving his hand impatiently. "That opossum on the stand, Mr. Albemarle — did you know the opossum is native to North America?"

"What's that got to do with the mask?"

Before answering, Mr. Strang slowly removed his glasses from his inside jacket pocket. After polishing them on his necktie, he held them in one hand, making jabbing motions in the air. The other hand was inserted deep in a jacket pocket. Although the ritual was new to Albemarle, the students of Aldershot High School were quite familiar with it.

Mr. Strang, having considered all facets of the problem at hand, was about to deliver A Lecture.

"Before I answer your question," he replied, "I'd like you to consider something, Mr. Albemarle. Since you first announced that the mask was missing, we've gone on the assumption that it was hidden on this floor. And yet we've searched everywhere and haven't found it. Isn't it obvious, therefore, that we were wrong — that the mask is somewhere else?"

"But it's got to be here!"

"Why?"

"Look, Mr. Strang, Talbot and I came up here at eight o'clock. That was two hours before the museum opened. You and your class got here about ten-fifteen. And nobody has left this floor this morning!"

"No?" Mr. Strang turned to Bradley Grier. "On the way up the stairs earlier, you had a slight altercation with a museum employee — the man in the leather apron. Do you remember what he said about his work, Bradley, something that might have a bearing on our problem?"

"I don't think so. Hey, wait a minute! He said he'd been from top to bottom of the museum collecting animals for cleaning."

"From top to bottom," repeated Mr. Strang. "And this is the top floor of the museum, isn't it? So we were not the only ones up here. That workman came up and left again. I further suggest, Mr. Albemarle, that in collecting the animals he had to use the elevator to take them to the basement, where he does whatever repairs are necessary."

"Hold on," said Albemarle. "Are you trying to pin this on old Ernie Frye?"

"Frye? Is that the man's name?"

"It is. And he's been working in this museum more than twenty-five years. He takes better care of the exhibits than most people do of their kids. Nobody's going to make me believe that Ernie stole — "

"You said the mask is extremely valuable?"

"Sure it is. But Ernie? Impossible! Besides, he never was actually on this floor. He waited in the elevator while Talbot and I brought him the things to be cleaned."

"What did you send down, Mr. Albemarle?"

"Why, let me see. There was a feather headdress, and a llama's-hair robe. I guess Talbot sent down a couple of animals — I heard him moving some things around after I got back to my post."

"I see. I don't suppose there's any possibility that you could have sent the mask down with the other things accidentally?"

Albemarle shook his head. "Ernie gave me a receipt for the headdress and the robe," he said. "He'd have spotted that mask right away if I'd had it. Besides, there are seven men working with him in the basement. One of them would have been sure to see something as big as the mask and ask Ernie about it."

Mr. Strang smiled. "Splendid," he said. "We can therefore eliminate Mr. Frye as the thief. I suspect, however, that he was the means by which the mask was taken off this floor."

"But how was it done without anybody seeing it?"

Mr. Strang took Albermarle by the arm and guided him into the Hall of Mammals. There he pointed dramatically to the niche containing the opossum, the koala, and the Tasmanian devil.

"Notice the empty space between the koala and the Tasmanian devil," said the teacher. "That space — about four feet wide — must have contained one of the animals that Mr. Talbot sent down for cleaning. I suspect the animal carried off the mask."

"You mean it was alive?" asked Albemarle in surprise.

"Hardly," said Mr. Strang. "But here, in a single group, are an opossum from North America and a koala, found primarily in Australia. Then there's that empty space, with the Tasmanian devil on the other side of it. It seems unlikely to me that these three animals were placed together haphazardly. If they weren't, then they must have had something in common, even though they come from different parts of the world."

"In common? Like what?" asked Albemarle.

"Remember what you said when I asked about the size of the mask? You said no one could conceal it unless he had oversized pockets. Do you know what a marsupial is, Mr. Albemarle."

"No, Talbot's the animal man around here."

"It's an animal that has a pouch for carrying its young. Or, if you will, an oversized pocket. All three of these animals are marsupials — that's their common factor, the reason the four of them were placed in the same niche. Now, what other animal with a pouch would fit into the empty space? It would have to be fairly large, since it obviously wasn't set on a stand like the others."

"A kangaroo!" cried Albemarle, snapping his fingers.

"Exactly, a kangaroo. An animal nearly the size of a grown man. The one animal with a pouch or pocket large enough to contain the mask."

"And nobody would notice if the mask was hidden in the pouch," added Albemarle. "But, look, the only one who could have hidden the mask there without being noticed is — "

"Mr. Talbot," replied the teacher. "He must have slipped through the rear door into the Indian Hall while you were at the elevator with Frye. After he'd taken the mask from the wall, he came back in here, hid the mask in the kangaroo's pouch, then moved the animal out to the elevator. You suspected nothing, because you didn't even realize anything was missing until we got here. You said yourself that, except for your one inspection when you first came on the job today, you didn't move from the entrance to the Indian Hall."

"Then the mask must be in the basement right now," said Albemarle. "And Talbot's got to get it before somebody down there starts working on that kangaroo."

"If you're looking for Mr. Talbot," said Bradley Grier, who was standing at the entrance to the Hall of Mammals, "you'd better hurry. He just started downstairs. He said something about calling the police and told us to wait — "

Albemarle looked around excitedly and finally yanked a bone from the skull of the burro's skeleton. Waving it over his head like a club, he dashed through the doorway and down the stairs, calling loudly for Talbot to stop. Mr. Strang, moving more slowly, arrived at the top of the stairs just in time to see Talbot overtaken by his pursuer, who brought the bone crashing down on Talbot's head.

Half an hour later, the missing exhibit had been retrieved from its unique hiding place. A tired but completely happy Mr. Strang stood with his class and watched Ernie Frye re-mount the glittering golden burial mask on the wall of the Hall of Indians. He felt a touch on his sleeve and turned to an equally joyful Mr. Albemarle.

"What a day this has been," said the attendant. "For a teacher, you're quite a detective, Mr. Strang."

"And you, Mr. Albemarle, were a veritable Samson," replied the teacher.

"Samson?"

Mr. Strang pointed to the bone still clutched in Albemarle's hand. "The burro's skull," said the teacher. "Didn't Samson also defeat his enemy with the jawbone of an ass?"

MR. STRANG VERSUS THE SNOWMAN

Wearily, Mr. Strang climbed the stairs of Mrs. Mackey's rooming house just as the hall clock chimed six. It had been a long day, and he still had three sets of chemistry tests to correct. Still, the weather report had predicted snow, perhaps several inches. Maybe Aldershot High School would be closed tomorrow.

The door to his room was slightly ajar. He started to push it open and then paused, sniffing several times like a hunting dog on a hot scent.

"Paul Roberts, what are you doing in my room?" he called loudly. Pushing the door open, he glared in mock anger over the tops of his black-rimmed glasses at the figure lounging in the easy chair in the far corner of the room.

Detective-Sergeant Paul Roberts slowly got to his feet, his huge body looming over that of the slender, gnome-like teacher. "Waiting for you," he said. "Mrs. Mackey was on her way out when I got here, but she said it would okay for me to come up. By the way, how'd you know I was in here before you opened the door?"

Mr. Strang rubbed the cold from his gnarled hands and then removed hat, scarf, and overcoat, hanging them on the ancient clothes rack behind the door. "Like Sherlock Holmes, I hate to reveal my methods," he chuckled. "But really, Paul, that shaving lotion of yours would gag a billygoat."

"I kind of like it," said Roberts. "It's called Boots and Saddle."

"Umm. The boots and saddle must have belonged to a Russian Cossack who hadn't bathed in six months," said Mr. Strang. "But what can I do for you, Paul? Has one of my students gotten himself into a jam?"

"Not exactly, but — " Roberts paused, uncertain how to begin. "Look, are you familiar with the name Simon Barasch?"

"If you've done your homework before coming here, you know good and well the answer is yes," replied the teacher. "His grandson Arthur is in my physics class. Arthur's been living with Simon since his father died three years ago."

"Simon," mused Roberts. "You're on a first-name basis with Barasch?"

"About six weeks ago, Simon Barasch broke his leg," said Mr. Strang. "Arthur was out of school for ten days to take care of him. During that time, he missed a good deal of work in physics. So, a couple of times a week, he's been staying after school with me for extra help. He lives way out at the edge of town, and I drive him home in my car. Quite often, I go into the house to see Simon. He's confined to a wheelchair and doesn't get many visitors."

"Yeah," said Roberts in a flat voice. "What do you two talk about, Mr. Strang?"

The teacher's mouth snapped closed with an audible click, and he shook his head vehemently. "Paul, we've been friends for a long time," he said. "But I'm not going to say another word about Simon Barasch until I find out what this is all about."

From the pocket of his overcoat, Roberts drew out a sheet of yellow paper. "Simon Barasch," he began, glancing at the paper, "alias Samuel Barr. In 1935, he served twenty months of a three-to-five-year sentence for smuggling. Paroled. Next heard of in '42, accused of bringing in narcotics from Mexico. He managed a hung jury on that rap.

"He got an acquittal on a charge of narcotics possession in '50, but in '54 he began serving five years of a seven-to-ten-year jolt for the theft of several ampules of morphine from a hospital in Seattle. Paroled again." Roberts stopped reading and looked at the astounded teacher. "Did Simon Barasch ever mention any of this during your visits, Mr. Strang?"

"No, I never knew. Is he wanted by the police now?"

"Not officially. But that's why I'm here. I want to talk about Simon Barasch."

"I'm afraid I still don't understand. If Simon's not guilty of any crime, I don't see that his past record can be held against him."

"Mr. Strang, during the past few months, one drug — cocaine — has been coming into Aldershot in a big way. Some people call it 'coke' or 'snow,' but, whatever name you use, it's pure poison. And most of it's being used by teenagers, your students over there at Aldershot High. They prefer it to other hard drugs like heroin, because it doesn't show up in urine tests, so they can take the school's screening physicals without having to worry.

"They start out sniffing it up their nose for a quick high, and, when that doesn't work any more, they use a needle to pop it into a vein. First thing you know, they're hooked. They've got a monkey on their back that would make King

Kong look like a midget."

"Is the problem really that serious?"

"In the past two months, we've found thirty-three kids who were users. Five were confirmed addicts, one of 'em a seventh grader. Those with big habits have had to be taken out of school and placed under treatment. And God knows how many teenagers are on the stuff that we haven't found out about yet."

"And because of his previous record, you think Simon Barasch is peddling the, uh, snow?"

Roberts wadded up the paper and thrust it deep into his pocket. "If pushers were all we were interested in, I could walk out of here and have the Aldershot jail full in an hour. But they'd just be replaced by others. The guy we're really after is the one we call the Snowman."

Mr. Strang removed his glasses and blinked at Roberts, a puzzled frown on his face. "The who?" he asked.

"Look, Mr. Strang, cocaine may go through a dozen hands before it gets to the eventual user. Each time, it's cut with sugar or milk powder to increase the volume — and the profits. But the process has got to start somewhere.

"In its pure form, cocaine comes in blocks the size of a small brick. Usually, each block is sealed in plastic. Somebody has to receive these blocks from suppliers and begin the process of breaking the cocaine down into smaller units. If we can make him — get a positive identification — the whole local organization could collapse."

"And you think this person — the Snowman — is Simon Barasch?"

"It figures. You can't just go out on the open market and buy cocaine. It takes connections, delivery techniques, means of payment. And the only person we've been able to come up with who'd know about these things is Barasch. On the other hand, we've got no real evidence of narcotics dealing by him since he moved to Aldershot."

"I see. And just where do I come in?"

"Aside from his grandson and a few delivery men — any of whom might be bringing in the cocaine — you're about the only one who can get into the house without making Barasch suspicious."

"And once inside, what do I do? Search the premises? Hold him at gunpoint?"

"Just keep your eyes open. See if there's anything out of the ordinary. A cupboard he keeps locked, a glassine bag in the trash — anything."

"Sounds like looking for a needle in a haystack."

Roberts gave a tired sigh. "It's all we've got going for us, Mr. Strang. And frankly, even if we locate cocaine in the Barasch house, we can't be certain of a conviction. What I'd really like to do is catch Barasch with his pockets full of the stuff in front of eyewitnesses. But anything you find might allow us to scare him into closing down his operation. That would be something."

"I'll try, Paul. That's the best I can promise. But Barasch, well, he just doesn't seem the type."

"They seldom do, Mr. Strang. And if he's clean, I'll be the first to apologize. Do you think you can get over there tomorrow?"

"Yes, if the blizzard they've been predicting holds off and there's school. Arthur's due in my room at three-thirty to complete an experiment. He should be finished by five o'clock. I'll have a visit with Simon when I drive Arthur home. But what's the hurry?"

"There's talk around that the supply of cocaine in town right now is kind of low. There's got to be a delivery in the next day or so. Maybe, just maybe, we'll get lucky."

The following morning, as Mr. Strang drove to Aldershot High School, the sky was heavy with gray clouds. The predicted snow, however, held off until shortly after lunch, when huge flakes began to fall, sticking wetly wherever they landed. By the end of the school day, the blizzard was in full blast, the air full of snowflakes and the ground covered to a depth of almost three inches.

In his room, Mr. Strang was just putting away a distilling apparatus in the storage closet when he heard the classroom door open.

"It's me, Mr. Strang," called a voice, "Arthur Barasch. I thought I'd get started with that experiment now."

In the doorway of the storage closet, Mr. Strang looked from the boy to the snow beating against the windows. "You didn't catch your bus," he said peevishly.

"No, sir. I thought I'd report here the way you said."

"Arthur," said Mr. Strang, trying to keep the annoyance out of his voice, "it's snowing outside, hard. You can't possibly finish in less than an hour. How were you planning to get home?"

"Couldn't you — I mean, you always drove me before."

"My car, young man, is not a snowplow. It tends to get stuck in anything worse than a heavy dew. Come on. We'll leave before the streets get any worse and — "

The teacher paused, remembering his conversation with Paul Roberts the previous evening.

"And then I think I'll wait out this snowstorm at your house," he concluded.

During the drive to the Barasch house, Mr. Strang's small purple car skidded alarmingly on the slippery streets, and its windshield wipers fought a losing battle against the falling snow. As the teacher pulled into the driveway and up to the side door, a rear fender struck a garbage can, adding still another dent to the car's battered exterior.

The teacher got out to examine the extent of the damage. "Nothing to worry about," he said, rubbing a gloved hand along a scratch where the bare metal was now exposed. "Hardly in the same league as the one I got when I collided with a fire hydrant in front of the school."

"Let's go in, Mr. Strang," said Arthur, his teeth chattering. "It'll be warm inside."

Half blinded by snow sticking to his glasses, Mr. Strang permitted himself to be led to the side door and pulled into the entranceway that led into the kitchen. Arthur slammed the door behind him, and the teacher stamped his feet to rid them of thick gobs of snow.

"Whew! What's that, Mr. Strang?" asked Arthur suddenly. "What's that smell?"

Mr. Strang sniffed the air, tentatively at first, but then breathing deeply of the pungent odor that filled the alcove. A beatific smile spread across his face.

"That, my boy," he said, slipping out of his overcoat, "is Scotch whisky. And not just a little bit of it, mind you. A whole ocean."

"Scotch? But how could — ?" Arthur Barasch took two steps into the kitchen. "Grandpa, are you all right?" he called.

"Careful, there, Artie! Don't get your feet wet. You and Mr. Strang stay over there in the corner, and I'll try to get this mopped up."

Simon Barasch, seated in his wheelchair with one plaster-covered leg stretched out before him, reminded Mr. Strang of a wounded walrus. His completely bald head was in sharp contrast to the fearsome mustache of bristling white hair that stretched across his jowled cheeks. In one pudgy hand he held a pair of tongs almost three feet long, the end of which gripped a paper napkin. With the napkin, he was making ineffectual passes at the flood of tan liquid on the kitchen floor. Behind him, an open window was admitting a blast of cold air.

"Spilled the whole bottle, I did," Barasch grumbled angrily. "I was gonna have a little nip, but it fell off the shelf." With the tongs, he retrieved the bottle, which was lying on its side on the floor, empty. "Not enough left in it to wet your whistle," the old man continued, tipping it to his mouth in a vain attempt to extract a few last drops.

"You and Mr. Strang go into the living room, Grandpa," said Arthur. "I'll clean this up."

"I'd be obliged if you would," replied Barasch. "And while you're at it, close the window, will you? I tried to air out the kitchen after the Scotch spilled, but the snow's coming in something fierce."

Mr. Strang wheeled Barasch into the living room, trying hard not to laugh aloud at the crippled man's mumbled outrage over the loss of his whisky. It was difficult for the teacher to equate this befuddled individual with the hardened criminal described by Paul Roberts the evening before.

"What brings you here this early?" Barasch finally asked. "Artie told me not to expect him until after five."

"The snowstorm. I was afraid that by five we wouldn't be able to make it." As if proving the truth of Mr. Strang's answer, the howling of the wind outside increased. There was a sharp click, and the front door banged open, admitting a flurry of snow.

"The confounded place is coming down around my ears!" roared Barasch, as the teacher slammed the front door and shot the bolt. "Whisky bottles jump off the shelf. Doors pop open by themselves. The house must be haunted."

Without answering, Mr. Strang looked about the room for anything that might be construed as incriminating evidence. He quickly ascertained that Simon Barasch was addicted to checkers, Charles Dickens, and wickedly strong cigars, none of which, the teacher was sure, would be of interest to the police.

Arthur Barasch appeared in the kitchen doorway, a mop soggy with Scotch whisky in his hand. "The radio says the storm ought to stop by nine," he said. "I guess you'll have to plan on eating here, Mr. Strang."

"I'd like that very much," replied the teacher. "Can I help with the cooking?"

"Naw," said Simon Barasch, sucking the end of his mustache. "We're having pork chops, and Artie cooks 'em better'n anybody. I'd offer you a drink, but there's nothing left in the house. Unless you'd care to wring out that mop."

Mr. Strang, however, insisted on helping in the kitchen. It gave him an opportunity to peer into all the cabinets and closets there. A quick taste was enough to assure him that even the soap powder was the real article.

When the meal was finished, he asked for a tour of the house. "Don't know why you'd want it," was Barasch's reply. "You aren't going to see anything but dust. I'm not much on housekeeping. But if you like, Artie'll take you around. In the meantime, I'll set up the checkerboard. I ain't been beat yet, but maybe you'll be the first."

A little after nine, the snow stopped. At almost the same time, they heard the roar of a snowplow cleaning the street in front of the house. By then, Mr. Strang had become convinced of two things: first, that he was a hopelessly inept checker player, and second, that there was no evidence of cocaine or any other drug stronger than aspirin in the entire Barasch house. Simon Barasch not only was unconcerned about the teacher poking into odd corners, he even went out of his way to show Mr. Strang all the hidden nooks and crannies.

And yet, as he put on his overcoat preparing to leave, Mr. Strang had the distinct impression that the old man was laughing at him.

"Artie will have you shoveled out in no time," said Barasch, shaking the teacher's hand. "Be sure and come back again, Mr. Strang. Any time. It's been real interesting having one of Artie's teachers come in and look us over."

He's a sly one, thought Mr. Strang. He knows what I've been doing. He's not the doddering old fool he pretends to be. Paul was right about him — he has to be the Snowman. But he didn't react, no matter where I looked. So either the cocaine hasn't arrived yet, or else he's already passed it on to someone else. Or —

The side door opened, and Arthur Barasch came back into the house, stomping snow from his boots. "All clear, Mr. Strang," he said. "Drive carefully, and I'll see you tomorrow."

"Well, Paul Roberts wanted snow, and now he's got tons of it," muttered the teacher as he got behind the wheel of his car and backed out into the street. Halfway to Mrs. Mackey's, he turned on the heater.

The blast of warm air melted the snow from his rubbers, and water formed a shallow pool on the car's plastic floor mats. He felt some of it soak into the cuffs of his trousers. He wished he were already in his room, where he had a half-full bottle of sherry hidden in a desk drawer. He wouldn't drink it all, of course. Just one glass to —

"*Brachiopoda!*" he shouted suddenly, his face twisting into a grimace. "Gotcha, Mr. Snowman!"

There was a telephone booth on the next corner. Mr. Strang, suddenly oblivious to the hazardous driving conditions, slammed on the brakes. The car skidded alarmingly, traveling almost fifty yards past the telephone before stopping inches from a giant maple tree. His joints cracking, Mr. Strang scuttled back to the booth, jammed a dime into the slot, and dialed Detective Roberts' number.

Twenty minutes later, Mr. Strang was seated on the passenger side of an unmarked police car across the street from the Barasch house. Paul Roberts was behind the wheel, and his sidekick, Detective David Bell, occupied the rear seat. The spot the teacher had chosen commanded a clear view of the house's side door and kitchen window — or it would have, had there been any light to see by.

"Are you going to tell us any more about what you saw in the house, Mr. Strang?" asked Roberts. "If I'm supposed to sit here and freeze to death, can't I at least know why?"

"Not yet, Paul," answered Mr. Strang. "You'd just barge in ahead of time and ruin the whole thing. Besides, there's the boy to consider. I don't think he has any idea what his grandfather's up to."

"I don't get it, Paul," Bell chimed in. "Where does this guy get off telling you what to do?"

"Sergeant Roberts asked for my help, and I'm giving it to him," said Mr. Strang in the same tone he used in dealing with an unruly schoolboy. "He said that, to be sure of a conviction, Barasch had to be caught with his pockets full of drugs. And that's exactly how I'm going to deliver him to you. Just be patient."

Ten o'clock and then ten-thirty came and went, with only the living-room lights on inside the house. It was nearly eleven when a lamp gleamed from an upstairs window and a figure was seen silhouetted against the curtains.

"That's the boy's room," whispered the teacher. "He's going to bed now. Keep that in mind, both of you. He's no part of your case against Simon Barasch."

A short while later, the lights in Arthur's room went out. Once again, only the living-room windows were illuminated. Forty minutes went by.

Suddenly Bell, who had been blowing on his hands to

warm them, tapped Roberts on the back. "You see that?" he asked.

"Yeah, the lights at the back of the house went on."

"Simon Barasch is in the kitchen now," said Mr. Strang, "and that's our cue to move closer. If we're careful, I think we can get to that forsythia bush just opposite the kitchen window without being spotted."

"He's probably just getting a snack or something," grumbled Bell. "Anyway, I'm glad I wore boots. This snow is deep."

The three men got out of the car, taking care not to slam the doors. They plodded through the snow, finally crouching behind the bush about fifteen feet from the kitchen window.

"Now what, Mr. Strang?" breathed Roberts.

"Now we wait. It shouldn't be long."

Even as he spoke, they heard the sound of a window latch turning. The inner pane slid upward, and the hinged storm window tilted out.

"Hey, what − ?" Bell began, but Mr. Strang silenced him with a gloved hand over his mouth.

A hand slid out of the window, holding a long object the teacher recognized: the tongs Simon Barasch used to retrieve objects dropped to the floor.

More of the object came into view, until the end of the tongs reached the pile of snow below the window. The tongs probed for a few moments. Finally they caught something − a small rectangular object that glittered in the light from the kitchen. Gripping their prize, the tongs were swiftly withdrawn into the house.

"Do you suppose, Mr. Bell," whispered Mr. Strang, "that when that arm appears again, you could get over there and grab it and not let go?"

"Count on me, Mr. Strang." Bell shifted his weight onto the balls of his feet.

Again the hand holding the tongs came through the window. Then Bell was running across the snow. A shout of anger and surprise was heard, followed by Bell's call: "I got him! Now what?"

Roberts and Mr. Strang ran to the window, where Bell was holding fast to Simon Barasch's wrist with both hands. Inside the house, Barasch was struggling in his wheelchair like a hooked fish.

From the pile of snow at his feet, Roberts picked up a small white block sealed in plastic. He tore open a corner and gingerly touched his tongue to the block.

"It's cocaine, all right," he said.

"Paul, do you think this will be enough to get a conviction?" asked Mr. Strang, pointing in through the window.

Roberts looked at the struggling man and then back to Mr. Strang. "I think so," he said with a grin. "Get a load of that, Bell."

From the pocket of Simon Barasch's sweater protruded another plastic-wrapped block of cocaine.

It was nearly three in the morning when all the formalities incident to booking Simon Barasch for narcotics possession had been complied with. Finally Roberts returned to the squad room, where Mr. Strang was trying without success to find a comfortable position in one of the hard-backed chairs.

"I sent Bell back to look after the boy," said Roberts. "He's the one I feel sorry for in this whole thing. Apparently he had no idea what old Simon was up to."

"Arthur once mentioned an older sister who's married and lives upstate somewhere," said Mr. Strang. "I'm sure something can be worked out."

There was a long silence between the two men, finally broken by Roberts. "Okay, Mr. Strang," he said. "Give. How'd you know old man Barasch had hidden the snow in the — well, in the snow?"

"A chain of deductions, Paul, that started with an empty bottle."

"The Scotch bottle you told me about?"

"Exactly. Barasch told Arthur and me that the bottle of Scotch had been on the shelf and had fallen off, spilling its contents. But that couldn't have been the case, because the bottle was empty."

"So it was empty. So what?"

"Think, Paul. Imagine that bottle lying on its side with whisky pouring out. The level inside the bottle drops. How far down does it go?"

"I guess it would keep going down until it was below the bottle's neck."

"At which point, there'd still be some whisky left in the bottle. And yet the bottle we saw was completely empty."

"Hey, yeah, that's right," said Roberts.

"Very well. So, deduction number one: Barasch was lying when he said the bottle had fallen accidentally. Therefore, he'd deliberately poured out the contents."

"But why would he do a thing like that?"

"Deduction number two: by pouring out the Scotch, Barasch was trying to conceal something. Another odor? Doubtful in this case, since the bagged cocaine would have no odor. Therefore, there was something on the floor that had to be hidden."

"Like what, Mr. Strang?"

"There seemed to be only one answer that made sense. Barasch poured out the Scotch onto the floor to hide the snow."

"Snow? You mean the cocaine?"

"No, I mean snow — small crystals of frozen water. You see, I believe Barasch had another visitor this afternoon, who entered the house just a minute or two before we arrived. Whoever it was had to have snow on his feet, which he tracked into the kitchen. Moments later, Barasch heard my car drive up. At that point, he made every effort to conceal the snow. Therefore, deduction number three: the visitor was there in secret, and Barasch didn't want his presence to be known to anyone. A secondary inference in the light of what you told me yesterday is that Barasch's visitor was delivering the blocks of cocaine."

"Wait a minute. Why would he plan a delivery when he knew you were coming?"

"The snow — the real kind — did him in, Paul. You see, Arthur and I weren't expected until after five. But because of the storm we left school early. We were more than an hour ahead of time arriving at the Barasch house."

"Slow down, Mr. Strang," said Roberts. "Let me get this straight. You mean when you came into the driveway with the boy, Barasch's connection — the one who delivered the cocaine to him — was in the house?"

"Exactly. Imagine their surprise when we pulled up and got out of the car. We'd undoubtedly have discovered them together if I hadn't stopped to examine a scratch on my fender.

"As soon as they saw us, the 'connection,' as you call him, ran out the front door. He didn't even latch it behind him; the wind blew it open shortly after we came in. At any rate, there was Simon Barasch with two blocks of cocaine, a snow-tracked floor, and only seconds to conceal it all.

"So he poured out the Scotch, making the mistake of emptying the bottle completely. Then, just as we entered the house, he opened the window and threw out the waterproof packages of cocaine. He didn't even have time to close the window; that's why he gave us that story about airing out the kitchen. And within a couple of minutes, the packages — as well as the tracks of the fleeing man — were covered with snow."

"But what made you figure Barasch wouldn't pick up the packages from the snow bank as soon as you were out of the house?"

Mr. Strang shook his head. "I know Arthur Barasch very well," he said, "and I was sure he wouldn't be an accomplice in his grandfather's dealings. Ergo, Simon had to wait until Arthur was safely in bed before retrieving the cocaine. He knew the packages were perfectly safe in the snowdrift."

Roberts shook his head in wonder. "You got all that by deductions from an empty Scotch bottle?"

Mr. Strang nodded, his wrinkled face beaming.

"Then how about coming over to my place?" said the detective. "I want to see what you can do with a full one."

MR. STRANG, ARMCHAIR DETECTIVE

The voice was like the scrape of a fingernail on a blackboard, cutting through the hushed atmosphere of the Bird and Bottle, Aldershot's poshest restaurant. "Glad you liked my little talk, Paul. I hope the men on your squad realize now that homicide investigation in the big city presents problems you just don't have out here in the suburbs." Stanley Holbeck took a sip from his martini and set the glass on the table with a thump.

Detective Sergeant Paul Roberts peered furtively at the *maître d'* in the far corner of the dining room and tried to shift his bulky body even lower in his chair. He was beginning to wish he'd never invited Holbeck out from the city. Oh, his talk to the Aldershot police had been all right. The man knew his stuff when it came to urban homicide. But his patronizing manner about everything outside the city limits was beginning to be a pain.

Mr. Strang sat in angry silence, fingering the stem of his wineglass and considering Holbeck in the same way he might examine an insect under a microscope. Even though Holbeck was a colleague of his friend Paul Roberts, the diminutive science teacher yearned to bounce his glass off the man's skull. He'd been pleased when Paul had invited him to join them for lunch – a teacher's salary didn't allow for meals at the Bird and Bottle – but now he was beginning to realize that payment would have to come, not from his wallet, but from his nervous system.

"You teach?" asked Holbeck, as if noticing Mr. Strang for the first time.

"Yes. Science. At the high school." Mr. Strang drained the last of his wine. He wished the waiter would bring their food. Not that a mouthful of meat and potatoes would do much toward shutting Holbeck up.

"That's nice. Especially for someone as old as you. Restful, if you know what I mean."

Mr. Strang had just struggled through a week during which he'd been forced to recalculate his budget request three times, had soothed the jangled nerves of a substitute teacher who'd dropped a beaker of sulfuric acid onto the floor of the supply room, had mollified a member of the school board whose son was failing chemistry, and had broken up innumerable fights between students, most of whom towered over him like teenaged colossi. Teaching could be described in many ways, but the term Holbeck had used wasn't one of them.

"Restful, Mr. Holbeck?" The teacher's self-control would have done credit to the Sphinx.

"Sure. Look, you're there in your school — your ivory tower. You read a few books and come up with a lot of theoretical stuff that sounds great. Trouble is, you're out of touch with the real world."

"Hey, Stan." Roberts finished his scotch and water as the waiter approached with a laden tray. "Back off, will you? The fact is, I asked Mr. Strang to join us because he's been able to give me quite a lot of help on some of my cases. Especially the ones involving school kids. I think he'd make a damn good detective."

Holbeck shifted as the waiter put his plate down. "Here in Aldershot, maybe," he said. "Back in the city, he'd last about two minutes on the force. Now, I'm not putting down teachers, mind you. It's just that they're not cut out to be detectives. Teachers have their heads in the clouds. The police need their feet on the ground."

"Oh ... *Annelida!*" snapped Mr. Strang, his patience at an end. "The analytical ability of the Aldershot faculty is in excellent working order, thank you."

Holbeck grinned at Roberts. "Feisty, isn't he?"

"If that means annoyed, I plead guilty," said the teacher. "I daresay that, given the same information you have, the faculty of Aldershot High School could handle any criminal case just as efficiently as you, Mr. Holbeck."

"Careful, Mr. Strang," said Roberts. "Remember, he's had training that you — "

"No, wait a minute," Holbeck interrupted. "Mr. Strang here has issued a challenge. I intend to take him up on it."

"Oh?" Mr. Strang looked at Holbeck, puzzled. "How?"

"We've got a case at work now that has some odd angles to it. We'll solve it eventually, of course, but maybe you figure you can come up with the answer without moving out of your chair. Want to try? Or will you admit that I'm right and you're wrong?"

Mr. Strang knew he'd been had. Holbeck had led him on and sprung the trap at precisely the right moment. Still, he'd give anything to wipe that self-satisfied look off Holbeck's face.

"You dare me to come up with an answer, Mr. Holbeck. Well, what's the question?"

Holbeck's expression was a cat-who-swallowed-the-canary smirk. "How do you hide a body in a fifth-floor luxury apartment − or get rid of it in some way − without anyone being able to figure out how you did it? Or, to be more specific, I want you to explain the disappearance of Mr. James Phillimore Earnshaw."

Mr. Strang and Roberts simply stared at one another for a long moment. Finally the detective shrugged. "You're carrying the ball on this one, Mr. Strang," he said.

"We've only been on the case since yesterday," said Holbeck. "A team of ten men is working on it, and so far we've come up with nothing. It'll be in all the papers tomorrow. But if you're as good as you say you are, Mr. Strang, you ought to be able to make like Sherlock Holmes or Ellery Queen or those other storybook sleuths who can solve every case without getting off their duffs."

"Both Holmes and Queen were allowed to examine − " Mr. Strang began.

"Got you worried, haven't I?" grinned Holbeck. "Come on. Did you mean what you said, or were you bluffing?"

Mr. Strang's eyes glittered. He pushed his chair back from the table. "I accept your challenge, Mr. Holbeck," he said. "You'll have a solution before we leave this restaurant. I do, of course, have one condition."

"What's that?"

"When comparing them with detectives, I used the word 'faculty' − meaning teachers, plural. I therefore reserve the right to call on any of my colleagues who I feel might be able to assist me. It's Saturday, and most of them ought to be available."

"Hey," said Roberts, "this could get pretty expensive. If we invite them here, they'll have to order a meal, and − "

"Exactly my point," said the teacher. "If I solve the case, Mr. Holbeck pays for everything. If not, I foot the bill."

"How about it, Paul?" asked Holbeck. "Mind spending a little more time here?"

"It's fine with me. I thought I was going to have to pick up the check. But, Mr. Strang, are you sure you can afford − "

"Mr. Holbeck will be paying," said the teacher with assurance. "Now, let's get on with it. What happened to Mr. Earnshaw?" He took a pen and a small notebook from a pocket of his jacket.

"The call came in about seven o'clock last night," Holbeck began. "A Mrs. Everett Keach, who lives in the Bartholomew Apartments. That's a fancy new place over on the East Side."

"I thought you said this involved a man named Earnshaw," said the teacher.

"It does. Give me time. Mrs. Keach lives in Apartment 4-B. Fourth floor, right next to the stairway. When the two officers — Berman and Pollard — got there, she was waiting out in the hall for them. She wouldn't let the men inside her apartment because she'd just had her rugs shampooed, and she wanted to keep them clean.

"She didn't say a word at first. Just kept puffing on a cigarette in one of those long fancy holders as if she was a volcano. And she was pointing up at the fifth floor. Berman and Pollard knew immediately what the trouble was."

"And what was it?" asked Mr. Strang.

"A terrible row going on upstairs. A man and a woman were shouting at each other, and you could hear things thumping on the floor. At the same time, a record was blaring away, *The Warsaw Concerto*. Berman's a music buff, and he recognized it. The whole thing must have sounded like the Normandy invasion."

Holbeck's expression registered wry amusement at humanity's foibles. "Mrs. Keach said the apartment was rented to a Rachel Earnshaw. She scarcely knew the woman. Mrs. Earnshaw kept pretty much to herself, apparently, and — "

"Wait a minute," said the teacher. "You said Mrs. Earnshaw. That's strange."

"Why?" asked Roberts.

"Paul, Mr. Holbeck just said the apartment was rented to Rachel Earnshaw. But if she were married, wouldn't it be more likely the place would be in her husband's name?"

"Not bad, Mr. Strang," said Holbeck. "Not bad at all. Mrs. Earnshaw is a divorcée. In fact, that's what started all the trouble. It seems her husband came back."

"Oh?"

"Yes. He got the wrong apartment at first. Mrs. Keach said he knocked on the door of her place and asked for his wife. She described him as a little guy, but stocky. It rained last night, and his coat and hat were soaked. She said even his mustache looked as if it had gone through a car wash."

"How long did he talk to Mrs. Keach?" asked Mr. Strang.

"Just a minute or so. She didn't even take the chain off the door. Sent him right upstairs."

"And how long after that did the fight start?"

"Not more than a couple of minutes. Mrs. Keach tried ignoring it for a while. Then she got hold of the doorman, who suggested she call the police."

"Is that when you entered the case?" asked Mr. Strang, finishing the last of his salad.

"Not quite. The two officers talked to Mrs. Keach for about five or ten minutes and – "

"With a violent argument going on right above their heads?" asked the teacher in amazement.

"Yes. They were kind of hoping it would end by itself, and I don't blame them. People in places like the Bartholomew Apartments are sometimes well connected politically. No sense getting them angry if you don't have to. And it looked at first as if it were going to work: all of a sudden, the argument stopped. No slowing down, no final remarks, the way these things usually end. It just cut off." Holbeck clapped his hands together. "Bang! Like that."

"But I take it something else happened."

Holbeck nodded. "The officers heard the door up there opening. Then Mrs. Earnshaw was screaming from inside the apartment: 'You get back in here! Don't you dare walk out on me!' Right after that, the door slammed shut again. And all that time the record was playing – loud. That's when Berman and Pollard went upstairs – on the double. Mrs. Earnshaw turned off the phonograph and opened the door as soon as they rang the buzzer."

"Could you describe her?" asked Mr. Strang, his pencil poised.

"Of course. I saw her later myself. She looked as if she were modeling for the Statue of Liberty. A tall woman. I'd have been scared to argue with her, if she were my wife. She was dressed as if she was going out for the evening: a long green gown with white stripes going up and down it, high heels, gloves, hair done up high on her head the way an expensive beauty parlor might have fixed it, the works. Anyway, the men asked her if she and her husband would please keep the noise down. And that's when she gave them a queer answer."

"And what was that?"

"'Why, officers,' she said, 'I haven't seen my husband in years. I live here alone.'"

"So the guy who came to see her wasn't her husband, huh?" chuckled Roberts. "I'll bet he was embarrassed when the patrolmen saw him."

"That's what I'm getting at," answered Holbeck. "Here's

where the case started coming apart. Mrs. Earnshaw took Pollard and Berman through her whole apartment."

"And?"

"And there wasn't anyone else there."

While Roberts and Mr. Strang looked at each other, the waiter came and cleared the table, leaving three cups and a fresh pot of coffee.

"The officers sat down with Mrs. Earnshaw and asked her what all the noise was about. She told them she'd been practicing a reading for a drama class. Only she couldn't show them a script – and, when they asked about the man's voice, she denied there'd been one. Finally they got on the subject of her husband, James Phillimore Earnshaw. Seems he walked out on her about three years ago. She swore she hasn't seen him since, except for the divorce proceedings, and she said nobody'd come to her door all day." Holbeck swabbed his brow with a napkin. "That's when I got called in."

"Earlier," said Mr. Strang slowly, "you mentioned something about a body. What was it that made you think this man, whoever he was, had been killed? Why couldn't he have just left the place?"

"Well, the stairs are out," answered Holbeck, "because the officers were one flight down, talking to Mrs. Keach. They'd have seen him, positively. And the elevator door is right across the hall from the Keach apartment. A light goes on and a little bell rings whenever the car passes each floor." He shook his head. "But no light and no bell."

"So no elevator," said the teacher. "But if he went to another apartment? Or upstairs?"

"We checked. Everyone else on the fifth floor heard the argument, too. But they didn't see anybody. And Earnshaw couldn't have gone upstairs, because there are only five floors to the building. And the door to the roof was not only locked but stuck tight."

"Fire escape?" suggested Roberts.

Holbeck turned thumbs down. "The windows of the apartments are all sealed. 'Total climate control,' they call it. You'd have to remove a whole pane of glass to get to the fire escape. And that can't be done without breaking off the plastic pins holding the panes in place. And every pin in the building was intact."

"Granted there was a mysterious disappearance," said Mr. Strang, "but I still want to know what made you conclude there'd been a murder."

"There's enough evidence to fill a truck," replied Holbeck,

"if only we could put it all together. First of all, we found a big carving knife in the middle of the living-room floor. And that wasn't the weirdest thing."

"What was the weirdest thing?"

"One of the living-room walls had just been repainted. I mean, it wasn't even dry. Bright red and still tacky. Whoever did the painting didn't bother to put down a drop cloth. The rug was all splattered, and the things that had been hanging on the wall were all piled in a corner of the room."

"You mean pictures?"

"Yes. Well, framed opera programs, really. Seems that, some years ago, Mrs. Earnshaw was a professional opera singer."

Holbeck took a notebook from his pocket and consulted it. "There were three framed programs. In one, Rachel Earnshaw was listed as Azucena in *Il Trovatore* at La Scala. Then she was Erda in Wagner's *Das Rheingold* for the Vienna State Opera. And there was a big one from Covent Garden that had her listed as Ulrica in *A Masked Ball*.

"According to her, at one time she'd been quite good. Then she got married, and her husband forced her to give up her career. She wanted to make a comeback, and that's why they got a divorce. She told Berman that she'd arranged a concert booking, and, if the critics were good to her, she might be able to join one of the city's opera companies. Her dream was to sing Carmen some day."

Mr. Strang was jotting down notes rapidly. "Let me get this straight," he said. "James Earnshaw — or whoever was impersonating him — had to be in the apartment, even though his wife denied it. I assume the place was thoroughly searched?"

"Yes, Mr. Strang." Holbeck looked at the teacher and sighed. "This is the kind of thing we're trained to do. First of all, Berman and Pollard went through the place, looking for a body. I mean, something that big, there aren't many places in an apartment to put it. Then I worked out my theory."

"I was hoping for a theory," exclaimed Mr. Strang delightedly. "What was it?"

"Theories are part of what I get paid for," said Holbeck with some annoyance. "Anyway, the playing of that record kept bothering me. I mean, when a couple of people are arguing, they usually try to keep it down, at least at first, so the neighbors won't hear. But these two sounded as if they wanted to wake the dead. So I figured maybe the music was just sound effects to hide any noises Mrs. Earnshaw made while disposing of the body. It even occurred to me the argument might have been faked — on tape or something — to conceal any screams during the actual murder."

Mr. Strang nodded his head appreciatively. "In your own words, Mr. Holbeck, 'not bad.' My respect for you is increasing by leaps and bounds. What did you come up with?"

"Well, being a singer, Mrs. Earnshaw had a hi-fi setup the likes of which you wouldn't believe. Turntable, AM/FM radio, tape deck — everything. There was a record of *The Warsaw Concerto* on the player, of course. So I put one man to checking all her records and tapes to see if he could come up with anything unusual."

"And?"

"Nothing. Just spot-checking every record and tape took him most of the night. She's got quite a collection. But, to tell the truth, I didn't expect him to have any success. So I put a team of men on another search of the apartment and even sent one man downstairs to examine the incinerator. This time we were looking for one of those cassettes like the ones that recording tapes come on. They're only about the size of a pack of cigarettes, but my boys are real pros. They gave that apartment the fine-tooth-comb treatment. Even opened up the sofa cushions and the plumbing. They didn't find anything. My point here is that they couldn't possibly have missed a body."

"What about blood?" asked the teacher.

"No blood anywhere."

Holbeck pushed his chair back from the table with a sigh. "She's got us up a tree. I had her go to a friend's place, and I set a police guard on her apartment. So we'll find him. Oh, we'll look a little foolish when the papers hit the streets tomorrow. But by this time next week, Mrs. Rachel Earnshaw will be booked and behind bars."

He poured a second cup of coffee. "Anyway, there's your problem, Mr. Strang. What happened to James Earnshaw? We have an eyewitness who saw him go up to the apartment, so he's got to be there. Where's he hiding? Or where did his wife put the body?"

The teacher didn't answer. Instead, he peered owlishly at his own scrawled writing in his notebook. "You're sure you haven't left anything out?" he asked Holbeck finally.

"Not a thing. How about it? Are you willing to admit you're stumped?"

"Stumped? With a knife in the middle of the living room and a whole wall sloshed with crimson paint? Why, I haven't had so much fun since I read *The Hound of the Baskervilles*."

"We figure the new paint was on account of blood on the

wall," said Holbeck to Roberts. "And her fancy get-up was to hide the fact that she'd been doing the painting."

Paul Roberts shook his head helplessly.

Mr. Strang signaled to the waiter.

"*Plus de café, messieurs?*"

"You can cut that out, Mickey," said the teacher, polishing his black-rimmed glasses on his necktie. "The luncheon crowd has left, and there's nobody here but us chickens. It's a pity your boy never inherited your ability with languages. As it is, it looks as if he'll be repeating Spanish next term."

"Yeah, I guess you're right, Mr. Strang," said the waiter sadly. "But at least he's improving in math. What can I do for you?"

The teacher tore a page from his notebook. "I want you to call these three people," he said. "Tell them I'd like them to come over here — within the hour, if possible. Mention my name."

"What if they can't make it?"

"Say there's a free meal in it. They'll be here like a shot. And you can move that next table closer. When my committee meets, I want them all to have enough room."

"Committee?" said Holbeck, looking curiously at the teacher. "What committee?"

"You said I could have faculty help solving this problem." Mr. Strang spread his hands wide. "Behold the first meeting of my Committee to Rebuke Uppity Detectives. I give you the acronym with my best wishes."

"Do you mean to tell me, Mr. Strang," said Roberts, "that you have actually made something out of what Stan told you?"

"Of course, Paul. That is, unless he left something out. If so, he pays the bill anyway, since one of the conditions of this whole exercise was that I know exactly as much as the police."

"I've told you everything we learned," murmured Holbeck. "But if you're so sure of yourself, why do you need the others?"

"Two reasons," Mr. Strang replied. "First of all, there are a few things I need to confirm. Second and more important, I'm certain all those I've invited would enjoy a meal in a fine restaurant, as long as somebody else is paying."

The first to enter the restaurant, some twenty minutes later, was a middle-aged man who seemed more than a little ill at ease in the suit he was wearing. "Mr. Holbeck, this is Edward Witkin of our school maintenance staff," said the teacher. "He's not exactly on the faculty, but I trust he comes under the terms of our agreement. After all, he is employed by the school district."

"Sure, sit down," said Holbeck. "Might as well get everybody into the act."

Alma Brubaker and Doris Nettles arrived together. Miss Brubaker, a gorgeous black woman dressed in the height of fashion, taught choral music. Mrs. Nettles, plump and matronly, was head of the Home Economics department.

The teacher directed the three newcomers to a corner of the room. There he spoke to them for several minutes in whispers. Finally the four returned to the table, where the two detectives were waiting impatiently.

When introductions had been completed, Mr. Strang saw that the others were seated, then tapped his glass for attention. "I'd like to get this whole affair completed as soon as possible," he began. "I'm sure Mr. Holbeck will want to be getting back to the city, if only to tell his colleagues how a group of schoolteachers solved his mystery for him."

Quickly he outlined the terms of the bet he'd made with Holbeck and, in greater detail, went over the story of the investigation into the disappearance of James Earnshaw.

Then he removed his glasses, holding them lightly in his right hand. His left was plunged deep into a pocket of his rumpled jacket.

"Now let's explore some possibilities concerning the missing man," he declaimed, for all the world as if he were speaking to a class of high-school students. "Assuming Mr. Earnshaw was killed by his wife, she was immediately faced with the problem of disposing of the body. Burial was out of the question — only moments after the argument ended, the police were pounding up the stairs. But could the body have been walled up inside the apartment, perhaps behind a secret panel? To see if Mrs. Earnshaw resorted to a method made popular by Edgar Allan Poe, I turn to my first guest expert, Mr. Witkin. What do you say, Eddie? Is the body moldering under the floorboards?"

Mr. Witkin looked up at the teacher and shook his head. "No way, Mr. Strang. These new buildings — even the luxury apartments — have walls as thin as tissue paper. Nothing more than some dry wall or thin paneling laid over the studs. Nowhere near enough room to hide a body."

"Wait a minute," interrupted Holbeck. "How can you be so sure, Mr. Witkin? Have you ever been in the Bartholomew Apartments?"

"Nope. But it stands to reason, don't it, that if that argument was heard so clear by all the neighbors, there ain't much thickness to the walls. In the old buildings, you could fire a cannon in one apartment and not wake up a baby sleeping next door. Ah, they don't make 'em the way they used to." He lowered his voice to a whisper. "How'd I do, Mr. Strang?"

"Admirably, Eddie. Enjoy your meal."

"Very well," said Holbeck, "so James Earnshaw wasn't in the apartment when Berman and Pollard got there."

"Ah, now we're getting somewhere. Secondary inference: he wasn't murdered. His wife simply had no time to dispose of the body."

"Well —" began Holbeck reluctantly.

"Oh, come on, Stan," snapped Roberts. "Give an inch."

Holbeck shrugged. "All right, no murder."

"And once we eliminate the murder theory," said Mr. Strang, "I hope that at least for the time being we can call a halt to further consideration of that painted wall and the knife. For muddling up a problem, those two factors take the cake."

"You have to explain them some way."

"All in good time, Mr. Holbeck."

"So James Earnshaw got out of the apartment under his own steam," mused Holbeck. "But how? He couldn't have gone downstairs without Mrs. Keach and the police either seeing him or hearing the elevator bell or seeing the elevator light."

"Then the conclusion is inescapable," said the teacher with a smile. "James Earnshaw did not leave the apartment."

"But if he didn't leave ... and he's not there — "

" — then we arrive at the only possible answer remaining to us: James Earnshaw doesn't exist!"

Mr. Strang looked around triumphantly at the small group of diners.

"Why — why he has to!" sputtered Holbeck.

"Really?" said Mr. Strang coolly. "How can you be so sure? Tell me, did you check whether or not Rachel Earnshaw was ever married?"

"No, I — " Holbeck groped about with one hand like a blind man. "I just assumed — "

"As did everyone else. You assumed there was a James Earnshaw for one reason only — because Rachel Earnshaw told you so."

"But he was seen by a witness," said Holbeck. "The little

man who talked to Mrs. Keach — what about him?"

"Isn't it obvious? That 'man' had to be Rachel Earnshaw herself."

"Aha!" Holbeck pointed an accusing finger. "There's where I've got you, Mr. Strang. There is no way I'm going to believe that. The person Mrs. Keach saw at her door was a man."

"Mrs. Keach," replied the teacher as if scolding a student for a minor infraction of the rules, "saw a figure she described as short and stocky. Aside from that, all she observed was a coat, hat, and mustache, all soaked with water. Nowhere in her account was there any mention of the person inside all this clothing and facial hair. And by her own admission Mrs. Keach and Mrs. Earnshaw were almost complete strangers to one another. It's no wonder the poor woman didn't recognize who was at her door."

"Come on! The man she spoke to was short. And I saw Mrs. Earnshaw myself. She's tall."

"I think it's now up to you, Mrs. Nettles," said Mr. Strang.

The Home Economics teacher got to her feet like a queen addressing her subjects. "Height, as I've told the girls in my classes, is a relative matter, Mr. Holbeck. A woman of five feet ten inches would be considered tall. A man of that height would be just above average."

"But — "

"Please don't interrupt. I further understand that, when you saw Rachel Earnshaw, she was wearing high heels and her hair was upswept, two things guaranteed to add several inches to a woman's height. Finally, the vertical stripes on her dress — designed to create the illusion of a taller woman. Under the circumstances, I'm surprised you didn't mistake her for the Jolly Green Giant. But in flat shoes, with her hair under a felt hat and crouched a bit in an overcoat, it wouldn't have been hard for her to appear to be a short stocky man. Especially if the illusion of masculinity were enhanced by a false mustache."

"Ummm. But how about the voice? I mean, a woman's voice is usually higher pitched than a man's. Wouldn't Mrs. Keach have noticed that?"

With a tiny smile, Doris Nettles sat down and applied herself to her filet mignon while Mr. Strang waved a hand in the direction of Alma Brubaker.

"I've never heard this Earnshaw woman speak, of course," said the music teacher. "But those framed opera programs rang a bell. Azucena, Erda, and Ulrica. All parts written to be sung in the same vocal range, Mr. Holbeck. And, while the Carmen role is usually sung in a higher register, Mme. Charles Cahier once − "

"What are you driving at, Miss Brubaker?"

"Mrs. Earnshaw was a contralto − the lowest female singing voice."

"You're saying she could sound like a man and bring it off? Is that it?"

"Right on, Mr. Holbeck. At least for a short time. Now may I get back to my lobster? It's delicious."

"Thus endeth the contributions of our guest experts," said Mr. Strang. "Enjoy your meals, one and all. And be sure to thank Mr. Holbeck."

"I'm not finished," said the detective. "What about the argument Mrs. Keach and the neighbors heard coming through the walls? It must have lasted at least fifteen minutes. And Miss Brubaker herself said Rachel could only make the man's voice sound convincing for a short time."

Mr. Strang shook his head in mock sadness. "Oh, Mr. Holbeck, you were so close to the answer." He held his thumb and forefinger with only a fraction of an inch separating them. "So very close."

"What do you mean?"

"The phony argument was − indeed, had to be − on tape, just as you suspected. And when it ended − Bang!, to use your own expression − it was merely the switching off of the tape deck as it was feeding in over the sound of the record. I have no doubt that the resourceful Rachel Earnshaw had little trouble in persuading one of her male acquaintances to dub in the man's part of the argument beforehand. On the hi-fi, with a little pounding of a chair on the floor and walls, it must have been most convincing. Your only error, Mr. Holbeck, was in assuming that, because 'Mr. Earnshaw' was seen and heard by the neighbors, he had to exist apart from Rachel herself."

Holbeck waved an admonishing finger at the teacher. "That apartment was thoroughly searched by some of the best men in the business, and no tape was − "

"Of course no tape was found. Confound it, man, I'm willing to concede the ability of your team of detectives. But they could search the Earnshaw place until doomsday and still find nothing. You persist in this hang-up that all the evidence is inside her apartment."

"But where else − ?"

"Cast your imagination back to the time when your uniformed men were first talking to Mrs. Keach. Just before they went upstairs, they heard — what?"

Holbeck wrinkled his brow. "The door upstairs opened. Mrs. Earnshaw screamed to her husband to come back inside. Then the door closed again."

"Ah, but according to our present hypothesis, there was no husband. Therefore, in spite of what she was heard to say, she must have opened the door to let herself out."

"You think the tape is in the hall outside her apartment? Out of the question! One look and you could see for yourself. That hall is all chrome and wood paneling. Even the carpet is tacked down. Once glance out there and we could tell — "

"You were looking for something out of place, an article you wouldn't expect to find in the hall. But if you'd reread 'The Purloined Letter' — "

"I tell you there's no place in that hall to hide — "

"Isn't there? You told me that Mrs. Keach, on the fourth floor, wouldn't let your men into her apartment because she'd just cleaned the rugs. An extraordinarily neat woman, wouldn't you say?"

"I guess so, but — "

"And yet she remained in the hall talking to your men for some five or ten minutes. And all that time she was smoking a cigarette. Certainly this paragon of cleanliness wouldn't allow herself to dirty the rug outside her own door. So tell me, Mr. Holbeck, what did she do with her cigarette ashes?"

"She put them in the ashtray, of course — one of those big aluminum things they have on every floor. Looks like a fancy bucket filled with — "

Suddenly Holbeck looked at Roberts and swallowed loudly. " — sand," he said, in an awed voice.

Mr. Strang nodded. "Usually those ashtrays are quite deep, too. A tape cassette pushed down far enough into that sand would still allow cigarettes to be snuffed out above it without danger of discovery, in the event your men used the one on the fifth floor. Even a quick raking with the fingers wouldn't uncover the hiding place. But I think if you pour out the sand from the ashtray outside the Earnshaw apartment, you'll find the missing 'argument' tape buried there. With the area under guard, it's unlikely Rachel Earnshaw has been able to retrieve it."

Roberts and the teacher grinned at one another.

"Let me get this straight," Holbeck said. "What you're saying is that, last night, Mrs. — or Miss, we've still got to check on that — Earnshaw dressed up in a man's clothes and went down to Mrs. Keach's apartment?"

"Yes. But first she painted the living-room wall and planted the knife. Red herrings, of course, simply to give your men some interesting and misleading clues to work on. Then, after donning her masculine disguise, she probably stood in the shower for a minute or so to get the proper degree of wetness to suggest that she'd come in from the outside."

"Wild, but certainly possible. And, according to your guest experts, she could have convinced Mrs. Keach she was a man."

"Exactly. Then upstairs and into her own clothing and a new hairdo. A wig, probably."

"Then, with all the false clues planted, she started the 'argument' tape. The record, too, for extra noise and confusion. And a little pounding on the floor to make sure Mrs. Keach got angry enough to call the police. And while they were talking to Mrs. Keach, Rachel Earnshaw hid the tape in the ashtray out in the hall."

"That's it. Naturally, it will prove I'm right if you find the tape. Well, are you satisfied, Mr. Holbeck? Ready to pick up the check for this little adventure in armchair detection? You now have a perfectly logical and coherent explanation of how James Earnshaw 'disappeared.'"

"Just a second. There's still the problem of the motive."

"Well, eventually you were bound to discover the truth — that she'd been putting you on. She had not, however, committed any crime. You simply drew some erroneous conclusions."

"But why did she go to all that trouble?"

"Purely as conjecture, I'd say the clue is that we have a woman who's attempting a comeback in an operatic career. Publicity will do her a world of good, and you yourself said the papers will be full of the case tomorrow. 'The Man Who Disappeared,' followed by 'Operatic Hopeful Outwits Police.' Why, people will flock to her concerts just to see the woman behind it all."

Holbeck considered this for a moment. "So the whole thing's a publicity stunt?"

Silence.

"All right, I concede," said Holbeck grudgingly. He signaled for the waiter and produced a well-worn wallet.

"*Merci, monsieur,*" said Mickey, eyeing the bills Holbeck placed on his tray. Then he swiveled his head and saluted Mr. Strang with a surreptitious wink.

"You'll have to excuse me," said Holbeck, heading for the door. "I've got a train to catch, back to the city. There's an ashtray at the Bartholomew Apartments I want to look into.

And, if I find what you say is in it, I'm going to sit down at my desk and write a hundred times, 'I will not open my big mouth to the teacher.' When you're in the neighborhood, Mr. Strang, drop in. Roberts was right. I wouldn't mind at all having you on my staff."

After Holbeck's departure, Paul Roberts leaned confidentially toward Mr. Strang. "You conned him," said the detective. "I don't know how you pulled it off, but you conned him."

The teacher's face was a study in wide-eyed wonder. "Why, Paul, I can't imagine what you're talking about."

"Yes, you can, you wrinkled old wizard. I know you. There's no way you'd let yourself be roped into a bet like that unless you were damn sure of winning. I have a feeling you knew all along that Rachel Earnshaw was pulling a fast one. That's right, isn't it?"

Mr. Strang's grin was that of a satanic imp. He slipped his glasses back on. Then, his eyes shining merrily, he nodded.

"What tipped you off?" Roberts asked.

"The name, Paul. It seems Rachel Earnshaw has a sense of humor."

"What name?"

"The one she gave her imaginary husband: James Phillimore Earnshaw. You see, it comes from one of those books your friend Holbeck accused us teachers of reading, up in our ivory towers."

"Books? What books?"

"The Sherlock Holmes stories, in this case. In several of them, Watson mentioned cases that he never got around to recording. One of those unchronicled tales was 'that of Mr. James Phillimore, who, stepping back into his own house to get his umbrella, was never more seen in this world.'"

Mr. Strang stoked up his briar pipe and tried unsuccessfully to arrange his wizened features to resemble the hawklike Holmesian visage.

"If memory serves, you'll find it in 'The Problem of Thor Bridge.'"

MR. STRANG INTERPRETS A PICTURE

The daylight robbery of the Gorham Savings and Loan in downtown Aldershot occurred shortly before 9 AM on the Tuesday after Labor Day. It was the most exciting thing to happen in that small suburban community since Honora Mc-Crea retrieved her husband from an all-night poker game at the point of a loaded shotgun.

The robbery became common knowledge throughout Aldershot within half an hour, having been passed along at incredible speed via the phone and the more personal "back-fence telegraph." Amid huge mounds of gossip and speculation, a few facts emerged. Some time before eight o'clock, the two robbers parked their car in the alley that ran alongside the venerable old bank building. After disabling the ancient outer alarm by filling its mechanism as well as its gong with heavy grease, the men forced open the side door and concealed themselves in a broom closet.

At exactly eight, Carl Felloes, the bank's president, arrived, accompanied by his daughter Sue, who was a teller. They entered through the front door, to which Felloes had the only key. "Those guys must have been looking out at me as I sat at my desk," Felloes told Detective Sergeant Paul Roberts. "And me not suspecting a thing."

Ten minutes later, Felloes admitted Norma Sanchez and Eddie Friedlander, the two other tellers. A few moments after that, the guard, Horace Cubb, arrived. Horace, it should be noted, was old and forgetful, and the job of guard was something of a sinecure. He was forbidden to put bullets in the gun he wore at his hip, a fact of which the robbers seemed to be aware.

Once the entire staff was assembled, the front door was relocked to await opening time at nine o'clock. As soon as the bolt was slammed home, locking the door, the robbers showed themselves. Each carried a revolver, and each wore gloves and a knitted ski mask that covered his entire face.

In the street outside the two huge floor-to-ceiling windows, each with its blind drawn, business went on as usual in Aldershot. Within the bank, the robbers worked smoothly and efficiently. The tellers at their stations, as well as Horace Cubb, stood with upraised hands. One of the robbers directed Carl Felloes to the huge vault door at the rear of the building. At 8:40, the time lock clicked, and the ponderous door swung open. Felloes was compelled to fill two pillowcases with all the available cash — about sixty thousand dollars.

The bank employees were bound and gagged. The robbers left by the same side door through which they had entered and drove off with their haul. Nobody outside the bank noticed anything unusual.

There's no telling how long the bank's staff might have remained on the floor in helpless bondage if JoAnne Hewes of the Ounces of Flounces Sewing Shoppe hadn't been impatient to make an early deposit. At 9:15, having waited ten minutes on the bank's front step with no signs of life from inside, she began banging on the front door. Getting no answer, she alerted the police. The damaged side door was discovered, and the bank's staff were found and released.

Beyond the evident fact that a robbery had taken place, the evidence developed by the local and state police over the next several days would have fit under a gnat's eyelid with plenty of room to spare. The robbers seemed to have melted into thin air with no signs — aside from the missing money — of their having been in the bank at all.

"We have no leads at this time" was all Paul Roberts could tell a group of reporters one morning ten days after the robbery. What the detective said to his pretty wife Bobbi when he arrived home that evening — exhausted, angry, and frustrated at having chased down yet another false lead — is best left to the imagination.

Mr. Leonard Strang steered his old maroon sedan into the parking area of the Eldrich P. Noble Elementary School. He got out stiffly, muttering in annoyance. Each year, two weeks into the fall semester, it was the practice of Aldershot High School to send one of its teachers to the district's elementary schools to speak to the fifth graders. The idea was to make the potential junior-highschoolers eager to begin the next level of their education.

This year, Mr. Strang had been unwillingly dragooned into service by his principal, Mr. Guthrey. And the gnomelike science teacher didn't have the foggiest idea what to say to the children he'd be addressing.

Much to his surprise, he did quite a creditable job at the impromptu assembly program. He decided to forego the "gee whiz" approach and simply describe the high school's science courses. Speaking in a soft voice and with no attempt at dramatic declamation, he nevertheless was able to communicate to the students his own sense of awe and wonder at the countless miracles to be found in the everyday world and in the heavens above. Even his few creaking attempts at humor were met by gales of laughter. He finished to a deafening round of applause.

He had more than an hour before he was due at the next school. Plenty of time to pay Margaret Lakmund a visit.

Margaret Lakmund had been hired as a part-time elementary-school art teacher for the district only a year after Mr. Strang himself. As art was considered a "frill," her beginning salary had been nineteen hundred dollars a year. Often she and the young Leonard Strang had shared meager suppers at the end of the month, while awaiting payday. There'd never been anything romantic in their relationship, despite the tittered gossip of other teachers. Maggie Lakmund was simply a good friend of long standing.

She was teaching a class of chattering third graders when Mr. Strang entered her classroom. The children had made bright designs on drawing paper with wax crayons. Now they were coating the paper with black paint, gasping in wonder as the watery pigment refused to adhere to the wax, allowing their designs to show through.

"Leonard, you old reprobate!" Maggie cried out with an earthy laugh when she caught sight of Mr. Strang. "What are you doing in these parts?"

"I just dropped in to see if you're keeping the kids up to the high standards we expect in high school," replied Mr. Strang with a grin.

"Standards!" Maggie wiped thin delicate fingers on her smock and then ran them through her mop of gray hair. "From what I hear, the only period when anything gets done over at that high school of yours is lunchtime."

Both Mr. Strang and Maggie chuckled at the children's awed reaction to their joking.

"Sorry if I disturbed your class," said the science teacher. "I'd better be on my way."

"You just got here," Maggie replied. "Sit down and take a load off those old bones. It's time for the kids to pick up, and I'm free next period. We can gab for a while."

She turned to the class. "Cleanup time!" she announced. "Meatball, Dizzy, you're class monitors today. Get those brushes cleaned and put away. On the double!"

A plump boy in short pants and a tiny girl with braided hair obediently began collecting brushes and taking them to the sink. "Meatball, I can understand," said Mr. Strang, eyeing the boy's paunch. "But Dizzy?"

"Desiderata Van Cleef," replied Maggie. "Everybody calls her Dizzy. If her parents hang a handle like Desiderata on the poor kid, what can they expect?"

The children were lined up at the classroom door, with Meatball at the head of the line. Before opening the door, Maggie patted his head. He looked up at her with an expression of total adoration.

"You haven't lost your touch, Maggie," said Mr. Strang, after the room had cleared. "You always had a way with kids."

"Yeah, I'm surrogate mother to a lot of 'em," Maggie said. "Broken homes, parents who'd rather be on the golf course than looking after their children. I'm amazed that some of the kids turn out as well as they do."

Mr. Strang turned his head to look at the artwork displayed on the bulletin boards that covered three sides of the room. "Those dogs are funny," he said, pointing to a display near the door. "They look like they're made out of soap bubbles."

"Look again," said Maggie. "They're horses. It's like I've always said: you high-school teachers have no artistic imagination at all."

A large picture at the front of the room caught Mr. Strang's eye. He shuffled over to it.

The picture had been done in thin lines of black paint with no color added. One horizontal line divided the top and bottom of the paper into equal sections. On this line, three circles about the size of quarters seemed to be resting. From each circle, two lines sprouted upward, resembling long ears. Every circle had a dome over it, somewhat like an inverted U. And a larger circle dominated the rest of the paper's upper area.

"Looks a little like three Hindus praying to the sun or something," murmured Mr. Strang. "What else have we got here?"

Below the bisecting line were two more small circles. Each rested on a horizontal line some three inches long. And two lines branched — downward, this time — from them both.

"Stick figures, probably," he mused. "But why blacken in the circles instead of putting faces on them?"

Finally, in the lower right corner was what looked like a shoebox supported by yet another pair of circles.

"Maybe those things on the dividing line are rabbits under bell jars," said Mr. Strang with a chuckle. "Anyway, this young genius seems to be into his Circular Period."

"Never guess about a child's drawing," said Maggie. "If you're wrong, he'll be crushed."

She came over and looked at the name printed on the back of the paper. "Oh, right. This one was done by the Mnemonic Kid."

"The who?"

"He's a little Vietnamese boy in the first grade. Hung Nguyen." The name came to Mr. Strang's ears as N'win.

"Why do you call him the Mnemonic Kid?"

"He's got a memory like a steel trap, that's why. He came here last spring not knowing a word of English. Now he can speak well enough to be understood, and he even prints a little – and he knows his numbers up to a hundred."

"I'm sure he's very bright," said Mr. Strang. "But mnemonics has to do strictly with memory development, Maggie, and –"

"And you ought to see this boy play Kim's Game, Leonard."

"Huh?"

"Kim's Game. It's a memory test. You put fifteen or twenty different items – common things, like coins and keys and pencils – on a tray. The child looks at the tray for exactly one minute. Then, after the tray's covered, he has to name everything he saw. Little Hung hardly ever makes a mistake. And he knew the names of all his teachers and classmates the very first day."

"He sounds like a most unusual youngster," said Mr. Strang.

"And polite as they make 'em," added Maggie. "His mother's a doll, too. She walked Hung to school the first day, and they arrived at 9:02. Two minutes late, and she was apologizing all over the place in that broken English of hers. Said she'd stopped off at Howland's Drugstore to buy Hung a little picture book as a birthday surprise. There were a lot of people in the store, and it took longer than she expected. Two minutes. Most parents wouldn't have bothered to apologize for being two minutes late."

Mr. Strang was considering the picture again. "Maybe that big circle in the background is the sun," he muttered. "I'll bet this shows some kind of prayer ritual in Vietnam."

Maggie shook her head. "You'd lose, Leonard. First art class of the year, everybody draws something they've seen that day. I haven't changed that first lesson in thirty years."

"Huh. I'd love to ask Hung what he saw."

"He won't be able to tell you for a while. He's in the hospital. His tonsils come out tomorrow. A public-assistance case, and the Nguyen family is having fits. They're as poor as church mice — the little shack they live in only has a few pieces of furniture in it — but they hate the thought of accepting charity."

"You know, Maggie, this picture fascinates me." Mr. Strang tapped the paper with the end of his pencil. "In all the other drawings in the room, I can make out what the child was trying to do. Okay, so a house looks like a box, and animals are so many sausages tied together. But at least you know what they're supposed to be. But here ... *Trematoda!* Didn't the boy say anything about the picture?"

"Well, I couldn't ask him directly what it was a picture of," replied Maggie, "but I did get him to talk a little about that thing down in the corner. The shoebox on wheels, or whatever it is."

"Oh? And what did Master Hung have to say?"

"The strangest thing. He told me, 'That's Katie Tennatey.' And then he wouldn't say another word about it."

Mr. Strang's forehead furrowed as he pronounced the strange name to himself. KAY-tee Ten-NAY-tee. A name that belonged in a limerick or other piece of comic poetry. A Vietnamese phrase, perhaps? But it didn't sound Oriental.

A high-pitched muttering outside the door signaled that Maggie's next class had arrived. Mr. Strang excused himself, gave the art teacher a peck on the cheek, and walked out into the parking lot.

As he drove onto the street, he began composing in his mind the talk he would give at the next elementary school. The same basic pattern would be used, of course. Why fiddle with success? Still, certain changes ought to be made in order to —

Katie Tennatey.

The name echoed in Mr. Strang's mind, almost as if he'd said it aloud. He shook his head in annoyance. This was no time to be hypothesizing about a child's daydreams. There was work to be done. Now if more stress were put on —

Katie Tennatey.

The name, and the picture connected with it, along with snippets of Maggie's story about Hung Nguyen, "The Mnemonic Kid," kept wriggling into Mr. Strang's consciousness like slippery eels he couldn't quite grasp. For a reason he couldn't comprehend, his brain would not relinquish its vision of a small boy coming to school with his mother and seeing — what?

Katie Tennatey.

By the time he was ready to go home, Mr. Strang's head was throbbing painfully. He arrived just as his landlady, Mrs. Mackey, was coming up the front walk, her arms loaded with paper bags.

"Gud day t'ye, Muster Strang," she said in a rich, peaty Irish brogue. "Been doin' a bit uv shoppin', I 'ave. First to the bank for funds, then next door to the drugstore, where they've a foin sale on toothpaste. Afterward the grocery, and I tell you, the price o' meat is a caution. Finally — "

"Mrs. Mackey, I have a bit of a headache," he told the talkative woman. "If you'll excuse me, I think I'll just go up and lie down."

"You do that, you poor thing," cooed Mrs. Mackey. "Some bug ye've caught, mebbe? If you want to stay home tomorrow, I'd be glad to call — "

"No, I'll be fine. I just need some rest, that's all."

Taking the afternoon paper with him, Mr. Strang went upstairs to his room. He stretched out on the bed and thumbed through the day's news. Another political scandal ... more trouble in the Middle East....

"No Progress in Gorham Bank Robbery" was the headline of a tiny article on page twelve. The teacher snorted his annoyance with the police. He'd followed the case closely in the papers for the past two weeks, hoping that some vital clue would lead to a dramatic recovery of the money.

"Scyphozoa!" he muttered. "Why, if I were one of those detectives, I'd — "

And then fatigue overcame him.

Mr. Strang slept. And, for one of the few times in his life, he dreamed.

In his dreams, richly robed Oriental priests faced the setting sun. Chanting in high voices and with arms outstretched, they bowed low to the slanting rays. Meanwhile, dusky-skinned children with sticks for arms and legs played and cavorted near a wheeled crate, from which a hollow voice proclaimed, "I am Katie Tennatey!"

The scene shimmered and changed. Three rabbits with long narrow ears sat beneath bell jars on a laboratory table. Two scientists, each wearing a dark surgical mask, were observing the animals. A small cart with KATIE TENNATEY stenciled on it stood in a shadowy corner. And illuminating everything was the huge sun. But it wasn't a sun. It was a —

Mr. Strang sat bolt upright in bed. His body was streaming with perspiration, and his eyes were wide as he peered into the darkness. He glanced at his alarm clock. It was 1:45 AM.

He reached for the telephone at his bedside and dialed a number. While the phone was ringing, he whispered a single word to himself: "Door."

"Paul Roberts speaking," said an exhausted voice at the other end of the line.

"Paul? This is Leonard Strang. I have to see you — now!"

"Mr. Strang, it's the middle of the night." There was more than a hint of anger in the detective's voice. "Can't it wait?"

"No. By morning I might forget some of the details."

"Details? What details?"

"I'll tell you when I see you. My place or yours?"

Twenty minutes later, Detective Sergeant Paul Roberts was still brushing sleep from his eyes as he admitted the diminutive science teacher to his house. "It's after two, Mr. Strang," Roberts mumbled. "There better be a good reason for getting me up at this hour."

"Paul, we've worked a number of cases together," said the teacher. "Have I ever let you down?"

"Well, no. But this better be good, that's all I'm saying."

Mr. Strang told his story. And it was good.

Within half an hour of the teacher's entrance, Roberts had the coffee pot on to boil and was at the telephone, shouting instructions first to his own men and then to the state police. "That's right, Kilowatt Tango. Get an APB out, right away. Yes, now!" He slammed the phone down and rubbed his hands together gleefully. "If only they haven't left the state," he muttered.

Two days later, there was a small ceremony at Aldershot General Hospital. Grouped around the bed of first-grader Hung Nguyen were the boy's parents, Mr. Strang, Paul Roberts, and Maggie Lakmund.

"We got 'em, Mr. Strang," Roberts announced. "They were in a little shack in the mountains upstate. A local cop up there spotted 'em. When the police broke in, they found most of the money. Some of it still had Gorham Savings and Loan bands around it. Open-and-shut case, the DA tells me."

"I — do — not — understand." Mr. Nguyen spoke in a halting voice. "You have apparently done some most successful police work. But what has this to do with my son?"

"Hell, your son — oh, excuse me, Mrs. Nguyen — your son

solved the case. Him and Mr. Strang, that is."

"Case? What case?" asked Mr. Nguyen.

"The robbery of the Gorham Savings and Loan." Roberts patted Hung on the shoulder. "He gave us the lead we needed."

"But — how?" Mr. Nguyen shook his head in confusion.

"I'd like an answer to that myself," said Maggie.

The detective's grin threatened to split his face in two. "You tell 'em, Mr. Strang," he said. "You're the one who figured it out."

"Let's hear it, Leonard," said Maggie in an amused voice. "How did you and Hung figure out whodunit? Astound us."

"It was the picture, of course," said Mr. Strang. "Did you bring it along as I asked?"

Maggie withdrew a folded sheet of paper from her purse. At the same time, the gnomelike science teacher whipped a pair of black-rimmed glasses from his pocket and put them on. He peered over their tops professorially.

"The bank," he began, "was robbed on the Tuesday after Labor Day. Does that particular day have any other significance, Maggie?"

"Sure, it's the opening day of school. But what — ?"

"Opening day." Mr. Strang raised a gnarled finger for attention. "The very day Mrs. Nguyen first walked her son to school. But they were two minutes late getting there. Why was that, Mrs. Nguyen?"

"I stop at store — drug store."

"And the drugstore, I hasten to add," said Mr. Strang, "is next door to the bank, as my landlady reminded me the other day. Why did you go into the drugstore, Mrs. Nguyen?"

"Buy gift — present. For Hung's birthday. Surprise."

Mr. Strang nodded. "And you didn't want Hung at your side while you bought him a surprise, did you?"

She shook her head. "Hung stay outside. I tell him to wait quietly. He good boy, do as I say."

"Mrs. Nguyen and Hung got to school just after nine o'clock," Mr. Strang told the others. "That had to mean they were at the drugstore before nine. When would you say you did your shopping, Mrs. Nguyen?"

"Maybe eight hours thirty, eight hours forty-five."

"Hey," cried Maggie, "that's just about the time the robbery was taking place!"

"You're catching on already to something it took me hours to realize," Mr. Strang nodded. "I had all the facts after I'd seen Hung's picture and heard you talk about him. But what a headache I got from my poor brain trying to make sense of it all."

"Sense?" said Maggie. "I still can't make sense of – "

"Think about little Hung, out there on the street while his mother's in the drugstore. He wanders about, a trifle bored. Finally, just for something to do, he peeks in a window."

"The bank window?" asked Maggie incredulously. "But the shades were down."

"True, so an adult passing by would notice nothing. But think of those tall windows in the front of the bank. They come down to within two or three feet of the sidewalk. Practically eye level for a first grader. And what if the shade hadn't been lowered quite all the way? Even an inch of clearance would have given Hung a front-row seat to everything going on inside the bank."

"But, if Hung saw the robbery, why didn't he tell the police?" Maggie asked. "Or at least let somebody know what was going on?"

"A little boy from a foreign country? Poor enough to be deprived even of the wonders of television? I doubt Hung knew there was anything wrong. He just saw some people inside the bank performing an odd ritual."

"Come on, Leonard," Maggie scoffed. "You're just guessing."

"No, I'm not," Mr. Strang replied. "Look at the picture, Maggie."

She unfolded the paper. "I don't see anything. There's that big circle at the top, probably the sun."

"Maggie, you told me yourself that you should never guess what a child has been drawing. But I'm not guessing. That circle isn't the sun – it's a door."

"Oh, Leonard, doors aren't circular!"

"The vault door in the Gorham Savings and Loan is. And the Mnemonic Kid remembered that. He remembered everything."

Maggie looked at the picture again, and her jaw dropped. "I told him to draw something he'd seen that day," she said softly. "And it's all there, isn't it?"

"Everything," said Mr. Strang with a smile. "The line across the center of the paper is the counter behind which the tellers stand. Those three circles on the line are the tellers themselves, and the 'ears' going up from them are their raised hands. The domes over them are the transaction windows at which they stand. Probably they had their backs turned, as there are no facial features in the picture."

"The stick figures with the circular heads at the bottom have to be the robbers," Maggie sputtered.

"And the circles themselves are blackened because the robbers were wearing masks," added Mr. Strang.

"But the box on top of the two circles — what's that, Leonard?"

"I suspect that, after looking in the bank window, Hung did a little more wandering around. He came to the alley next to the bank. That's when he saw Katie Tennatey."

"But who was she?" asked Maggie in exasperation.

"Why, the getaway car — drawn the way any child might draw an automobile. But this drawing gave Paul the lead he needed to catch the robbers."

Maggie frowned and shook her head. "I don't get it, Leonard. That box Hung drew could be any car in the world — if it's an automobile at all."

"Ah, but you asked Hung about the box he'd drawn. And he told you what it was, by giving you the label that was attached to it."

"The car had a label on it?" said Paul Roberts.

"Uh huh. And Hung was able to remember the label by a mnemonic trick. He turned what was on it into a name."

"A name?" said Maggie. "Oh, you mean Katie Tennetey." She again pronounced the name, slowly this time: "KAY-tee Ten-NAY-tee."

And then she stared fixedly at the science teacher. A dawning awareness widened her eyes, and suddenly her head bobbed up and down in understanding.

"The license plate," she whispered.

"Exactly," said Mr. Strang, "the license plate. Katie Tennatey. Or, more precisely: Kay Tee Ten Eighty. It's the license number of the car: KT-1080."

"So now you know what Mr. Strang told me the other night," Roberts chimed in. "I tried poking holes in his story, but, the more I thought about it, the more it made sense. So I called it in: Kilowatt Tango One Zero Eight Zero. And fortunately the two hoods hadn't left the state. In under twelve hours, we had 'em in custody."

Roberts reached down and patted the shoulder of the boy in the hospital bed. "Young fellow, you and Mr. Strang are probably going to share a nice reward from the bank for your work on this case. What are you going to do with your share? Get a TV? Or a new bike, maybe?"

The small boy beneath the white sheets pointed to his throat and spoke for the first time. In a harsh whisper, he

said the thing uppermost in his mind.
"Ice cream," said the Mnemonic Kid.

MR. STRANG TAKES A TOUR

"I'm Mindy MacGregor, your tour guide," said the uniformed girl with the microphone, as soon as the bus began to move, "and Sam Kent here will be doing the driving. For the next eight days, Sam and I will take care of everything you need or want."

Several of the male passengers grinned widely and moaned with feigned passion.

"Well, almost everything," Mindy went on, her face reddening. "We'll be crossing the border after lunch, and we'll arrive in Quebec this evening. Following a day of sightseeing there, we'll circle the beautiful Gaspé Peninsula, with overnight stops at the villages of Matane, Rivière Madeleine, Perce, and Carleton. From there, we'll return to the United States and end our tour with a couple of days traveling through New England. So just sit back, relax, and enjoy."

Mr. Strang intended to do exactly that. For the duration of the tour, he wanted no thoughts of Aldershot High School, boorish students, incessant paper work, or how alarmingly fast the summer vacation was coming to an end.

The young woman next to him — no more than twenty-five, if Mr. Strang was any judge of age — extended her hand. "It look like we'll be sitting together for the whole tour," she said. "I'm Sister Geraldine."

"I'm Mr. Str — make it Leonard." Mr. Strang took the proffered hand in his own gnarled fingers. But then he found himself staring at the girl's green ruffled blouse. "Sister Geraldine? You're a nun? But I thought — "

"I know, I know. You thought all nuns wear long black dresses and wimples and sensible shoes, and never go anywhere except in groups of a dozen or more."

Which is exactly what Mr. Strang had been thinking. He nodded. "I must say, Sister, that — "

"Please don't say it," she interrupted firmly. "You sound like every parishioner at St. Ignatius. For this tour, my name's just plain Gerry. And you're not to go all frosty and solemn on me, either. My parents gave me this tour as a birthday present, and I intend to have as much fun as I can."

Before Mr. Strang could reply, Mindy MacGregor was at

the microphone again. "Miss Ada Cermak?" Mindy pointed to a slender, birdlike woman who sat in lonely isolation in the rear seat of the bus. "Is that you?"

The woman mumbled something shyly and nodded.

"Good news, Miss Cermak," announced Mindy archly. "I have a note here that one more tour passenger will be meeting us in Quebec. A Mr. Daniel Gilfoil. So you'll have someone to share the ride with."

Miss Cermak twisted her hands nervously. "I'm not at all sure a man would — I mean, perhaps he'd rather sit somewhere else."

"The only vacant seat is next to you, Miss Cermak," said Mindy. "And I understand Mr. Gilfoil's a bachelor. Eight whole days. This could be your big opportunity."

"I'll take him if you don't want him!" shouted a female voice to a round of laughter.

In the tiny, self-contained world of the tour bus, the distinctive personalities of the tourists soon began to emerge. The three Nugent sisters appropriated as names the words which described Sam Kent on the sign above the windshield. For the entire tour, the plump one would answer only to "Safe," the slender sister became "Reliable," and the one with the jeweled glasses was "Courteous." In the seat behind Mr. Strang, Lola Pepperman extolled the beauty of the countryside in a bellow that threatened to drown out Mindy's electronically amplified lecture, and Herbert, her husband, contented himself with an occasional sigh and a more-than-occasional nip from a half-concealed flask. Across the aisle, the newlyweds — Harold and Joanne Wynn — ignored the scenery, gazing deeply into one another's eyes and generally behaving in the approved fashion for honeymooners.

The bus crossed the Canadian border without incident and reached Quebec City before seven o'clock. After getting settled in his single room. Mr. Strang quickly made his way to the hotel restaurant. The tour passengers were all seated in one area, and he found himself sharing a table with Gerry and the Peppermans. His enthusiasm for the French cuisine was somewhat tempered by the fact that Lola Pepperman turned the entire meal into a bleating recitation of the agonies of her first, second, and third pregnancies.

Afterward, as the four walked out of the restaurant, they passed a tiny table where Ada Cermak and a stout middle-aged man had their heads together and were talking in low tones.

Lola Pepperman leaned over the table. "I bet you're the new man on the tour," she proclaimed, with the delicacy of an avalanche. "You are the lucky one, Miss Cermak. I'd trade my Herbert in for this fella any day of the week."

The man turned and peered at Lola through rimless glasses, at the same time stroking his military mustache with an index finger. "I'm Dan Gilfoil," he said.

Lola made the introductions in a voice better suited for calling hogs. Mr. Strang squelched a desire to muzzle her with a napkin.

As the four walked through the hotel lobby, Herbert Pepperman nudged Mr. Strang and pointed to a rack of newspapers, whose headlines proclaimed *"Suspect du Vol S'evade"* and *"Canada, Etats Unis Sont d'Accord."*

"Terrible, ain't it?" Pepperman griped. "Nothing's written in your standard English."

The following day, as they strolled through Quebec's walled city, Mr. Strang and Gerry agreed that its quaint buildings, street vendors, and artists put them in mind of lithographs of nineteenth-century Paris. At a sidewalk booth, Gerry bought a cross of polished wood, perhaps a foot long, its two pieces joined by what appeared to be a hand-wrought nail. The vendor wrapped it in wads of newspaper before placing it delicately in a plastic bag, as if it were a rare antique rather than a simple souvenir. And when, at lunch, Mr. Strang was able to reach far back into past learning and request of the waitress *"L'addition, s'il vous plait,"* he was both gratified and dumbfounded when she brought the check straightaway.

Early the next morning, after a bountiful breakfast, the forty tourists trooped onto the bus, stowing their hand luggage in the overhead racks before taking their seats. Gerry kept the bag containing her cross on her lap. "Isn't it lovely?" she asked Mr. Strang, taking it from its bag and unwrapping the layers of newsprint. "Only five dollars, too."

"A bag," came a petulant voice from behind them. Lola Pepperman peered over the seat back. "You got a bag. I bought a pin and earrings, and I didn't get a bag. Herbert had to keep the things in his pocket."

"Perhaps if you'd asked," Mr. Strang began.

"It's not fair," Lola went on. "They should have — "

"Oh, here, take this one," said Gerry in annoyance.

Lola took the proffered bag and settled back triumphantly in her seat.

"Gerry," Mr. Strang whispered, "you didn't have to — "

"It's all right, Leonard. Anything to shut that woman up. She'll be asking for the cross itself next if I don't get it out of sight." She bundled the cross in its paper wrapping, got to her feet, and placed it in the overhead rack.

As the bus rolled on toward Matane, on the northern rim of the Gaspé Peninsula, there was much shuffling of luggage as the passengers retrieved their souvenirs of Quebec and passed them around for inspection. The bus's narrow aisle became increasingly crowded, and twice improperly stowed traveling bags tumbled down from the racks onto the heads of passengers beneath. Finally, Sam Kent pulled the bus to the side of the road and said something to Mindy MacGregor. She picked up the microphone.

"I know you all want to show off your souvenirs," she said, "but we're creating a very dangerous situation here. So please remain in your seats while the bus is moving. If you want anything from your luggage, I'll be happy to get it for you." Her eyes flashed as she looked about, daring anyone to defy her.

The tourists lapsed into guilty silence. The good fairy had suddenly turned into a harpy, and it was all their fault. Though he hadn't budged from his own seat, Mr. Strang was unaccountably ashamed of himself.

The rest of the journey to Matane was accomplished in silence, punctuated only by an occasional whisper.

As the bus approached the Matane Inn, where the tour group would stay that night, Mindy began hauling the hand luggage from the overhead racks and handing it to the owners. When the last bag had been lifted down, a puzzled look appeared on Gerry's face. She got up and looked in the racks on both sides of the aisle. Then she examined her seat and the floor beneath.

"Is something wrong?" Mr. Strang asked.

"My cross. It doesn't seem to be here. It's gone."

"Something that big doesn't just vanish," said Mr. Strang. He examined the luggage racks himself. Nothing.

The bus lurched to a halt in front of the inn, and Sam Kent reached for the handle to open the door.

"A minute, please," said Mr. Strang. "Gerry here is missing a wooden cross. It's probably just gotten mixed in with somebody's luggage, but if anyone runs across it she'd appreciate getting it back."

There were a few sympathetic words, but most of the

tourists were more interested in getting off the bus than in the lost cross.

When rooms had been assigned and the heavy luggage delivered and unpacked, the forty travelers got down to the business of entertaining themselves until dinnertime. Safe, Reliable, and Courteous headed for the inn's gift shop. Harold and Joanne Wynn twisted arms and disappeared down a winding woodland path. Dan Gilfoil stroked his mustache with one hand and held Ada Cermak's delicate fingers in the other as the two of them set out in the direction of a distant lighthouse. And Lola Pepperman trekked along the beach, searching for bright pebbles, while Herbert followed, literally holding the bag — the one Gerry had given up.

Mr. Strang sat in his small single room, staring at the wall. There was a knock on his door.

"It's me, Gerry," came a voice. "Would you care for a walk?"

Mr. Strang put on a sweater, and soon he and Gerry were strolling along the beach — in the direction opposite the one the Peppermans had taken.

"Leonard, you look as if you had all the cares of the world on your shoulders," said Gerry. "What's wrong?"

"I don't suppose your cross has turned up anywhere?" asked Mr. Strang hopefully.

"No, not yet. But I'm certain it will."

"I wish I could be that sure," replied Mr. Strang. "But everyone's had plenty of time to unpack. It ought to have been found by now."

"No big loss if it isn't, Leonard. I can afford the five dollars, so I'm not about to let it ruin my vacation. And neither should you."

"You don't understand." Mr. Strang pulled his sweater closer about his narrow shoulders. "The cross itself is relatively unimportant. But its disappearance confounds me. How could it have happened? It's not as if the thing is so tiny it could have fallen into a crevice somewhere."

"Leonard, I don't want you going on this way. It'll ruin your whole tour."

"Sorry, Gerry. But this brain of mine won't let loose of a problem until it's resolved."

Gerry strode to a huge boulder on the beach and sat down. "All right, Leonard," she said, looking up at him. "Let's talk about the cross. The last time I saw it was when I put it in the overhead rack after I gave the bag to Lola Pepperman. Perhaps it got snagged on a buckle or zipper of someone's luggage and — and —"

"And whoever it was carried a foot-long cross dangling from a bag or purse?" asked Mr. Strang. "And never noticed it, even when unpacking? You don't really believe that, do you?"

"No, I suppose not," replied Gerry tentatively. "But maybe it slid inside an open bag or something. I mean, the bus was bumping around a bit on those rough sections of road."

"And in that unlikely event, it would have been the first thing seen by the bag's owner when he unpacked after we arrived," said Mr. Strang. "Has anyone approached you to return the cross?"

Gerry shook her head. For a moment, she stared at Mr. Strang thoughtfully. "Leonard," she said finally, "are you implying the cross was deliberately stolen?"

"Can you give me any other explanation?"

"Oh, come on," she said. "I have some passing knowledge of the requirements for a conviction in a court of law." She ticked them off on her fingers. "Motive, means, and opportunity. There were means and opportunity aplenty, I grant you that. The aisle was full of people for a while there today, shifting luggage, opening and closing it. But there's no motive. Why would anyone steal a five-dollar souvenir? It couldn't be sold for enough to make stealing it worthwhile."

"But suppose someone wanted to get back at you for – for – "

"Revenge? Three days ago, I didn't know any of the people on this tour. And, since we started, I've been on my best behavior."

"Perhaps some kind of religious nut who – "

"Who goes on tours so he can snitch crosses? That's ridiculous. The whole idea of the cross being stolen is absurd."

"Nevertheless," said Mr. Strang quietly, "it's gone. *Infusoria!* The problem's enough to confound a Solon...."

That evening after dinner, a huge driftwood fire was lit on the beach in front of the inn. The tourists sat around it, some on chairs and others cushioned by the dry sand. A few couples held hands and whispered into one another's ears. Some inexpert singers began a round of *"Frère Jacques."* Now and then, someone got up and added more wood to the fire.

All of them – with a single exception – seemed to be enjoying themselves.

Mr. Strang leaned forward in his aluminum folding chair and glanced from one to another of the faces made ghostly by the flickering flames. Why? There was the rub. Why would anyone steal a souvenir worth next to nothing? Another five days, and the tour would be over.

Five days to answer a single question: why?

Breakfast was early the following morning, and then the bus was off to Rivière Madeleine, near the end of the peninsula. The scenery ranged from quaint little fishing villages, each with an elaborate church, to awesome cliffs that loomed above the narrow road like crouching giants. Dinner that evening was broiled lobster — which, as far as Mr. Strang was concerned, might have been cardboard. His mind would not release itself from the problem at hand.

Later, he sat by himself in the motel lobby, staring moodily at an Indian blanket hung on the far wall. The chair beside him creaked, and Gerry said, "I can't get over how easy it was coming across the border the other day. No luggage inspection or anything. Just show a birth certificate, and off you go."

"It's different in Europe," replied Mr. Strang. "I remember a trip I took when I was a good deal younger. At just about every border, they searched — "

"I knew you could do it if you tried," interrupted Gerry.

"Do it? Do what?"

"Get your mind onto something besides my cross. Isn't the tour fun, Leonard? Everyone's having a really good time."

"Except the Peppermans," he answered. "They'd have complaints about Paradise itself."

"But aren't Mr. Gilfoil and Miss Cermak cute? They must be well past fifty, and they act like a pair of nervous teenagers — him caring for that mustache like it was some kind of pet and her always patting her hair and making sure her skirt hangs just right."

"And wandering off by themselves every time they get off the bus," added Mr. Strang. "In the romance department, they're giving the Wynns a run for their money."

"You know, Leonard," said Gerry, "Joanne Wynn told me this tour cost more than they could afford, but they wanted a honeymoon they'd always remember. I wonder if they're really being wise about their finances."

"The Fates — perhaps in the form of doting mummies and daddies — will undoubtedly provide," replied Mr. Strang. "Anyway, that's the Wynns' problem. I'm still working on one of my own. Gerry, why would anybody steal — "

"Oh, Leonard!"

Next morning, it was on to Perce at the very tip of the
Gaspé. The raw beauty of Perce Rock, rearing out of the water like a huge, surrealistic sperm whale, and the cliffs of Bo-
naventure Island, inhabited by millions of gannets, sea par-
rots, and other birds, were in distinct contrast to the town
itself, where every second building seemed to house a souvenir shop filled with grotesque shell figures and mechanical
pencils inside of which swam plastic fish.

A boat trip around the rock and the island was part of
the tour. It was here that Mr. Strang and Gerry were again
trapped by the bombastic Lola Pepperman. "Where have you
two been hiding?" she bawled, as the boat roared seaward. "I
haven't seen you in a coon's age."

"We've been around," replied Gerry.

"Not any of the places Herbert and I were," Lola went on.
"I was saying to him just this morning how we see so little
of you — and nothing at all of the lovers."

"The Wynns?" said Mr. Strang. "They're right back there in
the last seat."

"Naw." Lola dismissed the Wynns with a wave of her hand.
"I mean Dan and Ada. The way those two old goats carry on,
I reckon it's wedding bells before fall. You won't find them
aboard. They're too interested in one another to come sightseeing with the rest of us."

Mr. Strang paid mental homage to the wisdom and fore-
sight of Mr. Gilfoil and Miss Cermak.

The last stop on the Gaspé Peninsula was at Carleton. After unpacking, Mr. Strang found himself with an hour before
dinner and nothing to do. Across the street from the motel
was a gift shop, where he hoped to find some picture post-
cards.

As he entered, he could hear Safe, Reliable, and Courteous
Nugent chattering in the rear of the store.

"It's not as if the perfume's any good," Courteous was saying. "I wouldn't buy — "

"It's not the perfume I want," Safe answered. "It's the bottle. See, it's shaped just like the lighthouse we saw yesterday.
It's my money, and I want it."

"Then you go right ahead and buy it," Reliable assured her
sister. "You don't even have to open it. Just leave it sitting
on your dresser to remember the tour by. Chances are the
bottle's worth more than the stuff inside, anyway. I've heard

that the bottles are the only real difference between — "

In Mr. Strang's mind, the voices of the Nugent sisters seemed to fade away. For several minutes, he stood rigidly, seeing and hearing nothing, his nose only inches from a red plastic lobster hanging on a string.

"May I 'elp you, *monsieur?*"

With a start, Mr. Strang returned to reality. Beside him stood the shop's proprietor, a tiny woman with deep wrinkles and a broad smile.

"No. I mean yes," he told her. "Do you have a phone here?"

From the small office at the rear of the shop, he made several calls, the recipients of which were happy to accept the reversed charges. Returning to the motel, he located Mindy MacGregor and asked a favor, which she granted with some reluctance. Then he told the man at the desk he was expecting a telephone call sometime that night, and he was to be awakened no matter what time it came.

With those chores behind him, he entered the dining room whistling a French *chanson* and ate a delicious and most satisfying meal.

It was nearly three in the morning when Mr. Strang's call came through.

Next morning, the bus had been on the road for more than two hours — heading over back roads toward the Canada-Maine border — when Mindy took up her microphone and pressed the switch.

"We'll be crossing into the U.S. in half an hour or so," she announced. "Be sure you have your identification ready for Customs."

There was a general shuffling through pockets and purses.

"It'll be a long day on the road," Mindy went on. "And this isn't a very scenic part of the trip. But Mr. Strang has something he wants to say that might keep us entertained. So come on up front, Mr. Strang, the microphone's yours."

With a popping of knee joints, Mr. Strang got to his feet and shuffled forward. He took the microphone from Mindy. "Good morning!" His voice boomed through the bus, and several of the tourists covered their ears.

Mr. Strang moved the mike away from his lips and tried again. "Good morning," he repeated. "You'll recall that, a few days ago, Gerry — my seat partner — lost a cross. That disturbed me. Though the cross itself had little value, I couldn't get its disappearance out of my mind. So yesterday I dreamed up a little story which — farfetched though it may be — would

202 | William Brittain

account not only for the missing cross but for several other things I've noticed during the tour."

There was a confused babbling among the passengers.

"I remembered a newspaper headline I'd seen back in Quebec. *"Suspect du Vol S'evade,"* it said. Or, if my high-school French isn't too rusty, Robbery Suspect Escapes. I phoned the Quebec police, and they very kindly gave me the whole story.

"It seems that, eleven days ago, a Georges LeClair walked into one of Quebec's larger banks with a gun in his hand. When he walked out again, he had — in addition to the gun — some sixty-eight thousand dollars of the bank's funds. Within hours of the heist, Mr. LeClair was apprehended, identified as the robber, photographed, fingerprinted, and held in custody. In the meantime, however, he'd stashed the money in some unknown place. The police never did find it."

"The police told you all that?" hooted Lola Pepperman. "It sounds fishy to me, Mr. Strang."

"Well, I do confess to letting them in on a few things I thought they might be interested in before they opened up," replied Mr. Strang, with a trace of a smile. "But to go on, LeClair was remanded into the custody of officials from the *Pavillon Cellulaire de Montreal* — a Montreal prison — to be held for questioning. However, shortly after the car taking him to prison left Quebec, his guards got a bit careless. To make a long story shorter, Georges LeClair escaped.

"Interestingly enough, Mr. LeClair was described to me as having one of those bland faces that can assume almost any personality and a wide range of ages, making identification extremely difficult. Equally interesting is the fact that he speaks four languages flawlessly. One of them is English."

"The cross," said Joanne Wynn. "What's this LeClair got to do with the missing cross?"

"All in good time," replied Mr. Strang, in his most professorial manner. "Let's consider the bind that LeClair found himself in after the escape. His photograph and description were being given wide circulation. He could hardly walk the streets, much less make use of any available transportation. How, then, could he avoid being retaken?

"LeClair was a member of Quebec's criminal fraternity. As such, he must have had friends who'd help him go about getting new clothes, false documentation of a new identity, et cetera — especially for a price. And he certainly had funds. Sixty-eight thousand can go a long way, even in this age of inflation." He cleared his throat and continued. "What I've told you so far are facts. But here, I'm afraid, we must enter the gray area of conjecture. What if — and I'm only supposing now — what if LeClair decided to leave Quebec, and Canada itself, on a bus full of tourists?"

"What?" Lola Pepperman jumped to her feet, banging her head on the luggage rack. "Mr. Strang, are you saying this LeClair fella is one of us? That's downright crazy! We all started out from the good ol' U.S. of A., same as you."

"Easy, Lola," replied the teacher. "I'm simply trying to tell an entertaining yarn. But I submit to you that there is one among us who did not cross the border with us when we came into Canada."

All heads turned toward the rear seat, where Dan Gilfoil sat stroking his mustache, an amused smile on his face. "You're quite right, Mr. Strang. I joined you in Quebec. That hardly makes me a criminal. And I'll remind you, sir, that there are laws against slander in Canada."

"I don't recall mentioning the name of anyone here present," answered Mr. Strang innocently. "My story concerns a man named LeClair. And LeClair's escaping in a tour bus would be a stroke of genius. What better method? To the local residents along its route, bus tourists are transitory and anonymous. Among ourselves, we're pleasant and charming. Yet who in our group — couples excepted — really knows anything about the others, beyond what each one has divulged about himself or herself? I say I teach school. Yet I could be an ax murderer for all you know. Oh, by the way, Mr. Gilfoil, it's my understanding that, when your tour reservation was made in Quebec — through the tour office, rather than a travel agent — it was paid for in cash."

"You were a busy little bee yesterday," said Gilfoil sarcastically. "What's wrong with cash?"

"Nothing, nothing," Mr. Strang said, half to himself. "Odd, though, that you didn't use a credit card like most people. The clerk remembers the transaction quite well. She was unaccustomed to handling such a large amount of money, according to the Quebec police. And it seems a woman made the original booking."

"My secretary," explained Gilfoil.

"Yes, of course. Certainly no one wishes to accuse you of not wanting to show your face in public — or of wearing glasses that would tend to disguise your appearance — or of constantly stroking your mustache, not to groom it but simply to reassure yourself that it hadn't dropped away from where you'd glued it."

"This is outrageous!" Gilfoil roared. He glared at the passengers on either side of the aisle and then leveled a finger at Mr. Strang. "There stands a madman! I'm just a tourist like the rest of you. You've observed me for days. Can you possibly believe that — "

"The fact is, Mr. Gilfoil," snapped Lola Pepperman, "we haven't seen much of you at all. Oh, I'm not saying I believe this hogwash of Mr. Strang's, but having that rear seat, Mr. Gilfoil, you're off in a corner like. And, every time we stop, you and Miss Cermak walk off by yourselves."

"True love, of course," said Mr. Strang. "Yet, if you were LeClair, you might want to cut down on the chance of being recognized, even through a disguise. Certainly keeping away from the rest of us as much as possible would diminish the risk of accidentally being exposed by someone who'd seen your picture somewhere."

"Mr. Strang," piped up Gerry. "I'd laugh if this accusation weren't so serious. But what has all this got to do with my missing cross? You did say that was the point of this fantastic tale."

"Ah, yes, the cross. A possible reason for its being taken came to me yesterday, when the Nugent sisters were discussing how a perfume container can be more valuable than the scent inside it."

"I don't see — "

"Imagine LeClair on this bus during the ride from Quebec to Matane, when the cross disappeared the other day," said Mr. Strang. "Passengers were milling about in the aisle, taking souvenirs from their luggage. LeClair might pretend to do the same, just to give the appearance of being like everyone else — and, glancing into the luggage rack where your cross lay, Gerry, perhaps he saw — "

"Saw what, Mr. Strang?"

"Perhaps he saw himself."

"What? Mr. Strang, that's insane."

Mr. Strang shook his head. "I think LeClair saw a photograph of himself, along with the story of his crime, on the newspaper wrapped around the cross. And he knew he had to get rid of that incriminating sheet before anyone else spotted it. He couldn't take a chance on unwrapping the cross. With so many people around, he'd be noticed. So he stuffed the cross, still wrapped, into his own bag and got rid of it later. It's my theory that LeClair wanted the newspaper in which your cross was wrapped, Gerry, not the cross itself."

"Then where's the cross now?" asked Gerry blankly.

"The Canadian police are extremely thorough," Mr. Strang

answered. "Seems they did a bit of digging and sifting among the ashes of our campfire on the beach at Matane. They came up with what looks like a hand-wrought nail."

"Mr. Strang," Mindy MacGregor said. "This is all supposition, you know. I'm responsible for this tour, and I couldn't possibly allow charges to be brought against Mr. Gilfoil or anyone else on the basis of what you've said. It would look bad for the company if he were even detained for questioning. So, if you don't have anything in the way of proof — "

"Proof?" Lola Pepperman chimed in. "There ought to be proof aplenty. We could start with that cute little mustache and see if it comes off, like Mr. Strang said."

"Not conclusive, I'm afraid," replied the teacher. "Oh, would a couple of you gentlemen back there see that Mr. Gilfoil doesn't endanger himself by reaching for his bag on the overhead rack? For his own safety, of course. I doubt LeClair would bring a gun on a bus tour, but I think that bag will contain all the necessary proof that Mr. Gilfoil is either an innocent tourist or the criminal Georges LeClair. If you're the former, Mr. Gilfoil, you'll have my abject apologies. If you're the latter — well, I'm afraid the authorities will have to take over."

"Proof? What are you talking about, Leonard?" Gerry asked.

"I hardly think LeClair would attempt his escape without sufficient funds," was the reply. "If Dan Gilfoil and Georges LeClair are one and the same, it's my guess his hand luggage will contain wads of money rather than just a change of underwear."

"Lay off that bag," growled Gilfoil. "All of you. You're not going to pry through my bag just because of some crazy old man's story!"

"Quite correct, Mr. Guilfoil," Mr. Strang replied. "Your bag is quite safe from us. But I see we're coming up to some people who have every right to make as thorough a search as necessary."

The bus hissed to a stop. On a wooden building at the edge of the road, a sign read: CANADA-UNITED STATES BORDER CUSTOMS INSPECTION. Cars of both the Royal Canadian Mounted Police and the Maine State Police lined the sides of the road.

"Good," said Mr. Strang to Gilfoil. "We're expected."

Dan Gilfoil's traveling bag was found to contain two handkerchiefs, a bottle of spirit gum, and forty-six thousand dollars in Canadian currency.

Two days later, as the tour ended and last goodbyes were being said on the sidewalk beside the bus, Mr. Strang approached a thin woman standing forlornly on the corner of one of the city's busiest streets, choking back tears while attempting in vain to flag a taxi.

"Miss Cermak," he said, removing his hat, "I don't think either one of us is in any great hurry to get home to an empty house. I'd be honored if you'd have dinner with me this evening."

AFTERWORD
by Susan Brittain Gawley

The first story my father ever sold was "Joshua," to *Alfred Hitchcock's Mystery Magazine*. He framed the acceptance letter and kept it.

Having a father who wrote seemed very natural to me. His office was his inner sanctum, and woe betide the unfortunate who went in without permission. There were always piles of onionskin, foolscap, and carbon paper and plenty of typewriter erasers around.

When it was time for him to write, he wrote. He developed a discipline, and was able to write his stories in a certain time frame. When I was in high school, I remember he wrote one story a month.

My bedroom shared a wall with his office, and I often went to sleep to the sound of a Royal manual typewriter. One memorable Friday night, after Bill and Ginny had been out for the evening, he got an idea. So at 3 AM he was back at the typewriter. I was asleep in the next room. He finished the story, went to bed, retyped it the next morning, sent it in, and had a check by the following Wednesday. It was not always that easy.

Fred Dannay was a great teacher and mentor, and Bill tried to pay it forward by helping others. Last fall, Josh Pachter contacted me and told me how Bill had helped him early on, and that he wanted to do something now for my mother. That "something" includes the book you have just read.

Thank you for your interest in my dad. I hope you've enjoyed his stories.

Susan Brittain Gawley
April 2018

A WILLIAM BRITTAIN CHECKLIST

In the following list, EQMM= *Ellery Queen's Mystery Magazine,* and AHMM= *Alfred Hitchcock's Mystery Magazine.*

An asterisk preceding a title indicates that the story is collected in *The Man Who Read Mysteries.*

The "Man Who Read" series (11 stories, all first published in EQMM)

*The Man Who Read John Dickson Carr	(12/65)
*The Man Who Read Ellery Queen	(12/65)
*The Man Who Didn't Read	(05/66)
*The Woman Who Read Rex Stout	(07/66)
*The Boy Who Read Agatha Christie	(12/66)
*The Man Who Read Sir Arthur Conan Doyle	(08/68)
*The Man Who Read G. K. Chesterton	(04/73)
*The Man Who Read Dashiell Hammett	(05/74)
*The Man Who Read Georges Simenon	(01/75)
*The Girl Who Read John Creasey	(03/75)
*The Men Who Read Isaac Asimov	(05/78)

The "Mr. Strang" series (32 stories, all first published in EQMM)

*Mr. Strang Gives a Lecture	(03/67)
*Mr. Strang Performs an Experiment	(06/67)
Mr. Strang Finds the Answers	(11/67)
Mr. Strang Sees a Play	(03/68)
*Mr. Strang Takes a Field Trip	(12/68)
Mr. Strang Pulls a Switch	(06/69)
Mr. Strang Takes a Hand	(04/70)
Mr. Strang Lifts a Glass	(05/71)
Mr. Strang Finds an Angle	(06/71)
Mr. Strang Hunts a Bear	(11/71)
Mr. Strang Checks a Record	(02/72)
Mr. Strang Finds a Car	(07/72)
*Mr. Strang Versus the Snowman	(12/72)
Mr. Strang Examines a Legend	(02/73)
Mr. Strang Invents a Strange Device	(06/73)

Mr. Strang Follows Through	(09/73)
Mr. Strang Discovers a Bug	(12/73)
Mr. Strang Under Arrest	(02/74)
Mr. Strang and the Cat Lady	(05/75)
Mr. Strang Picks Up the Pieces	(09/75)
*Mr. Strang, Armchair Detective	(12/75)
Mr. Strang Battles a Deadline	(06/76)
Mr. Strang Accepts a Challenge	(11/76)
Mr. Strang Buys a Big H	(04/78)
Mr. Strang Unlocks a Door	(06/81)
*Mr. Strang Interprets a Picture	(08/81)
Mr. Strang Grasps at Straws	(11/81)
Mr. Strang and the Lost Ship	(06/82)
Mr. Strang Takes a Partner	(Mid-July/82)
Mr. Strang Studies Exhibit A	(10/82)
Mr. Strang and the Purloined Memo	(02/83)
*Mr. Strang Takes a Tour	(Mid-July/83)

The Standalone Stories (29 stories, all in EQMM unless otherwise noted)

Joshua	(10/64, AHMM)
Mr. Lightning (as by "James Knox")	(07/66)
The Zaretski Chain	(06/68)
The Last Word (as by "James Knox")	(06/68)
The Second Sign in the Melon Patch	(01/69)
That Day on the Knob	(09/69)
Hand	(10/69, AHMM)
Just About Average	(06/70, AHMM)
Falling Object	(02/71)
A Gallon of Gas	(04/71, AHMM)
The Driver	(01/72, AHMM)
Wynken, Blynken and Nod	(04/72)
The Artificial Liar	(04/72, AHMM)
The Sonic Boomer	(02/73, AHMM)
The Scarab Ring	(05/73, AHMM)
A State of Preparedness	(09/73, AHMM)
The Button	(10/73, AHMM)
The Platt Avenue Irregulars	(11/73, AHMM)
He Can't Die Screaming	(02/74, AHMM)
Waiting for Harry	(03/74, AHMM)
The Impossible Footprint	(11/74, AHMM)
I'm Back, Little Sister	(12/74, AHMM)
Aunt Abigail's Wall Safe	(05/75, AHMM)

Yellowbelly	(10/75, AHMM)
Historical Errors	(02/76, AHMM)
A Private Little War	(05/76, AHMM)
One Big Happy Family	(09/76, AHMM)
The Second Reason	(02/77)
The Ferret Man	(Spring-Summer/77, *Antaeus*)

The Children's Books

All The Money In The World	(1979)
Devil's Donkey	(1981)
Sherlock Holmes, Master Detective	(1982)
The Wish Giver: Three Tales of Coven Tree	(1983)
Who Knew There'd Be Ghosts?	(1985)
Dr. Dredd's Wagon of Wonders	(1987)
The Fantastic Freshman	(1988)
My Buddy, the King	(1989)
Professor Popkin's Prodigious Polish: A Tale of Coven Tree	(1990)
Wings	(1991)
The Ghost from Beneath the Sea	(1992)
The Mystery of the Several Sevens	(1994)
Shape-Changer	(1994)
The Wizards and the Monster	(1994)

ACKNOWLEDGMENTS

Thank you, thank you, thank you to Ginny Brittain and Susan Brittain Gawley, William Brittain's widow and daughter, for their friendship, encouragement, and support.

Thanks always to the late Frederic Dannay and Eleanor Sullivan, the first and second editors-in-chief of *Ellery Queen's Mystery Magazine*, who gave each of the stories included in this volume its original publication.

Big ups to Doug Greene and Jeff Marks of Crippen & Landru for instantly recognizing that *The Man Who Read Mysteries* was a book that needed to exist, and for shepherding it through the publication process.

A tip of the fedora to Charles Ardai, Jon Breen, Mike Nevins, and Bill Pronzini, who helped track down some of the stories included here, and to Robert Lopresti, who suggested the addition of the checklist.

Special thanks to Arthur Vidro, who provided both a typescript of "The Man Who Read Ellery Queen" and a copy of the Summer 2012 issue of his own excellent publication, *(Give Me That) Old-Time Detection*, which has a photograph of Bill Brittain on the front cover and, inside, a fascinating selection of letters between Brittain, Fred Dannay, Eleanor Sullivan, and *EQMM*'s Clayton Rawson and Connie Di Rienzo. It was from Arthur's article that I learned that Dannay had removed the last names of the two characters in "The Man Who Didn't Read" prior to its publication in *EQMM*. I have restored those last names here, and readers familiar with Poe's "A Cask of Amontillado" will understand why Dannay deleted them and appreciate why I've put them back where the author originally had them.

Most of all, my thanks, love and respect to Bill Brittain for writing these wonderful tales — which gave me many hours of enjoyment when I read them on their original publication and did so yet again when I reread them during the preparation of this collection — and for the many kindnesses he and Ginny showed me when I was a punk teenager. This book is a long-overdue expression of my appreciation, Bill, for your talent and your friendship.

Josh Pachter

THE MAN WHO READ MYSTERIES

The Man Who Read Mysteries by William Brittain is printed on 60 pound paper, and is designed by Jeffrey Marks using InDesign. The type is Fontin, a semi-serif typeface design by Jos Buivenga recently. The printing and binding is by Thomson-Shore for the hard cover and the trade paperback version. The book was published in May 2018 by Crippen & Landru Publishers, Inc., Cincinnati, OH.

Crippen & Landru, Publishers
P. O. Box 532057
Cincinnati, OH 45253
Web: www.Crippenlandru.Com
E-mail: info@crippenlandru.Com

Since 1994, Crippen & Landru has published more than 100 first editions of short-story collections by important detective and mystery writers.

This is the best edited, most attractively packaged line of mystery books introduced in this decade. The books are equally valuable to collectors and readers. [Mystery Scene Magazine]

The specialty publisher with the most star-studded list is Crippen & Landru, which has produced short story collections by some of the biggest names in contemporary crime fiction. [Ellery Queen's Mystery Magazine]

God bless Crippen & Landru. [The Strand Magazine]

A monument in the making is appearing year by year from Crippen & Landru, a small press devoted exclusively to publishing the criminous short story. [Alfred Hitchcock's Mystery Magazine]

]

Recent Publications

Challenge the Impossible: The Impossible Files of Dr. Sam Hawthorne by Edward D. Hoch. Full cloth in dust jacket, signed and numbered by the publisher, $45.00. Trade softcover, $19.00.

Ten Thousand Blunt Instruments by Phillip Wylie, edited by Bill Pronzini. Lost Classics Series.
Wylie's stories were, in the words of editor Bill Pronzini, "controversial, provocative, iconoclastic." His detective fiction was among the most ingenious and innovative of his generation. Full cloth with dust jacket, $29.00. Trade softcover, $19.00

The Exploits Of The Patent Leather Kid by Erle Stanley Gardner edited By Bill Pronzini. Lost Classics Series.
The Patent Leather Kid is an elegant crook, hiding his identity with mask, gloves, and shoes made out of black patent leather. In truth, he is a wealthy, seemingly indolent socialite, who becomes a terror to the underworld. Full cloth in dust jacket, $29.00. Trade softcover, $19.00

Valentino: Film Detective by Loren D. Estleman.
Valentino has a perfect job for a film buff – he is a film detective who locates lost movies so that they can be preserved for future generations. And often he has to become an amateur sleuth as well. Full cloth in dust jacket, signed and numbered by the author,
$43.00. Trade softcover, $17.00.

The Duel Of Shadows: The Extraordinary Cases Of Barnabas Hildreth by Vincent Cornier, edited By Mike Ashley. Lost Classics Series.
"One of the great series of modern detective stories." So

wrote Ellery Queen when he introduced American readers to the writings of Vincent Cornier. Full cloth in dust jacket, $28.00.

Shooting Hollywood: The Diana Poole Stories by Melodie Johnson Howe.
Melodie Johnson Howe was "one of the last of the starlets," making movies with Clint Eastwood, Alan Alda, James Caan, James Farentino and others. Hollywood is brutal, and it is a place, as Marilyn Monroe said, "where they'll pay you a thousand dollars for a kiss, and fifty cents for your soul ..." Diana Poole finds crime in that world of glitz, glamour, and greed. Full cloth in dust jacket, signed and numbered by the author, $43.00. Trade softcover, $17.00.

The Casebook Of Jonas P. Jonas And Others by E. X. Ferrars, edited By John Cooper. Lost Classics Series.
Stories by a mistress of the traditional mystery. "She remains," wrote one reviewer, "one of the most adept and intelligent adherents of the whodunit form." Full cloth in dust jacket, $29.00. Trade softcover, $19.00.

Nothing Is Impossible: Further Problems Of Dr. Sam Hawthorne by Edward D. Hoch.
Dr. Sam Hawthorne, a New England country doctor in the first half of the twentieth century, was constantly faced by murders in locked rooms and impossible disappearances. *Nothing Is Impossible* contains fifteen of Dr. Sam's most extraordinary cases. Full cloth in dust jacket, signed and numbered by the publisher, $45.00. Trade softcover, $19.00.

Night Call And Other Stories Of Suspense by Charlotte Armstrong, edited By Rick Cypert And Kirby Mccauley. Lost Classics Series.
Charlotte Armstrong introduced suspense into the com-

monplace, the everyday, by writing short stories and novels in which one simple action sets a series of events spiraling into motion, pulling readers along, breathless with anxiety. Full cloth in dust jacket, $30.00. Trade softcover, $20.00.

Chain Of Witnesses; The Cases Of Miss Phipps by Phyllis Bentley, edited By Marvin Lachman. Lost Classics Series. A critic writes, "stylistically, [Bentley's] stories ... share a quiet humor and misleading simplicity of statement with the works of Christie .... Her work [is] informed and consistent with the classic traditions of the mystery." Full cloth in dust jacket, $29.00. Trade softcover, $19.00.

Swords, Sandals And Sirens by Marilyn Todd.
Murder, conmen, elephants. Who knew ancient times could be such fun? Many of the stories feature Claudia Seferius, the super-bitch heroine of Marilyn Todd's critically acclaimed mystery series set in ancient rome. Others feature Cleopatra, the olympian gods, and high priestess Ilion blackmailed to work with Sparta's feared secret police. Full cloth in dust jacket, signed and numbered by the author, $45.00. Trade softcover, $19.00.

The Puzzles Of Peter Duluth by Patrick Quentin. Lost Classics Series.
Anthony Boucher wrote: "Quentin is particularly noted for the enviable polish and grace which make him one of the leading American fabricants of the murderous comedy of manners; but this surface smoothness conceals intricate and meticulous plot construction as faultless as that of Agatha Christie." Full cloth in dust jacket, $29.00. Trade softcover, $19.00.

The Purple Flame And Other Detective Stories by Frederick Irving Anderson, edited By Benjamin F. Fisher. Previously uncollected stories by one of the premier mystery writers of the 1920's and the 1930's. Full cloth in dust jacket, $29.00. Trade softcover, $19.00.

My Mother, The Detective: The Complete "Mom" Stories by James Yaffe. Second edition enlarged. Trade softcover, $19.00

All But Impossible: The Impossible Files of Dr. Sam Hawthorne by Edward D. Hoch. Full cloth in dust jacket, signed and numbered by the publisher, $45.00. Trade softcover, $19.00.

Sequel to Murder by Anthony Gilbert, edited by John Cooper. Full cloth in dust jacket, $29.00. Trade softcover, $19.00.

Subscriptions

Subscribers agree to purchase each forthcoming publication, either the Regular Series or the Lost Classics or (preferably) both. Collectors can thereby guarantee receiving limited editions, and readers won't miss any favorite stories.

Subscribers receive a discount of 20% off the list price (and the same discount on our backlist) and a specially commissioned short story by a major writer in a deluxe edition as a gift at the end of the year.

The point for us is that, since customers don't pick and choose which books they want, we have a guaranteed sale even before the book is published, and that allows us to be more imaginative in choosing short story collections to issue.

That's worth the 20% discount for us. Sign up now and start saving. Email us at crippenlandru@earthlink.net or visit our website at www.crippenlandru.com on our subscription page.